CROW'S HAUNT

Rachel Wade

Fisher King Publishing

CROW'S HAUNT

ISBN 978-1-914560-10-1

Fisher King Publishing
The Old Barn
York Road
Thirsk
YO7 3AD
England

fisherkingpublishing.co.uk

In memory of Richard and Elma

Part One

Chapter One

Mrs Holden had never intended to sell everything she owned. It began mid-morning, August 17th, 1862, a date well remembered by residents for its smothering heat, which had turned the stinking stale air of York's most notorious thoroughfare into an abusive haze. Clinging a sullied shawl to her shoulders with elongated fingers more bone than flesh, Mrs Holden lumbered to her front door to study the scene.

Summer always brought strangers to the Shambles. They journeyed from the surrounding towns touting for business or shopping for specialities scarcely available elsewhere. Peering out from squinted slits, her mouth a silent curve, Mrs Holden's expression was one of permanent distaste. While neither pretty nor polite, her steely stare and sharp tongue meant she excelled as a shopkeeper, with stories of her customer encounters becoming local legends. Her first was nicknamed Lanky Luke.

Nearing seven feet tall and as slender as a poker, Luke moseyed through the city with swaggering limbs and the odour of clams. He had taken advantage of the balmy weather to make the lengthy trip across the moors seeking more profitable markets. As he searched for such a place in York's city centre, he noticed a most uncommon building. Mrs Holden was perched at its entrance inspecting the tidal flow across the cobbles.

She spotted the boy like a magpie to jewels, eyeing him with curiosity and caution as he began fondling the fishing nets tangled against the wall.

The old woman wrinkled her nose. She could smell salt on him and noticed the pale stains on his clothing and boots. He was perhaps from Whitby, Staithes or Scarborough. She had never been to the coast herself, nor even outside of the city, but buried somewhere behind the furniture was a drawing she had always loved, a watercolour depicting the crashing waves and gnarled cliff face of some local coastline. She had often become lost in its markings, pondering on how the fishermen managed to pluck their catch from the murky depths and how many had sunken into its callous embrace.

The visitor tugged the nets to test their strength before asking the price. Mrs Holden's customary stare swiftly masked her surprise. It seemed this stranger had assumed her house was a shop and that the items she had amassed along its exterior were there for sale rather than convenient storage. She was momentarily amused but hid it well. Instead, she locked eyes with him, a challenge to offer what he dared. With a brief nod, Luke rummaged in his pocket and held out four coins. Mrs Holden eyed them in turn, mutely mouthing each number.

"'ave 'em then," she barked, swiping the money from the open palm before her. Luke released the nets with a chuckle and swung them over a shoulder before making his way back towards the square. He paused at the end of the street for one last look at the rummy residence he had just visited.

"Quite the haunt you got 'ere, missus!" he called over the hubbub. Luke was never seen again, but the old woman had had her first successful sale and Holden's Haunt – for the name had stuck – was officially in business.

The building was barely visible behind the dense smog belched from the bellows of the newly industrialised city. Slumped on the furthest corner of the Shambles, it was the only residence to survey both the cobbled street stretching down to the left and the church square on its right. Centuries-old, the area had long been the commercial heart of the neighbourhood, known for its many butcher's shops as well as providing a bakery, tobacconist's, grocer's, pawnbroker's, draper's, goldsmith's and two inns, all inherited businesses with prolific histories of successful trade.

By day, the din of toil punctuated the conversations of customers in the coarse regional dialect. Smoke and soot choked the air as a persistent fog pervaded with the reek of rotting matter and flooding sewers. At night, the beer louts, brawlers and busty maidens came out to play, roaring obscenities into the black beyond as they stumbled down the sodden cobbles, splashing fluids from orifices and receptacles. The inhabitants took cold comfort in the street's unfaltering familiarity sheltered from the rapidly changing world. Happy in their ignorance, they failed to notice the building on the corner as it took on a life of its own.

Unbeknown to the neighbourhood, the outside of

Holden's Haunt gradually shapeshifted over the course of many months. What were once empty walls thickly stained with grime became steadily concealed by all manner of intriguing oddments. There were pails of tarnished metal hung from their handles on nails hastily bashed into beams. Below, nesting tables, milking stools, chicken coops, lobster traps and mismatched leather boots squatted haphazardly. Under the window ledges rested tall vases of cracked clay filled with wooden canes, metal pokers and walking sticks topped with carved characters: a fox, a serpent, an owl and a grimacing gargoyle. More curios swung attached by ropes hooked through rusted loops: wreaths of dried flowers, fishing nets, giant chains and matching manacles intertwined with bold hued bird feathers and scraps of cloth.

Inside, the collection was no less captivating. In the gloom permitted by the windows caked with greasy residue there was a maze of furniture and scattered knickknacks: worm-eaten wash stools and sagging bookcases, glass-fronted cabinets and chipped enamel sinks, dainty jewellery boxes, framed oil paintings, and a vast oak bureau with ivory inlays. Glistening trinkets lined the bases of pewter bowls alongside ornaments of pottery, porcelain, glass, wood and silver. Moulding books replaced absent furniture legs and countless kinds of clothing wavered in disorderly stacks. Even the ceiling was arrayed with nets, lamps and birdcages. It seemed that every surface had been used for this exceptional collection, a rare assemblage of the practical and commonplace alongside the peculiar and exotic.

Enveloping the interior of the house and its belongings was a permanent and pungent odour of rot, damp, smoke and rat droppings, with the greatest whiff of them all coming courtesy of a pile of precariously balanced stained chamber pots to the left of the fireplace. On the opposite side was a shabby armchair from where the equally aged owner surveyed her empire with a stern glare, seemingly oblivious to the smell but very much aware of the private world she had somehow created.

Widowed and childless, Mrs Holden had withdrawn from the community following the death of her husband. Unable to remain in the same house as his ghost and her grief, she had taken to moving the furniture around and covering it with the objects she had kept hidden for so long. While the four walls remained unchanged, the atmosphere became entirely altered, even revitalised. It had been a purging process and while her sorrow and loneliness remained ever present, she had somehow found a sense of purpose, a new reason for being.

By the time her home came to be a shop, Mrs Holden was in her sixth decade. While her mind had been kept attentive and engaged by the daily demands of her collection, the passing of time had been less sympathetic to her body. Since the demise of her spouse, she had visibly withered year on year, becoming hunched and heavy, frail and worn. There were broad bands of silver within her remaining wisps of hair, deep creases and puckers covering her face, and her once elegant hands now resembled the talons of a bird. Only her eyes retained the glint of youth.

Although she may not have turned heads with her appearance, Mrs Holden was still quite capable of attracting attention with her personality and reputation. Smart, observant, determined and dedicated, she had achieved a level of success that had taken other city establishments generations to attain. From a single opportunity, Mrs Holden had steered her former family home on the journey to becoming a reputable business, one which was unique among the city's other industries. She was without question a formidable woman.

Soon enough, thanks to her entrepreneurial talents, each object at Holden's Haunt became coveted and haggled over. Despite their distaste for change, the locals eventually found a fondness for this novel venture, regarding it as a magical place where they could escape the monotony of normality through the purchase of a single scrupulously hunted out object. Some even visited once or twice a week to try their luck at discovering something new. There were the summer visitors too, and the many more who journeyed to the city tempted by tales of the famous shop, each longing to discover its secrets for themselves. For Holden's Haunt was not a place one explored on a whim. It could take hours, days, even weeks to uncover a real treasure. The lure of competition and the promise of reward kept customers coming back.

Chapter Two

Aging, alone, and now the owner of an unusual business, Mrs Holden could quickly have become a novelty or a source of ridicule, particularly within a city that seemed to thrive on gossip and controversy. It was true that in the early days of the shop, folk would come simply to stare and marvel with a combination of disgust and wonderment at the ever-changing arrangements before scurrying back to their work, home, or to the pub to share what they had seen. There were frequent debates as to whether Mrs Holden was mad or marvellous. After all, on a street like the Shambles, only the highest quality of merchants could have a hope of survival. The competition was fierce and even more so for a woman. Despite the progressive politics of many of the new and developing city industries, it was still a rarity to find a female unaided at the helm of a prosperous business. Mrs Holden, however, was more than capable of handling herself and her customers. If there had been any advantage to her long and troubled life, it had been the formation of a very thick skin.

Mrs Holden had moved into the property on the eve of her twentieth birthday, which also happened to be her wedding day. She had taken only a few steps from the exit of Holy Trinity Church to reach the front door of her new home. Her husband, Matthew Holden, had inherited the quaint property from an unfortunate uncle who had lost three wives and several children to various illnesses. The old man had relied on his nephew for care and company, leaving his house and numerous possessions along with a small amount of savings to him when he passed away a week before the wedding.

The couple felt truly blessed to have acquired such a fine home at the ideal moment, but their joy was not to last. Mrs Holden befell the same curse that had struck the old uncle; twenty years after moving in, she found herself entirely alone. Unable to work and with a dwindling inheritance, it was a welcome relief when Lanky Luke became her first customer, with more quickly following as word spread of the shop's many treasures. While the possessions she had so meticulously preserved had become a form of substitute family, she could not afford to be sentimental when her stomach cramped with hunger. Every item sold meant another day of survival.

While the 'haunt' was Mrs Holden's livelihood, to many of the locals it was merely a source for their storytelling. Pubs were particularly rife with such gossip and none more so than the Eagle and Child Inn. Folk would take up an argument practically every night about the old woman and her trading, with a blacksmith named Dan Chelten invariably at the source of such debates. Though not exceptionally skilled at his profession, Dan had gained notoriety and most of his work through the many tales of his plucky endeavours, for this was a man who would never turn down a dare, especially with a decent pay out. With his mammoth muscular arms, broad pockmarked nose and his rosebud ears, Dan resembled a failed boxer still trying to win a fight. And competition was what he routinely pursued.

It had been a typical Saturday evening at the pub with Dan and his regular gang barking at one another across a table ladened with empty glasses. He seemed to be in a particularly conceited mood, so his associates decided to set him the ultimate test. He would fetch a pony for a pail purchased from Holden's Haunt, but this was to be no ordinary vessel. They wanted Mrs Holden's very own cleaning bucket, suds and all. The eager bidders placed their bets, all fuelled with the curiosity of discovering whether the rumours were true – that everything in the shop was for sale, even something the old bat might need for herself. Dan readily accepted the challenge, already dreaming away his winnings as he downed his eighth and final pint.

The following day, Dan arrived at Holden's Haunt shortly before lunch. He had slicked back his tresses and wore a fine tweed waistcoat with newly polished leather boots that squeaked as he walked. Forcing a wide false smile, he gave a sharp knock against the door before entering the threshold of Mrs Holden's abode, glancing around nonchalantly. His expression quickly changed as his eyes attempted to take in the mass of objects. While he had heard numerous stories about the contents within, he still found himself struck with awe at the sight of such a vast collection.

Mrs Holden glanced up briefly to take in the stranger before swiftly returning to her needlework without a sound. She knew by now not to bother with idle tourists, instantly recognisable by their body language and daft expressions. Dan was unperturbed; he was busy scanning the room for the cleaning bucket, but every pail he saw was bone dry. He walked around, peering behind furniture, opening cupboard doors and drawers. He even rummaged around the stinking chamber pots, but there did not seem to be a bucket anywhere.

Dan returned to the exterior of the shop and began shifting chains and nets and sticks and pots in his search, but there was nothing resembling a cleaning pail. He slipped back inside where the old woman was still sat in silence darning a sock little more than a scrap. Convinced she was unaware of his return, he took his chance to sneak through to the back room, finding a tiny kitchen fitted with an empty hearth. He then headed upstairs to a single room so dim and filthy that it looked like it had not been used in years. Save for a broken broom and a thick layer of dust, it was completely empty. With a heavy heart, Dan crept back downstairs, cringing as the final stair creaked. Mrs Holden smirked fainty, her fingers still working the thread.

"Broomstick's f'sale an' all," she called out, clearly aware of Dan's prowling but by no means concerned by it.

He, on the other hand, was becoming increasingly frustrated. How easy it had seemed only last night. He had boasted to the entire pub about how he would 'mop the floor' with his conquest, basking in the bawling laughter of his friends as they egged him on. He could almost taste the triumph, thick and hot on his tongue. Dan kept searching, watching Mrs Holden out of the corner of his eye until an idea crept into his head.

"That sock..." he began, pointing a stubby finger towards Mrs Holden's lap. As the thought became fully formed, Dan's finger extended further, his eyes bulging as his rising confidence sent blood surging through his body. He kept his hand steady and his gaze determined, locked on the old woman as she continued to darn. Like a fighter seeing his chance for victory, Dan's purpose had become clear. He needed that sock, for what could be a more fitting prize to take back to the pub than an object once worn by Mrs Holden? They could even hang it above the bar.

A lengthy moment passed before the old woman paused in her activity. She raised her eyes to the tip of the protracted finger, scowling at its presence as if it were a nuisance bluebottle. Dan felt a lump form in his throat – guilt or fear? He could not tell. He lowered his hand, reached into his pocket and produced several coins, which he released into a lopsided earthenware bowl balanced on a bedside cabinet. They both listened to the rattle of metal against clay. It sounded like an absurdly large amount for a dirty old rag. As they both waited for the din to settle, Mrs Holden sewed a final three stitches then rose to her feet. She shuffled towards a tatty wooden cabinet with two mismatched handles and inched out the bottom drawer, taking it to where Dan was standing. With a great heave of effort, she upturned the contents. Out they tumbled, thudding in a towering heap in front of Dan's shiny shoes; at least thirty threadbare socks, pungent with age and squalor. Mrs Holden retrieved the one she had been working on and tossed it onto the pile.

"There y'are. Tek y'pick," she called, walking back towards her chair.

Dan wrinkled his nose before tentatively plucking one from the assortment with a finger and thumb, tucking it into his recently emptied pocket before leaving in silence. Mrs Holden did not say a word of goodbye nor even look in his direction, though she did allow herself a private chuckle once he had departed. Back at the pub, the single sock did not earn Dan the reputation he had hoped for, but the dare had proved a long-contested point. The local folk now knew for certain that the old woman would be willing to sell everything she owned.

Rumours continued to flourish regarding Holden's Haunt, but what Dan thought he had discovered was not strictly true. These were not objects Mrs Holden could easily replace simply by ordering more as a regular shop might. Many of the items had belonged to her husband, his uncle or her parents. Some were purchases the couple had procured for their future: a crib, a rattle, knitted booties and a hat. They should have been hers to keep. Instead, Mrs Holden had little choice but to sell them, to say farewell not only to a wooden stool or a pewter bowl but to her history and hopes, to pieces of her soul. Even her wedding ring was now for sale. Seeing so many memories casually picked through, coarsely handled, waved about by someone offering a mere two bob, made her pulse quicken. She would rather they sit gathering mould and dust in her cramped house on the corner for the next decade than see them wasted on wonton characters like Dan Chelten and the countless others like him.

One item Mrs Holden was particularly fond of was a letter opener, eight inches long with a blade of silver-plated metal barely half an inch wide and a cutting edge like a razor. The bone handle was exquisitely carved and featured some form of a runic emblem in the centre, the provenance of which was unknown. It had quickly become the old woman's most treasured possession, though she had never had cause to use it for its intended purpose. Of all the many family heirlooms she had owned, this was the only one she would never part with – the recollections it evoked were too strong and too important.

She could still remember the precise day she had first laid eyes on it – Monday, June 20th, 1835. Concealed within a blanket on the kitchen table of her parents' home, it had been innocent curiosity that had nudged the young Mrs Holden into opening the folds of fabric to reveal the blade within. The letter opener had appeared on the same day as the new baby, and it was for this reason that she now clung to it so fiercely like some magical talisman. It had remained in her ownership ever since, providing the only way of ensuring her memories of that time would remain.

Mrs Holden, or Agnes Dartton as she was formerly known, had permitted the little boy to use the letter opener for his many games and adventures. She had revelled in watching young Benjamin charge around with the object held tightly in his chubby hands, grinning with glee as he galloped about the garden or their shared bedroom. It had been a trusty sword for a brave knight, the enchanted key to an unknown kingdom, and a medical tool for dissecting dead frogs. Each time Mrs Holden now pressed her fingertips to the emblem and traced the length of the blade along her palm, another joyful reminiscence surfaced and swam like a ghost released from purgatory.

The letter opener had been a secret between her and the boy throughout their childhoods, both managing to keep it hidden from their parents lest they think it an unsuitable toy. Later, Mrs Holden would conceal it from her husband, fearing that he might take a fancy to it himself or else sell it and squander the money at the pub. Now she did not have to worry about its theft, though she still preferred to keep it hidden while the shop was open. She could not imagine life without it, just as she could not live without the pictures in her mind of her darling Benjamin and his chirping laughter as he played.

Now that Mrs Holden was alone, she was able to stash the letter opener away close to her person and take it out each evening to indulge in her memories, having formed a long-standing and comforting ritual for doing so. She would wait for the sun to set and the street to empty of its daily crowd before pushing the door closed and setting the bolt. After finishing a light supper, she would let the embers settle in the fireplace and tentatively reach her slender fingers down along the cushion of her armchair to produce the prize. Sometimes she would sit for hours staring at and stroking its puzzling symbol, wondering what history it held, recalling the charm it had possessed for her and the little boy.

There was only one other person alive who had ever seen the letter opener and whom many considered to be Mrs Holden's only friend. His name was Tobias, but everyone called him Mr Michael.

Chapter Three

Living on the Shambles, with its boundless commotion and unceasing cacophony, Mrs Holden could not describe herself as lonely. Other than the few private moments with the letter opener, her days were fully occupied negotiating with patrons, silently scrutinising the activity on the street, and taking the occasional jaunt to the nearest market for supplies. The moments Mrs Holden found herself unaccompanied became increasingly rare, as it seemed everyone wanted to browse her collection searching for that one exceptional item to transform their lives. The only visitor who did not come in the hope of making a purchase was Mr Michael.

A carpenter by trade, Mr Michael spent most of his waking life in his shared workshop on Micklegate where he carved furniture for local businesses and private commissions, with the occasional requirement of conducting trade outside of the city every few months or so. Each day, he would leave work before dusk and arrive home just as night had settled in time for his supper. It was during the commute home that he would take the opportunity to watch the barges on the River Ouse making their final journeys, purchase a loaf from the bakery, or see Mrs Holden at her shop.

The old woman could always hear the arrival of her friend before she saw him. Reaching nearly six foot five inches tall, Mr Michael would accidentally announce himself by cracking his head on one or several hanging objects. As if to balance out his height, he possessed two abnormally elongated ears that dangled from his head, which was topped with a mound of sandy hair usually sprinkled with sawdust. As with Mrs Holden, it was his eyes that said more about his character than words ever could. The colour of chestnuts and just as lustrous, they were the first and last thing people remembered about him.

As he would visit directly from his workshop, Mr Michael frequently arrived at Holden's Haunt with something he had been working on to show his friend. Often it would be a prototype of a larger work, though he also enjoyed forging small decorative objects for pleasure. While the rest of her body had wilted like a plucked flower, Mrs Holden still possessed a fine eye and deft hands. She would work the objects across every fingertip, carefully considering her friend's handiwork before offering a candid critique. As the daughter of his former mentor, Mr Michael trusted her feedback implicitly as if it were the ghostly echo of Mr Dartton's own wise words.

Even now, years after the old man's passing and longer still since he had seen him, Mr Michael would feel a swell of pride in his chest whenever he heard the name Edmund Dartton uttered, always with great reverence. Perhaps there was something in the renewed friendship he had formed with Mrs Holden that had brought the spirit of the famed carpenter to life; could it be that he saw his mentor within her? Perhaps she too saw her father within Mr Michael? It was a comfort for both to remember his legacy through the pieces Mr Michael now created.

When the fateful day came that saw Mrs Holden's home become a business, the proffered carvings then became gifts and were added to the assemblage to await discovery. With or without his contributions, the whole throng of goods seemed to swell and shrink in immeasurable quantities every time Mr Michael visited. He had frequently wondered how his friend was able to support herself, and while the thought of her having to sell her possessions had initially caused him concern, he now felt proud that she had taken her financial matters into her own hands. It was such a simple thing, yet seeing his carvings alongside Mrs Holden's existing collection filled Mr Michael with gladness. From time to time he would even be present for a sale, the pair watching in awed silence as a proud father took away a toy soldier for his boy or a new mother selected a miniature pony for her baby's bedside. Neither could quite believe how much joy his wooden carvings could bring.

When Mr Michael was not there to witness first-hand the purchase of his creations, Mrs Holden never forgot to recall each transaction whenever her friend came by to visit. She was an excellent storyteller and would always go into intricate detail about the event, shrewdly tapping her nose whenever he asked how much she had made. Like most people, Mrs Holden thought it vulgar to discuss money, but it intrigued Mr Michael to know just how much his friend was making at the shop and how exactly she was recording each purchase. He had never seen any till nor leger in the room and could not believe that she relied on memory alone to keep track of trade, though perhaps it was possible. Over the years, Mr Michael had learned that his friend was full of surprises.

There was also the unspoken truth, the secret that lingered in the back of both Mrs Holden and Mr Michael's minds which neither would speak of. While others may not have considered Mr Michael's lot to be remarkably lucky, he himself had always been thankful for his wife, his daughter, his home and his career. They were his reasons for being, but Mrs Holden had not been so fortunate. So much loss, so little hope. In bringing her items to sell, Mr Michael felt that he was able to provide for his friend when no one else could. She would never have taken his money, so bestowing the carvings seemed the only alternative, a way to resolve his concern.

Mrs Holden of course knew exactly what Mr Michael was doing, but she would not turn away his objects. They both knew that she needed them and so long as they could each maintain their ignorance, she would have some security for her remaining years. She was not a rich woman and had already been pray to many forceful angry gentlemen brandishing illegible pieces of paper as they tried to cajole her into signing her property away. After all, it was positioned on one of the most lucrative streets in the entire city, thereby possessing an almost unique commercial opportunity, if only they were at its helm and not some barmy spinster.

Despite their threats and shouts, their fists and forked tongues, Mrs Holden had not succumbed. This was not just a shop. This was her livelihood, her security, the solid four walls within which she now kept every one of her most private and powerful memories. She would not leave it willingly.

As their time spent together increased and their friendship strengthened, Mrs Holden reached the point where she felt trusting enough of Mr Michael to be able to reveal to him her most precious possession, the letter opener. While she was reluctant to share its personal history, she had long wished to understand more about its past and what the symbol might represent. On being cautiously handed the object, Mr Michael studied it with great care, as intrigued and as clueless as his friend. He did not think its pattern to be anything other than decorative, though he did wonder as to whether it could have a Viking connection given the city's history.

Though he was by no means well-travelled, Mr Michael had had the opportunity to visit several neighbouring towns and villages for commissions over recent years. He could remember seeing similar runic designs carved into ancient stones by the roadside or on wooden beams on the exterior of buildings, each example weathered and worn, seeming to have been there for centuries. While the letter opener was indeed fascinating, the most interesting matter for Mr Michael was the extent to which Mrs Holden seemed attached to this one object, particularly when she had a shop full of far more unusual finds. There was a secret, he was sure, but the old woman would never divulge it to him, just as she would never give up the letter opener. It would likely have to be prised from her cold dead hands before it found itself a new owner.

Chapter Four

Much like young Agnes, Tobias Michael had always preferred a life of solitude. In his adolescence, he would frequently escape to the nearest cluster of woodland or find a secret hiding place down by the river where he could feel calm and content in his own company. He grew up in a crowded and competitive household with a mother and father, one set of grandparents, an aunt, and three older brothers, all boisterous louts who differed noticeably from Tobias in appearance and personality.

His siblings relished their daily dares, challenging one another to climb the highest, dive the deepest and fight the dirtiest, looking like triplets with their identical squat statures, muscular limbs and wide square jaws. Tobias in comparison was willowy and gaunt, even as a baby. He sensed from a young age that he looked and felt different from the other children and took solace in escaping his brethren.

Concerned for their youngest son's wellbeing, Mr and Mrs Michael sent eleven-year-old Tobias to a family friend who lived on the outskirts of the city just beyond the Bar Walls close to a narrow stretch of river with a cluster of trees behind. They had a daughter called Margaret who was a few years older than Tobias, with hair the colour of soot and dark oval eyes like a deer. Having had no siblings to play with, Margaret had developed a selfish attitude and a brutal tongue that her parents hoped to soften with an appropriate playmate before it led her to trouble.

Meek and well-mannered, Tobias seemed the ideal choice to tame the daughter and the pair were left to play together three or four times each week. Margaret had been quick to assert her authority from day one, with Tobias hastily learning that no amount of diplomacy or polite refusal could appease his new friend. His only choice was to comply with her wishes or else face a tirade of yelling and stomping, so he begrudgingly joined in with her favourite pastimes: tag, catch, and hopscotch. The girl had an enviable collection of skittles, marbles, a board game and some picture books, but Tobias was forbidden from touching them.

One game Margaret especially enjoyed was that of spying on the next-door neighbours. They also had an only child around the same age, but instead of forming a sisterlike friendship with Margaret, the girl had apparently shunned her attentions in favour of solo adventures by the river. Still pained by this rebuff, Margaret would drag Tobias to various vantage points and whisper cruel comments about the girl in his ear as they observed from afar. Tobias held no interest in girls nor in bullying and was thankful to find somewhere else to direct his attention. From one of Margaret's favoured positions, he could see into the workshop of the carpenter next door. While Margaret gossiped about the girl, Tobias would gaze in amazement as the man carved, sanded and polished a lump of wood into a beautiful object. On realising he was being watched, the neighbour kindly invited Tobias to take a closer look, and soon enough he was being taught the trade on a regular basis, his games with Margaret long forgotten despite her numerous protests.

After completing his house chores, Tobias would race as fast as his bandy legs could carry him to the workshop. He would put on an old apron – adult size, though it still only reached mid-thigh on Tobias – and carefully position himself next to the older gentleman, whose name was Mr Dartton. The boy was fascinated by the tools, techniques and materials, watching intently as his mentor guided him through each process. Eventually, Tobias was encouraged to have a go himself, and soon enough he was able to work as a proper apprentice helping to finish various items of furniture under the old man's observant eye.

Sometimes Mr Dartton's daughter would come to watch them both through a narrow gap in the door, silent as a mouse but always softly smiling. Though the two children were never introduced, Tobias learned that her name was Agnes and that she was far from the evil creature Margaret had made her out to be during their spying games. Agnes did not look like she would hurt a fly. He never once heard her speak, though she often hummed a playful tune before scurrying barefoot back out into the garden, disappearing into the trees that led to the water.

A year later and with the help of his mentor, Mr Michael was able to secure an official apprenticeship position with a carpenter on Micklegate, his childhood spent as fast as the flick of a coin as he found himself a working man. Despite the long hours, Tobias would occasionally have opportunity to visit Mr Dartton with samples of his work and the odd small carving as a gift. The Darttons now had a little boy in addition to Agnes, so he would whittle the siblings matching toys: knights on horseback, princesses in fine dresses, fairy-tale monsters and majestic beasts.

Mr Michael noticed that the pair liked playing with the animal figurines the most, so he began to make them a collection of woodland creatures, taking pleasure in finding images in old newspapers, borrowed books and even on advertisements to use as inspiration. As his workload increased, however, Tobias – now known as Mr Michael – had to cease both his models and his visits to the Dartton family. Soon enough, he and Agnes were strangers once more.

It was during the second year of his apprenticeship when Mr Michael first met Winifred Alice Bow. Her parents owned one of the pubs further down the road, and he was often taken underarm by his employer and dragged along for a swift half following a hard day's graft in the workshop. Wincing as he sipped at yet another foamy pint, Mr Michael watched the young girl behind the bar mopping away the sodden surface with the skill of someone twice her age. It did not take long before the pair were introduced and soon enough Mr Michael understood what all the raised eyebrows and low whistles of his workmates had been about. He was in love.

Though he was by no means a wealthy man, Mr Michael was at least skilled in a craft and fairly certain of a prolonged career within the trade. Both his employer and his clients were always in praise of his work and he was equally willing to put in the extra time and effort to please them. The coins mounted, diligently saved for the day when he would be able to buy a small ring and propose properly to Winifred in the grounds of the ruined abbey where they had shared their first kiss.

Another year on and Mr Michael was offered the opportunity of a lifetime; the chance to be an independent carpenter in his own right, working alongside the men who had helped him to develop his skills on Micklegate. He quickly grew into a well-established businessman with a reputation as one of York's finest carpenters. Folk would often comment on his ability to source, repair and make almost any wooden household item from scratch, with his dining tables and chairs becoming the most coveted for their prettiness as well as their practicality. It was one such grateful customer who gifted Mr Michael with something much more valuable than money. He paid for his new piece of furniture with a solid gold ring.

It had been a gloriously sunny day in the early spring of 1840, the sky an almost unnatural shade of blue as the usual dank fog had miraculously lifted. As if anticipating the unseasonal weather, Winifred was wearing a blue dress, matching the shade of her eyes. Her cheeks were flushed with exhilaration and Mr Michael too seemed to bounce as they walked. He produced the ring that he had so proudly worked for and did the honourable deed as onlookers whooped and clapped. Winifred, giggling into a gloved hand, accepted his proposal without hesitation. Three weeks later, they were married.

With his remaining earnings and the inheritance he had reserved for many years, Mr Michael procured a small terraced property between the streets of Walmgate and Fossgate, a short walk from the city centre and within easy reach of his workshop. For a young man with barely any education and having lost his parents and brothers when he was sixteen, Mr Michael was proud of his purchase, especially when he carried his bride over the threshold. It was dark and damp and permanently filled with dust, but it was theirs and theirs alone – a house where the newlyweds could raise a family and live in modest comfort, grateful and content with their lot.

Though their union was a happy one, Winifred suffered greatly as a married woman. For as long as she could remember, she had aspired to be a dutiful mother with a bustling brood beneath her feet, tending a stove and keeping a respectable house. Fate, however, had had other plans; over the course of eight years, she gave birth to six children, all male and each dead within days of delivery. They had been sickly and weak, emerging with a strange greenish hue to their skin and their eyes fixed shut, struck with an undiagnosed condition in the womb that no doctor seemed able to name nor cure.

Despite her growing anxiety and bodily discomfort, Winifred persevered with the tender nurture of each child before they died in their sleep, the turquoise tinge becoming black and blue bruises, their eyes having never opened. None of the brothers lived long enough to see another of their siblings born, and so close were their deaths that only a single gravestone was needed to mark their demise.

The young woman withered with every pregnancy, birth and death, her body becoming a bowing bony husk that tottered rather than walked, her hands constantly shaking and her forehead permanently damp. More than this, it was her eyes and her heart that had begun sinking like a ship run aground, fading to faint shadows. When Mr Michael met her gaze and tried to hold her hands steady, he could only see emptiness in her weary eyes, a never-ending grief with no solace or hope. Her fingers became so thin that the gold ring would not stay on. It sat by her bedside as she slept, day after night after day. In his own sad state, Mr Michael retreated to the familiarity of his workshop until man and wife were barely speaking.

By some small miracle, there came one last chance at happiness. Despite reaching the age of thirty-six and long having given up on the hope of children, Winifred discovered that remarkably she was once again pregnant. Nine months later in the autumn of 1859, she gave birth to a perfectly healthy blonde-haired baby girl, her blue eyes the same shade as her mother's while the infant's ears protruded outwards just like her father's. Overwhelmed by their luck and joy, the couple named the baby Irene after Mr Michael's mother, the girl marking a new beginning for a family that had very nearly lost faith in life and love.

Renewed by her changed status, Winifred ignored her tender state and threw herself into the duties of motherhood. She wanted her daughter to be everything that a good little girl should be; not only courteous and helpful but independent and bright too. She would show her how to darn socks and knit blankets, pluck chickens and bone fish, make pastry and remove stains, walk gracefully and say 'how do you do'. Irene was loved but she was also expected to fill the immeasurable empty void that had been left by her brothers.

Mr Michael doted on his daughter. While he lacked the luxury of time to spend with her, he made sure that the evenings and rare days off he did have free were taken in her company. As Irene grew older and proved herself to be mature and capable beyond her years, Mr Michael was confident enough to bring her along with him on the jaunts he occasionally made out of the city for commissions and deliveries further afield. Irene was never happier than when she was in her father's shadow and would delight in the thrill of boarding a borrowed trap to accompany her father on his adventures, far removed from the bustle, noise and smoke of York.

After one such excursion in the early autumn of 1864, Irene returned full of wonder and inspiration, eagerly recalling to her mother the tale of the cook she had witnessed preparing a most marvellous pie. Charmed by her daughter's enthusiasm, Winifred aided the youngster in creating their own variant of what later became a much-loved family recipe. The three dined that evening in peaceful contentment, having second and third servings of pie before heaving their weary feet and bulging bellies beside the fire where they rested until bedtime.

During that night, Winifred was awoken by agonising

pains. She tried to race down the stairs in time to reach the privy, but ended up tripping and tumbling down, landing awkwardly and in even greater anguish at the bottom. Mr Michael awoke at the noise and hurried to reach his wife, who was crying and shuddering on the floor in what seemed to be a pool of water. Mr Michael was at first confused by the arrangement but the odour told him all he needed to know. It tugged at a distant memory he had thought, had hoped, was long gone. Winifred had miscarried again.

The birth was so early that there was nothing to bury. Mr Michael cleaned his wife, dressed her, and carried her to the bedroom upstairs. He held her as she wept through the dark hours and through to the dawn of the following day. Eventually she fell asleep, pale and still trembling, just as Irene had begun preparing breakfast downstairs. Mr Michael could hear the dull clatter of pots as she set water to heat and eggs to fry, but there would only be two diners that day. He did not know how to explain what had happened to his daughter, so he chose not to say anything.

Winifred remained in bed day after day, usually sleeping, though sometimes she simply kept her eyes closed as if she did not want to remind herself of the reality of living. On learning of her mother's unnamed illness, Irene went to her bedside and did everything she could think of to help. She sang, brought flowers, made sweet coffee and fresh bread; she even baked the pie, though it did not taste the way it had when the three of them had shared it together. Mr Michael continued with the only routine he knew, keeping his hands active in his workshop while his mind rolled over the same thought. His wife and his future hung by a single thread.

By the time Irene reached the age of eight and began attending Fishergate School, Winifred had not moved from her bed in nearly three years. Her body had reduced to a pallid husk, her hair falling out in wiry strands as the dark rims under her eyes blackened and sagged. She barely spoke and only then with a basic request for a glass of water or the chamber pot. She seemed to hold no interest in her daughter or husband, usually falling asleep at their words if she were not already in slumber.

Irene took on the daily chores with a neighbour occasionally popping over to help her with the tasks she had not yet mastered. The girl was a quick learner and eventually the woman stopped visiting, leaving Irene to run the household. Mr Michael meanwhile worked harder than ever at the workshop in the hope that more money would provide further opportunities and freedoms for his daughter and wife. Extra clothing and bedding, better food to help them grow strong and healthy, and funds for medicine to help Winifred's state, even though the family physician, Doctor Pruce, had warned that there might not be a cure.

In the face of little hope, Mr Michael resolved to remain positive. After everything his family had been through, he was never once regretful of his situation. On the contrary, he considered himself the luckiest man in the world to have Winifred and Irene. It was a happiness he only wished Mrs Holden could have known.

Chapter Five

Even though Mr Michael and Mrs Holden lived only a short walk away from one another, their paths as young adults never seemed to cross. They had their families and homes to focus on and rarely had the time to reflect on their pasts, though there was the odd memory that still managed to resurface and raise a smile. The days when a customer would purchase one of the very first carved animals ever given to Mrs Holden, or the clement summer evenings when Mr Michael would make use of the extended daylight hours to recreate the squirrel that Agnes Dartton had adored. Only then would they each remember the final day of his apprenticeship and wonder how nearly thirty years had gone by.

When the two former friends finally did meet, it was as if a lifetime had passed; indeed, they were not the same people they had been before. It was entirely by chance that Mr Michael overheard a conversation outside his front door one morning on his way to his workshop. A neighbour was commenting to another across the cobbled street about the 'Holden death'. He had known his friend's married name for some time, but this was the first he had heard it uttered aloud. Most treated the knowledge of the latest deceased as some source of competition, but for Mr Michael on this occasion, it served to send cool shivers along his limbs.

Though he rarely spoke to his neighbours, Mr

Michael was curious enough to enquire directly to the two women for details. With solemn faces they took turns to inform him that the Holden family residing on that there Shambles had been struck a most devastating blow; the loss of their first and only child, who would be commemorated and buried at Holy Trinity Church the following week. Mr Michael's face fell, his whole body suddenly filled with a most unexpected grief. Though he had barely known Agnes and was now a stranger to the married Mrs Holden, he was surprised to realise that he still cared deeply for the Dartton family and, if questioned, would not have hesitated to have called Mrs Holden a friend.

As he continued along the street with the neighbours still prattling on behind him, Mr Michael could not help but recall his own personal situation and the dull sickening ache he had experienced at the deaths of his own dear children. Their tiny faces and curling hands had been etched in his memory like carvings on wood, handmade and unique. His heart stung like a fresh wound for his loss and for the pain he knew Mrs Holden would be going through.

They may not have known one another, but Mr Michael still felt the urge to help his former acquaintance. It was therefore a most fortunate coincidence that the bereaved parents were looking for an experienced carpenter and had been given the recommendation of one particularly talented workman who lived close by. When approached by Mr Holden regarding the commission of the stillborn child's wooden coffin, Mr Michael did not hesitate to accept. He postponed all his other commitments and began toiling intensively in his workshop to create the tiny box that would be the final resting place of Mrs Holden's infant. Mr Michael later learned that a doctor had informed the family of Mrs Holden's now delicate state, advising them that she would not be able to conceive again. His former friend would never experience the joy that he and Winifred had known when they were blessed with Irene.

As he worked, Mr Michael attempted to recall what Mrs Holden had looked like all those years ago. It struck him as strange that despite the many times she had stood watching him work, he could not remember her height, build, or even whether she was pretty. His impression instead was of a confident and carefree young woman in loose floral dresses and bare feet, even in winter, with a bashful smile and long fingers that curled around the workshop door. And the eyes, he remembered, were an unusual shade of grey, like polished pewter or a well-thumbed silver coin.

Once complete, Mr Michael delivered the coffin himself. It was exquisite work, its edges carved with ornate flowers and birds that had taken hours of concentration. When Mr Holden received the finished piece, he looked overwhelmed and at a loss for words. He simply turned the creation over and over, staring at every detail. He muttered a thank you before cradling the box in his arms and walking back through into the house, leaving Mr Michael waiting by the open door. There were muted whispers from inside followed by a sharp sobbing hastily hidden.

Mr Holden returned, his face pale and eyes swollen,

and handed over a cluster of coins, more than the amount they had agreed, but he was insistent. Mr Michael wished the family well and turned to make his leave, but as he did so, he glimpsed past Mr Holden's shoulder and caught sight of another figure standing in a doorway. A woman, her round face partially concealed by the long fingers of one hand over her mouth. The dress she wore had once been decorative but now looked thin and worn, stretched taut across her broad shoulders and sagging at the neck. Mr Michael caught her gaze, her eyes rimmed with red but identical to the ones he could remember from his childhood, like pebbles coated with dew. He knew then that he had finally come face to face with Mrs Holden.

As he left the couple to their grief, Mr Michael tried to think of another way in which he could acquaint himself with Mrs Holden. He did not want to intrude on her privacy after such a terrible ordeal, and in the end the idea that they might become friends again faded into a fantasy. It would be a further ten years before he would meet Mrs Holden again and, with the cruelty of fate, it would be caused by another family tragedy; this time, the death of Mr Holden himself.

The story was in all the newspapers, across every billboard, and on the lips of each inhabitant in the city within a day of its occurrence. Seven workmen had been killed and another ten injured by the partial collapse of a new bridge that was being built just beyond the railway station. Mr Holden was one of the masons helping to complete the ambitious project and had been crushed under the rubble along with several co-workers, though he was considered one of the luckier men. He had been taken to hospital where he passed away, the exact cause of death unclear.

Once again, Mr Michael had been struck with intense emotion on hearing the news and decided he could not pass up the chance to express his condolences to Mrs Holden. As the door opened, Mr Michael was taken aback by the stranger stood before him. He stared at the unfamiliar figure before realising with great sadness the cruel and unforgiving impact of grief and the dramatic effect it had had on his friend. Mrs Holden was now squat and round like a contorted turnip, covered with layers of mouldy rags, her face crumpled, her hair a matted mass. Yet despite her aged appearance, there was one feature that remained; her eyes, clear and almost twinkling, brimming not only with sadness but also, Mr Michael believed, with hope.

He had decided to bring with him one of his recently completed wooden figures, a small bird with its wings outstretched, each delicately carved as if fluttering in flight. He thought perhaps it could serve as a symbol for Mrs Holden's lost loved ones, something she could keep and remember them by. Though quiet and reserved, Mrs Holden welcomed Mr Michael into her home, muttering a timid thank you for the gift as she tucked it safely inside her pinafore pocket. She made a pot of strong tea and brought out a small dish of walnuts, her favourite, setting them down on a waist-high stack of folded textiles. Mr Michael was surprised to see the surroundings in such seeming disarray, with furniture, ornaments and random objects piled up on every surface, some gleaming with polish while others were thick with dust.

From the assortment, Mrs Holden produced a mahogany chair with a green cushioned seat and placed it opposite her own armchair for her guest. Settling into the somewhat surreal situation, they sipped tea and commented on the quality of the nuts before Mr Michael told his friend all about his daughter and her famous pie. Realising his mistake only too late, Mr Michael attempted to divert the conversation onto the weather and the likelihood of the river flooding again, but Mrs Holden did not seem upset. If anything, there was a flush to her face that softened the wrinkles. He continued with his stories of Irene.

While it took some time for them to feel comfortable speaking with one another, after many visits the pair began to share more and more tales about the separate paths they had taken. They began to meet regularly at Mrs Holden's home where the chair became fixed in its position and where there would always be a fresh pot of tea and some tempting treats waiting. Mr Michael would bring figurines or examples of his work to show her and some leftovers to sample of Irene's cooking. They spoke most often of the seasons and of the Shambles, of good food and high prices, and the ever-changing landscape of the city. These were idle observations of everyday life, trivial small talk without purpose or emotion, but it was precisely the form of conversation they both needed and appreciated.

When Mrs Holden came to tell the tale of Lanky Luke, it began an unexpected chapter in not only her life but also in her friendship with Mr Michael. They were now both business owners, creating names for themselves despite the fierce competition. While one made objects, the other sold them, and no matter how rich or poor folk were, they could always find a bob or two to spare for the finest handmade wooden dressing table or the dirtiest second-hand chamber pot. They may have been few with their words, but Mr Michael and Mrs Holden both knew the language of commerce, and with it their bond grew stronger.

Chapter Six

Following four months of successful trading, Mrs Holden commissioned Mr Michael to make a wooden sign for the shop. He set to work immediately, selecting a strong oak board which he stained with a dark water-resistant lacquer before carefully etching the words 'Holden's Haunt' in gold paint across the front. Mrs Holden eyed it carefully before giving a curt nod of approval. He managed to remove a ladder from the assemblage of oddments outside the shop and hung the sign above the entrance, one of many that ran the length of the street. This newest addition looked by far the most appealing, thought Mr Michael, with its surface shining even in this dimmest part of the city, as if it were providing a beacon for passers-by. Almost bouncing with enthusiasm, he coaxed his friend out of the confides of her gloomy room to admire his handiwork.

As soon as Mrs Holden stepped over the threshold, an almighty squawk caused the entire street to come to a rare and momentary standstill. Shoppers and residents crouched in terror, clinging their purchases or infants against their chests, shielding them from the unknown. Mrs Holden remained perfectly still, her eyes fixed above where an enormous crow had perched atop the newly hung sign. It was so perfect in shape and so dark in colour, it was as if it too had been carved from wood.

Its slender black plumage gleamed like polished coal, its talons curving around the etched wood while its beak clicked as if in communication. While the street returned to its business, Mrs Holden listened. She seemed to understand it.

"Come now," she nodded, a small lopsided smile appearing as she turned to head back into the shop. The bird obediently followed, flapping its way to the top of the bookcase in the far corner of the room, and there it stayed.

The crow became as notorious as Mrs Holden thanks to its unnerving stare and the distinctive chip at the end of its beak. It would watch customers in silent accusation as they perused, snapping its mouth open and shut with great ferocity if it suspected any unsavoury activity. More often than not, the visitor would hurriedly pay for their item before fleeing the scene, the bird casually returning to preening its feathers once the threat had dissipated. Mrs Holden would watch the creature fondly, remembering how in her younger years she had once saved a hatchling crow that had fallen from its nest.

It was not unusual for birds to scavenge along the Shambles when there were so many easy pickings, but this specimen did not come to be fed. Every day, Mrs Holden attempted to persuade it with bits of dry bread, meat fat and apple cores, which it would fly down to inspect, pick at, then revert to its perch. It seemed simply to enjoy the old woman's company and the calming solitude, along with the novelty of watching each newcomer as they searched the shop for buried treasure. It did not take long before the crow became yet another excuse for more curious bounty hunters to venture in and explore Holden's Haunt.

On the odd occasion, particularly if the weather was fine and the smog had lifted a little, the crow would go outside to spend a few hours flying in the rare air. As the sun began to fall, it would find its home once more and take a convenient rooftop perch from where it could watch the final comings and goings of the day along the street. It had been known to swoop down with a sharp shriek to protest some unsuspecting cat, pigeon or child that had crept too closely to the old woman's wares outside the shop, serving to strengthen the growing suspicions of the local residents.

There were still those who believed in black magic and suspected the existence of witches in the city; they were among the first to suggest that the bird had been enchanted in order to protect Mrs Holden against thieves and tricksters. Others argued that the crow was the old woman's familiar, committing evil deeds on her behalf. Some saw the bird as a symbol of death, haunting the old woman in her deteriorating health, and a few claimed it to be a sign of prophecy used to predict the future. Tall tales quickly became engrossing legends across every street corner, shop counter and dinner table. Indeed, Mrs Holden and the bird even looked alike, the same unflinching stare, the crooked smile, the blackened tattered coverings, so much so that 'the crow' quickly became used as a nickname for both of them.

For Mrs Holden, there was no mystery. Her new

guest was simply a visual pleasantry as one might keep flowers in a jar or a pebble from the beach. She had always loved wildlife and birds in particular. They had offered her companionship throughout her childhood, a beating heart to remind her of her own. When little Benjamin grew old enough to walk and talk, they had spent hours exploring the woodlands that surrounded the family home. They loved to listen to the morning chorus high in the trees above them, to feel the damp dew beneath their bare toes, to watch the scurrying beetles, wriggling worms and silken fish journeying through life, oblivious and free. When the charming crow with its damaged beak had flown in through her open door, she had welcomed it gladly.

Ten years later, it felt as if the bird had always been with her. Perhaps in a way it always had. As Mrs Holden allowed the memories of her youthful adventures to grow ever more vivid, the crow continued to attract more and more visitors to the shop. The neighbourhood children began daring one another to enter, taking turns to creep through the door and throw vegetable peelings or scraps from the gutter in the hope of watching the bird feed or fly. Mrs Holden quickly grew weary of their games. She was eventually forced to intervene by clanging a huge metal spoon against an even larger soup tureen, which let out the most appalling sound and sent the children scattering with fright. They never returned, except one.

The only child permitted to enter Holden's Haunt was Mr Michael's daughter, Irene. She was ten years old when she first met Mrs Holden and it was at her own request. She had prepared one of her famous pies using some choice cuts of beef her father had bought earlier that day. As it was cooking in the oven, she decided that she would take the very first slice and meet her father at the shop where she knew he would be visiting after work. Little Irene stood with the cooled dish in her hands on the furthest end of the Shambles, waiting for the bob of his head. Mr Michael had been surprised to see her standing there amid the commotion of the street, but he had always known this day would come. Like him, his daughter was curious in spirit and good-natured in heart, with the generous slab of pie before her as evidence. It would be the first of many visits, with Irene's joyful smile and happy chatter bringing some much-needed vitality to Mrs Holden's life.

The old woman needed no introduction as the child was the spitting image of her father. Willowy and strong with long limbs, Irene's distinctive ears were hidden by lank soft curls the colour of hay, her blue eyes always wide and gleaming as if constantly searching for something new. Mrs Holden quickly became fond of her, though she found it difficult to express as much. Instead, she would look toward the fading light of the windows and listen to Irene's stories, often taking up needlework as the tales unfolded. Irene barely noticed Mrs Holden's seeming indifference; she was far more interested in the crow and the travels she imagined he had taken. Like the old woman, she too possessed a great interest in the natural world and the many curiosities it contained.

During one visit, Irene took with her an oyster shell

filled with seeds, nuts and berries she had collected from a favourite spot down by the river. It was a gift for Mrs Holden and the crow to share, she said, carefully balancing the offering between both palms. The old woman muttered her thanks but was secretly pleased to have been brought bounty from the outside world, a place that now only existed in her distant memory. Though neither she nor the crow ate the contents, it was a welcome reminder of her former life, a time when she would source the same treats herself to scatter around the garden or across the surface of the river. There she would sit with Benjamin, both mesmerised by the birds plucking from above and the fish gawping from below.

While Mrs Holden and Irene were enamoured by the crow, Mr Michael did not feel at all comfortable in its watchful presence. He had heard the rumours regarding the bird and its mistress, fanciful stories growing ever more macabre, muttered musings of dark forces and evil shapeshifting creatures. He did not believe in fairy tales but was still unnerved by such suggestions and in particular the use of the word 'witch'. The subject of religion had never entered his conversations with Mrs Holden, though he had often wondered why she never attended church nor even visited the graves of her loved ones. Mr Michael tried to cast such queries from his mind and ignore the spiteful remarks, but it did not prevent the crow from appearing in his dreams, pecking at his shoulder, his neck, his face, before finally finding his eyes.

While the residents of York may not have been particularly devout, the majority remained proud traditionalists with an unquestionable commitment to the age-old doctrines of the Christian faith. Those who lived on the Shambles and in the surrounding areas attended the church of Holy Trinity, or Christ Church as it was also known, which seemed to have existed since the dawn of time. As the rest of the city swelled with industry, innovation and population growth, the squat grey parish found itself under chisel and hammer once more and was almost entirely rebuilt in 1861. The congregation were divided between those who had lived through its transformation and those who only knew of its modern incarnation, but all were one and the same under the eyes of God. They each recited their vows of holy matrimony beneath the silhouetted shape of its wooden cross, christened their children at the ancient font, before finally finding themselves inside a wooden box as woeful wails echoed around the stone walls.

The church represented the circle of life from cradle to grave, a daily reminder of the virtues of faith and the importance of a wholesome existence. Week after week, the pews would fill with parishioners under the watchful gaze of the vicar, the same set of faces raised in reverence. The Sunday bells would chime and Mrs Holden would listen through the tiny tarnished windows of her shop, never moving a muscle from her armchair, the inclination for worship now entirely absent. She was of course conspicuous by her absence, but eventually most of her neighbours came to forgive and forget the old woman of her sins. Many had watched from afar as she had become fragile and infirm following the death of her husband, their prayers occasionally filled with her name. For a few others, however, they surmised she was past repentance and were glad she had chosen to exclude herself from their worship. The audacity, they cried; if only they could stay at home on the Lord's Day and not have to make a wasted donation to someone else's pocket!

The neighbours would never know the number of times Mrs Holden had wished herself a disciple of God. She would sit every Sunday and allow the sound of the bells to absorb her, images moving through her mind as she imagined the joyful families attending the service in their finery. Wives holding hands with their husbands, their adorable children running on ahead as the whole neighbourhood became one welcoming congregation united to give thanks to the Lord for love and life. What did she have to be thankful for, she would remind herself, wiping the stains from her cheeks. Would she ever find it in her heart to forgive Him for taking her little boy away? Could she ever forgive herself?

In her youth, Mrs Holden had loved to teach Benjamin songs, including one that she had learned from her mother as a baby. It was based on a Bible story about two men who had made their homes on different types of land, her mother holding her tiny hands as they mimed the motions. As she retold the tale, the little boy would sit attentively on her knee and rock merrily along to the melody. She would hum the tune before beginning the words and they would take turns to slap their hands on top of one another's as if forming their own abode. Up and up they would climb, the houses stretching ever higher until they could no longer strain their arms. His laughter had been like poetry to her ears.

Chapter Seven

It happened in the September of 1872. As the subtle heat of the summer began to ease, the residents wrapped extra layers around their limbs and their fires burned a little longer each day, their appetites beginning to crave the satisfying stodge of root vegetables, hearty meats and dense breads that would soon stock the shelves. Winter was coming, they all knew. All except Mrs Holden. It had been weeks since she had ventured outside, instead relying on what little scraps she had accumulated over the summer to keep her fed and warm. She could not leave for fear that it would happen again. Someone was stealing from her, and not just one or two odd items. Day after day, she had begun to sense the growing loss. While she could not always place her finger on what precisely had been taken, she was still consumed with a persistent feeling of unease and suspicion. Her gut instincts were rarely unfounded.

At first, the missing goods were barely noticeable. Trinkets that had long been hidden in the grand mass of curios, ornaments that left little space when removed, and other possessions that were of so small a value that barely any visitor had even regarded their presence. Objects that had once been combined in multiples were taken one by one, the difference between a couple or a handful being almost indistinguishable. There were also several missing wares that had once been displayed on the walls outside the property, long obscured under the weight of other similarly forgotten features. The disappearances were so incremental that customers, neighbours and passers-by noticed nothing, but Mr Michael had.

With each return visit to Holden's Haunt, he pondered over the whereabouts of the many items that had so often caught his eye during his visits. The squat ceramic jug with the daisies painted on its handle, the worn photo frame made from thickly varnished oak, the ostrich feathers that had once snaked through the hanging chains by the door, the length of fake pearls that would have reached to the floor if worn around a woman's neck. If these had all been recent purchases, then the shop was doing better than he or even Mrs Holden could have hoped, with such a varied assortment finding new homes within such a short space of time. Though Mr Michael hoped for the best, there was an increasing concern causing a dull ache in the pit of his stomach. Something was wrong, but all he could do was wait for the truth to reveal itself.

Whenever he asked Mrs Holden about her recent customers, she would furrow her brow and squint at the ceiling in careful consideration. There was the chap she remembered with an unusually large moustache that looked peculiar, the strands thick and dry. Then there was the man of similar height and build who looked almost identical were it not for his round glasses and daintily patterned waistcoat. She could recall a third gentleman who had visited wearing a thick leather cloak and who had walked as if his shoes were too big for his feet. Mrs Holden could not recollect what they had each bought, but why should she? So long as they had purchased their items for a good price, she had no need to dwell on their motives. Mr Michael was not quite so sure.

One week later, Mrs Holden closed the door of her shop earlier than usual so that she and Mr Michael could be alone. She swore him to secrecy before carefully fishing a hand under her chair to produce a rusted tin. Just as he had always suspected, there was no till or any form of written account of each purchase, merely Mrs Holden's memory and this, an old metal box that looked to have once contained tea or flour. She gave it a hearty shake, the contents jangling loudly in proof of her stories regarding the unusual-looking men and their unknown purchases. For Mrs Holden, a sale was a sale. The sound of the tin was all the confirmation she needed that everything was as it should be. Mr Michael kept his suspicions to himself.

While he still had his reservations about the recent purchases, Mr Michael chose not to question his friend any further about her business transactions. It was none of his concern of course, and she had already proven herself quite capable of maintaining her enterprise independently. Nevertheless, Mrs Holden seemed insistent on proving her success and began to report every further sale with as much detail as she could remember. There had been nothing out of the ordinary, she reassured him, shaking the tin as evidence. Yet Mr Michael did not like what he heard, both his friend's recollections and the sound of the metal din, identical to the time before and the time before that. Either she was spending the money as soon as it had been earned or she was not receiving any at all. Whichever scenario was the truth, Mr Michael was helpless to do anything about it.

Day after day, more and more items vanished from view, and this time several were immediately noticeable, including the wooden chair Mr Michael would usually take up. He returned to visit Mrs Holden as often as possible, continuously checking for the missing items and occasionally trying to draw his friend into a conversation about their whereabouts, though without response. Instead, he waited patiently for the opportunity to employ a little more cunning. It took two weeks before the distraction came in the form of a particularly haughty and awkward new customer who required Mrs Holden's personal assistance. She rose reluctantly from her chair to attend to the enquiry, leaning on the front door frame to look out at the man as he searched through the jumble of items hanging up outside.

As the customer spoke, Mrs Holden kept shaking her head. This purchase would take some time, Mr Michael realised – it was now or never. Swiftly and silently, he stole behind the weathered old armchair in the far corner of the room and retrieved the tin container, prising off the rusted lid as noiselessly as he could manage. Peering inside, he had to suppress an audible gasp. It contained several disks of pressed metal and that was all; there was no money or coins of any kind. Just rubbish, mere scraps. This was no form of payment. This was robbery.

Mr Michael suspected that his friend had known all along that the tin was empty, but what he needed to know was why.

On his following visit, the question spilled from Mr Michael's mouth before he could prevent himself; why had she not told him about the stolen objects? He did not mention the tin for fear of upsetting his friend further, though Mrs Holden knew full well he had already discovered it was empty. After returning indoors with a profitable sale, she had carefully removed the tin to add her latest earnings and knew instantly that the lid had been tampered with. As for the missing possessions, she had nothing to say in the way of an explanation. She shrugged and turned her head away as if looking out of the window. Mr Michael followed the direction of her gaze only to notice that the two panes were now entirely obscured by grime. A darkness was beginning to envelop Holden's Haunt in every sense. He had no alternative but to go to the police.

After speaking with the officer at the front desk of the police station, Mr Michael was ushered into a small room by Inspector Falmer. While still relatively new to his senior position, the inspector was already well known across the city. Unlike his forebears, he appeared committed to patrolling the streets by day and often long into the night flanked by his favoured officers, though how many criminals they actually caught was still hotly debated. He was instantly recognisable and seemed to like it that way, taking great pride in his pristine uniform, perfectly pert helmet and coiffured moustache, which would always twitch in various directions as he spoke.

Mr Michael was quite distracted by its activity as he tried to listen to the inspector's decision regarding Mrs Holden's predicament.

The inspector had promised to accompany Mr Michael to the property the following day, where a reluctant Mrs Holden eventually allowed two officers to examine the property for evidence. An hour later, the inspector brought an end to the search as his officers had still found no clues nor explanations among the remaining possessions. Mr Michael hovered in the corridor listening in as Mrs Holden was then questioned by the inspector himself, but she had been unable to recall any unusual occurrences worthy of notice. The officers left to take their enquiries to the street, asking the old woman's neighbours as well as several of the regulars at the Eagle and Child Inn on the corner if they had noticed anything suspicious. Not a single soul seemed able to provide any information.

It was not in Mrs Holden's nature to accept defeat. If the cruelty of her past had taught her anything, it was to instil a sense of resourcefulness in times of need. When Mr Michael next visited a few days later, he found his friend attempting to drag what little remained outside of the shop into her front room along with the few items she had stashed elsewhere in the house and the backyard in the hope that they might make a sale, however small. A few neighbours had brought unwanted items to add to the declining collection, and Mr Michael had managed to hastily carve a few more figurines in contribution.

Holden's Haunt was far from its former glory but its owner remained adamant that she would keep the business going. She stayed in her armchair day and night with the crow perched beside her, both refusing to leave what remained of the last few possessions. Mr Michael and Irene provided what little food and fuel they could spare and assisted with keeping the fire going and preparing simple meals. They both noticed that the rusted tin remained, faithfully wedged under the chair despite its lack of contents. Nevertheless, Mrs Holden was hopeful that it would one day soon come in useful. After all, the police were continuing to review the case and may perhaps be successful in locating the missing objects. Mr Michael and Irene nodded enthusiastically, though in their hearts they were losing hope.

As soon as she awoke and before she slept, Mrs Holden would touch each of the objects she still had left in turn, running her fingers up and down, back and forth, as if committing their shapes and textures to memory. She would test their weight in the cup of her hand. She would bring things to her ears and mouth, sensing their sound or temperature. She grew to know every remaining belonging intimately, readying herself for their departure. Despite her optimistic words to her friends, she knew the last of the shop's contents would not be hers for much longer. Someone somewhere had a plan, and so far it had worked. She was losing her livelihood, and very soon she was sure she would lose something much more valuable – her life.

While Mrs Holden was not old in years, her ailing body and rapidly weakening mind told her otherwise. There was a persistently painful ache deep within her bones and her flesh sagged, covered in cuts and sores.

Her reactions had slowed so that she had become clumsy and she could barely remember what she had done the day before. There grew to be a dullness in her head that made the world around her seem frightful and intense. She would no longer look out onto the street to take in the traffic nor eagerly anticipate the next customer through the door. Every sound, motion and memory felt like torture. If she were to die in her sleep, right there in her armchair, she would be grateful.

Chapter Eight

A flurry of important commissions prevented Mr Michael from returning to Holden's Haunt for another fortnight. Irene too was preoccupied with caring for her mother, who had taken a turn for the worse and was now sweating in her sleep. The pair hoped the police would take care of Mrs Holden and prevent any further thefts, though it did not stop their silent suppers being consumed with troublesome thoughts. Mr Michael spent every day wondering how he could help. His overriding concern was for his friend's wellbeing, as he had noticed her looking ever frailer with each of his visits. The last remaining possessions could well be all she had left in the world and he did not know how she would survive without them.

As Mr Michael approached Holden's Haunt, he was immediately struck by the absence of objects outside. It looked like a completely different building, and a sad and sorry one at that. His concerns bounced around his head as he instinctively ducked to avoid the usual paraphernalia that had previously delayed his entrance, but now there was nothing left to disturb him. The realisation brought a rare smile to his lips before his jaw fell on entering the main room. Gone. Everything had gone. All that remained were the four walls, the floorboards and an inconceivable amount of dust. Dust in every crevice, along every edge, even lining the ceiling. And there she sat exactly as he had last seen her. Mrs Holden in her armchair.

She greeted him pleasantly enough, passing a few general comments about the increasingly inclement weather before reaching for the metal box underneath. Mr Michael felt the smallest flicker of hope within his gut. Either his friend had been robbed, or she had been shrewd enough to sell the last remaining possessions and was about to show him her earnings. With quaking hands, he watched as she wriggled opened the lid and shook out the contents onto her lap. Bowing her head towards the fallen remnants, Mrs Holden carefully picked up the fragment from her sullied pinafore. A matted clump of dust. Mr Michael watched as the realisation finally overcame his friend. Her face grew so pale as to be translucent and her shoulders began to heave up and down as if she were fighting for breath. Again, she shook the tin as if expecting the money to have lodged itself within, but there was not a scrap. Not even a sound.

Mr Michael watched in silence, wondering how Mrs Holden had not noticed anything, worrying what she would now do. He felt helpless as the tragedy revealed itself. Her head moved in multiple directions as if she were searching the room, but it was too little too late. Replacing the tin, she slowly rose from her chair and began pacing the empty space, her hands tremoring as her feet slowly slid across the grubby floorboards. She was not crying but her face was scrunched up as if tears would fall at any moment. It was as if she had been in a dream and was now awakening to the dreadful reality.

There was nothing Mr Michael could do, no words that would provide comfort or advice, least of all an explanation. He could hardly bear to see her in such a state, vowing to help in any way he could. Mrs Holden seemed oblivious to his words, still slowly spinning in the barren void as Mr Michael left Holden's Haunt and closed the door behind him.

Inspector Falmer returned to the property, his officers resuming their searches and questioning but with even fewer leads than before. Mrs Holden could not even answer the most basic of their queries; they feared she had lost her mind. Word soon spread of the appalling crime and within hours became the talk of every street corner in the city. The old crow had finally been had, the locals gossiped eagerly, though there were no smiles nor titters of laughter to accompany the joke. The majority were genuinely saddened to see such a defiant woman reduced to a penniless and pitiful position, with not even a whisper of the likely culprit of the crime. There was no one who could help Mrs Holden now: no husband, children, parents, or siblings. They lamented her demise as if she were already dead, drinking readily to her memory and to the former magnificence of Holden's Haunt.

Unlike the rest of the city, Mr Michael had very little to say, especially to Mrs Holden herself. He continued to visit but their conversations had quickly dwindled to brief comments concerning the changing seasons, devoid of purpose and conviviality. He had provided his friend with a small sewing kit so that she could try to maintain the few clothes she had left, with Mrs Holden eagerly darning away on each occasion afterward. As he reported on the days when they were to expect rain, Mrs Holden sat silently absorbed in her needlework. At first, Mr Michael thought she was merely keen to keep busy as a distraction from the reality in evidence around her. As time wore on, however, he came to realise the key advantage of her toil. He could never see her face nor expression. Perhaps she had ceased feeling at all.

Everything was in decay, especially Mrs Holden herself. Her clothes and hair looked like they had not seen soap or water in weeks, her hands scabbed, split and cut from the constant scratching as she tried to relieve the worry that kept her awake at night. Though most of her face was kept hidden by a permanent downwards stare as she darned, the skin that was visible had taken on a greenish tinge, drooping off the bones, her wrinkles caked with dirt. She looked like she had already been thrown out onto the street, destitute and forgotten. Mr Michael watched her in silence, the swollen fingers gripping a sock and needle with forced effort, her head bowed down and yet not at the right angle to be able to see into her lap where she was working. She was moving from memory, the same spot over and over. She enquired in a hurried mutter after her friend's daughter and wife, a polite formality rather than a genuine wish to start a conversation. Mr Michael answered with as much enthusiasm as he could muster but he could not take his eyes away from her. Something was amiss.

Perhaps it was intuition. Perhaps he had come to know Mrs Holden more deeply than he had realised. He could sense the disturbance in the blood pumping through his neck, in the unnerving whisper created by her working fingers, within the dense and decaying air all around them. Short and sharp, Mr Michael told his friend to stop. A moment of stillness, then Mrs Holden slowly ceased her stitching and heaved a huge sigh, as if she had been expecting this and somehow welcomed it. She raised her head to face her friend so that he could finally see into her eyes for the first time in weeks. They were sunken and thickly filmed, pearlescent white as if a spider had woven its web across them. A single tear rolled off her cheek, falling into her lap and readily absorbed by the sock. Mr Michael left immediately to call for a doctor.

Chapter Nine

Doctor Hughes was the resident physician on the Shambles. Though he had never met Mrs Holden in a professional capacity, he had long been aware of her reputation. His own wife had even procured a household implement or two from Holden's Haunt and always remarked on her visits with great fervour. Doctor Hughes had heard plenty more tales besides of the elaborate treasure trove within the establishment and was almost glad of the excuse to visit, until he entered and saw the famed proprietor herself. It took him several moments to regain his composure and attend to the patient, such was her decrepit state. Mrs Holden remained silent throughout the examination, though the expression on her face suggested she was far from comfortable. Having concluded his tests, the doctor rose and gave a solemn nod of confirmation. Mr Michael's suspicions were indeed correct; Mrs Holden was blind and would never regain her sight.

In desperation, Mr Michael sought a second opinion from his own family physician, Doctor Pruce, but the diagnosis was repeated word for word. He tried other experts including an optician, a pharmacist, even a neighbour who dabbled in herbal remedies, but all they could offer were sympathetic shrugs. There was no cure. There was nothing that could be done. This remarkable woman had turned into a shell, liable to break at the smallest touch. The only relief Mr Michael could provide was a loaf of bread and the company of his daughter in the hope that the sound of her gentle voice would bring comfort to his friend.

Irene did not hesitate to join her father in his visits to Mrs Holden in her time of need. She had watched him grow pale and fatigued in the past few weeks from so many sleepless nights filled with concern for the old woman's safety and his frustration at the lack of progress made by the police. Together they began tending to Mrs Holden as often as they could, her father taking dry wood and spare food while she saw to everything else: dusting, mopping, cooking, darning and emptying the chamber pot day after day. Sometimes Irene would seat herself on the floor next to Mrs Holden's armchair and sing melodies she had overheard in the street, or else perform tales of her own invention about the woodland animals she had seen in picture books.

It was as Irene came to the end of one such story that she noticed the crow too had vanished. It seemed that they had been so consumed by their thoughts that no one had noticed the creature missing. Irene and her father searched the local surroundings, peering into trees and across rooftops in the hope that the bird had merely decided to watch the house from afar, but it could not be found. They even asked neighbours and fellow shopkeepers on the Shambles but were met with either impassive shrugs or stifled laughter.

"So the crow's flown the nest, eh?" smirked Dan Chelten to his pals down the pub, his prize-winning sock still pinned to the wall, "Serves 'er right. One crow's enough for this street."

When Mr Michael broached the subject with Mrs Holden herself, he saw the immediate contortion in her face and the supreme effort with which she tried to conceal it. She muttered something about going to a better place before returning to her darning, the same sock now nearly twice as large with repeated stitches. Walking across and crouching at the foot of her chair, Mr Michael listened to the faint echo of her movement, wishing he could take her hands in his own, wanting nothing more than to provide a solution or some form of relief.

"What can I do?" he asked anxiously, "How can I 'elp?" He searched her face studying the deep crevices, the downturned crescent of a mouth, the milky white spheres of her eyes that had once been so bright and inquisitive. Mrs Holden shook her head, dropping the work into her lap before wringing her hands together tighter and tighter. Little red streaks began appearing across her skin as the dried knuckles cracked and bled. She was trembling head to toe.

"It were me," she replied in the softest of whispers, "And there's nowt they can do. I were 'ere the whole time. I let 'em in, I let 'em tek it all away. Even m'bird's gone." She buried her face in her hands, wrapping the long fingers around the taunt bones, feeling for the first time in years the dense and weathered skin underneath. She was not crying, merely ashamed, sorry to be seen at her very lowest, lonely and desperate in an empty house. Void of possessions, of family, of life. What had she to live for now?

Mr Michael waited, time standing still in the silent Holden's Haunt. He tried to think of a reply but could summon no words. He did not know how to convince Mrs Holden otherwise for he did not know the answers either. If he himself had discovered he had been robbed, if he had lost his wife and every single one of his children, would he not despair just the same? Would he not place his head in his hands and weep? He was certain he would not be as strong as the woman sat opposite him, who despite her admission still did not shed a single tear. He swallowed the lump that had formed in his throat and rose to his feet. As he paced the empty space, his shoes tapping against the floorboards, he tried with all his might to think of a single word of hope. His mouth remained mute.

As Mr Michael turned his attention back to his friend, he watched Mrs Holden replace her hands in her lap and lift her chin, a strange expression playing across her face. A grimace of pain, he thought at first, or even the wince of concentration? His gaze fell from her face to her hands in which she held something, an object. It seemed his friend had not been robbed entirely; he would have recognised that emblem anywhere. She turned and stroked the letter opener between her fingertips as if convincing herself of its existence while he struggled to stifle a smile. Something akin to relief washed over him, making his skin flush with a warmth that was sorely absent from his surroundings. The hopeful flame was quickly extinguished by the reminder that winter was approaching. The blade would not save his friend. She would die of cold if starvation or grief did not consume her first.

Nor did the object offer Mrs Holden any form of physical protection. Though neither spoke of it, they were both well aware that the thief could easily return to claim this final prize. For now, it was the old woman's comfort as well as her only source of funds, but for how much longer, neither could know nor predict. Coal, food, clothes, blankets and a few items for the kitchen were all that Mr Michael could provide in the meantime, along with his companionship. The knife, on the other hand, was solely Mrs Holden's responsibility. Before leaving, Mr Michael implored his friend to keep the object out of view.

"Until we find who did this, you mustn't 'ave it in plain sight." He tried to keep his voice steady and measured but could not help the subtle note of fear that tinged his words. "It'll not protect you if they return. You must 'ide it an' listen, always listen. I'll send Irene t'help an' I'll return meself as often as I can."

Mrs Holden had her face turned towards the far wall as if sensing the threat beyond. She gave a few slow shakes of her head, batting her friend's worry aside, but she could tell by the severity of his voice that he was serious, even scared. It was a feeling she knew all too well, though she had had many more years of practice in its concealment. She breathed slowly, counting in her mind, listening to the whistle of the wind as it whipped around the corner of her property, the shop that could no longer trade. The business that had failed. She wanted to ask Mr Michael to stay; not to protect her from the villain but to save her from herself, from her own ghosts. But she remained silent, too proud and too timid to admit her pitiful thoughts. As Mr Michael bade his friend farewell and closed the door firmly behind him, Mrs Holden blew out the candle beside her and clung the letter opener to her chest.

Chapter Ten

Mrs Holden could not sleep. Instead, she listened to the barrage of noise outside on the street, a wavering racket of drunks swearing and singing dirty songs along with gaggling girls baying for their attention and weekly earnings. Irene had visited a few hours earlier with a piece of meat pie she had made but Mrs Holden could not bring herself to eat it. Her mind was on other concerns. She could live without decent meals, a constant fire or a change of clothes. She could survive the coldest of nights and the overwhelming darkness that now seemed to envelop the room without a lamp or fire. She had become used to the absence of the crow and had resigned herself to the woeful emptiness of the money tin. But the one thing Mrs Holden could not cope with for much longer were the memories.

They grew daily, nightly, in number and in strength. They filled the void left by her belongings, swelling in the shadows so that she could hardly breathe. Though blind, she had still sensed the loss of her possessions as they had been taken in turn and in their place had flooded in the many painful moments of the decades of her life. She wanted to weep, then to sleep, before finally forgetting, but she could do none of these things. She could only sit in her threadbare armchair, her fingers clinging onto the letter opener in her lap despite Mr Michael's warning to keep it well hidden. Her thoughts tumbled agonisingly through an already wearied mind.

Irene continued her visits, bringing provisions and cleaning the barren room. She noticed that the food would sit there untouched for days, threatening to harden or mould. She would prepare it as best as she could into something more palatable, but it was difficult when she did not have the time nor the equipment. The only thing Mrs Holden would touch was her letter opener. Irene often saw her reach the spindly fingers of one hand down the side of her chair to check it was still there. The look of relief and comfort on her face reassured Irene that it was. Mrs Holden had at least managed to hold on to something, a symbol of her former life.

Concerned about Mrs Holden's lack of appetite and without wishing to worry her father, Irene decided to call on the services of Doctor Pruce. Having already seen to the old woman to confirm the diagnosis of her blindness, the doctor was glad to attend at the polite request of the young girl whom he had known for many years. After having to bear the terrible news of another infant death to Mr and Mrs Michael, it had come as a welcome relief to assist in the pregnancy and safe birth of their only living child. He had visited on several further occasions since that day to try to help Winifred's symptoms, but to little avail. He was only too sorry that he could not complete the family's happiness by bringing their mother back to her full state of health, particularly for the sake of the girl.

It had taken some time before Irene had felt confident enough to approach the doctor regarding Mrs Holden. She had always felt uneasy in his presence on account of his inability to cure her mother. However, he was still one of the few adults whom she knew reasonably well and felt she could trust.

Doctor Pruce was a tall man but seemed to have no shoulders, his coats always hanging off him in an odd manner despite his consistent smartness. He wore tiny round spectacles balanced impossibly on the end of his nose and his head was entirely bald. Irene used to have to hide her giggles whenever he positioned himself by the window to see to her mother, the light bouncing off his head to cast a dancing shape against the ceiling.

Having thoroughly examined Mrs Holden on his previous visit, Doctor Pruce was quite certain that Irene's concerns were nothing to worry about. Though she looked aged beyond her years and had lost her sight, he was adamant that Mrs Holden still possessed enough strength and mental awareness to be able to care for herself. He was sure that the girl would be reassured once he had made a quick repeat visit and, on that particular day, he had ample time between his afternoon appointments to do so. He followed Irene down the street, bobbing and weaving past the daily shoppers until they finally arrived at Holden's Haunt.

On entering the room and seeing his patient, Doctor Pruce's usual calm and professional countenance quickly took on a look of simultaneous astonishment and sadness. The situation had indeed become dire. The famous shop, once home to so many intriguing treasures, had been stripped bare of its contents save for the old woman in her solitary chair, bloated and blind, living off scraps of food like a mouse. Reluctantly, Mrs

Holden followed the doctor's instructions, allowing him to rest two fingers against her neck which bulged under his touch, followed by the protrusion of her tongue, its surface revealing a profusion of red welts.

The doctor stretched open each eye with his thumb and first finger, water seeping from the sockets, causing his hands to slip and his patient to growl in indignation. Doctor Pruce then opened her hands and found the insides sliced repeatedly, as if she had tried to defend herself from an attack. The only thing Mrs Holden had to fight off were her own demons, thought the doctor. After such hardship in her life, he suspected she was finally becoming depressed, perhaps even mad. The self-inflicted wounds on her palms were irrefutable evidence, but he was reluctant to provide her name to the notorious Bootham institute just yet. Even if she had lost her mind, Mrs Holden was not a danger to anyone. Only to herself.

Doctor Pruce departed with a few well-meaning words of advice, given to both Mrs Holden and Irene. He instructed his patient to eat and drink as much as possible, to try to keep the fire going and wrap up well, and to occasionally leave the door ajar for air to circulate. Irene had hoped he might be able to offer some pills or remedies to help with the old woman's appetite and perhaps even improve her eyes, but he had nothing of use. "It would take a miracle," he shrugged as he closed his case shut with a snap. He told Irene that he would be back in a few days to check on Mrs Holden if he could spare the time. She nodded politely and thanked the doctor with as much sincerity as she could muster, already knowing that he would not be returning. Not until it was too late.

After leaving some bread and cheese on a plate along with two extra blankets, Irene bid farewell to Mrs Holden, who was tenderly fondling her letter opener now that the doctor had departed. Her face was vacant, her mind in another time and place. Remembering the doctor's words, Irene left the door open and shouted a reminder to Mrs Holden to close it again in half an hour's time, though she was fairly certain that not a wisp of fresh air would even come close to entering the front room, especially not on a street like the Shambles. She said a silent prayer as she headed for home, still in two minds whether to tell her father about Doctor Pruce's visit.

Once Irene had turned the corner of the street out of view, Dan Chelten arrived at Holden's Haunt carrying the sock he had purchased all those years ago. He had heard the sad tale of Mrs Holden and wanted to return the item along with his condolences, a rare deed but one which had been keeping him awake for too many nights. Finding the door already open, he slipped in and saw the old woman with an intriguing object. It was like nothing he had ever seen and worth a fair bob, no doubt. He had never coveted anything as much as he did that letter opener in that moment. It was almost as if it possessed him. He wanted it, needed it, and who was Mrs Holden to stop him?

Chapter Eleven

It was not the first time Irene had been threatened with the cane. Teachers had been banned from using such a punishment at Fishergate School, but Master Timmel still liked to keep his own at the front of his desk so that each of his pupils could see it and contemplate its use. Sometimes fear was just as effective as force and Master Timmel believed strongly that a firm hand was what every child needed, particularly when they came from a broken home like Irene Michael.

Though her father was a well-liked and successful workman capable of producing some of the finest carpentry in the city, it could not be denied that Irene was far too independent for her age. Master Timmel was sure he was not alone in his observation and he knew the cause; a distinct lack of parental discipline, no doubt the result of the girl's failure of a mother and indifferent father. That day during class Irene had been particularly distracted, refusing to answer the teacher's questions on three occasions and declining to complete her sums. She had been staring out of the window for most of the morning, daydreaming.

Most of the other children had heard about Mrs Holden by now. They whispered and poked Irene, urging her to share the secrets they suspected she was hiding. Even Master Timmel would look up from his desk and pretend to survey the classroom, hoping to overhear a choice piece of gossip they longed for Irene to reveal. She could almost see his beetroot red ears visibly twitching behind his whiskered mutton chops. They were all like a pack of wolves baying for blood, tantalised by the sordid stories they had already learned from their parents over breakfast. Irene remained silent except for a few sharp stares that warned her classmates to leave well alone. She had never been in a fight or even an argument, but she was different from the other children and therefore something to be feared. They believed they could sense an energy in her, a repressed anger that was sure to reveal itself eventually. It was always the quiet ones. The teacher kept brandishing his cane in warning at her but Irene no longer cared. She felt so numb that she doubted she would even notice its whip across her bare hands.

Irene had never heard of a burglary so brutal as the one at Holden's Haunt. She shuddered to think what kind of a man, or even a woman, could have done such a thing. A house entirely emptied. Such a crime was unheard of, especially in a city that everyone always said was so friendly and welcoming. They were a community where people looked out for one another, where they each knew each other's first names, sat side by side in church every Sunday, wished their neighbours a good morning in the street. Yet no one had looked out for Mrs Holden.

While she was optimistic by nature, Irene was also aware of life's cruelties. She understood that people could be pushed to commit terrible crimes in moments of weakness – fights, thefts, stabbings and even murders. To be able to rob an old woman of her entire house though was an altogether different kind of offence, a violation of a woman's right to an independent livelihood. Irene had decided that whoever the culprit was must be very troubled. She could only hope that they would not return for the letter opener or for something far worse; Mrs Holden's life.

Irene had discussed her concerns with her father the previous evening, explaining that she did not think Mrs Holden was eating or keeping herself warm enough. Though she usually told her father everything, she had decided not to mention Doctor Pruce's visit. Irene was still upset that he had been unable to help Mrs Holden, not even offering one single vial of medicine to make her a little more comfortable. Day after day, the old woman sat in that reeking old chair, the air clogged with smog, the dust growing ever denser as if it were burying her alive. Doctor Pruce, like so many others, seemed to have given up on Mrs Holden, just when she needed support the most. But there was one man she knew who would not give up.

Mr Michael had listened attentively to his daughter's fears, silently reflecting on how much she had matured in just a matter of months. No child should have to endure this kind of physical and emotional toil, he realised. He did not know what he would have done without her. After patting her hand in reassurance, he offered to clear the dishes away himself and prepare a cup of hot chocolate for them to share. Irene gasped in delight at the suggestion, her previous worries vanishing up the chimney as Mr Michael set a small pot of milk to heat.

The tiny packet of finest sweetened cocoa had been a token of appreciation from a client he had built a bookcase for, which had then found a home in the man's office at the new Terry's factory. The chocolate works had been one of several exciting new developments in the city and stories of its products, production methods and proprietors were the only kind of gossip that Mr Michael enjoyed overhearing. He intended to take Irene to the factory one day just so that they could stand outside and inhale the aroma of the sweet treats being made, but for now the single cup filled with the warm and fragrant beverage would be just as pleasurable. The pair took turns to sip at the indulgent liquid, savouring the lingering bitterness on their tongues as they listened to the wind and rain rattling outside. They finished the contents just as the embers faded into darkness in the fireplace.

Heading to bed with her stomach full, it was the first night in many weeks that Irene managed to sleep soundly, though the anxiety returned almost immediately on waking. She had hoped school would provide a welcome distraction but only found herself filled with anger and frustration as she was forced to endure the constant titters and whispers around her. Her classmates seemed to consider Mrs Holden's situation as just another source of chatter and ridicule. Irene could hardly bear their cruelty but had always managed to conceal her tears until the journey home, though her eyes felt tight and sore that day with the effort. They did not known Mrs Holden like she and her father did. They would never understand.

Despite her sadness, Irene finished her calculations and was able to recite the poem they had been learning for the past week. As the hours passed, she pushed harder and harder against the nasty words and the eager pokes of the other children. She now realised that just because no one else would help Mrs Holden, it did not prevent her from doing so. She could not offer any form of advice or compensation for the loss of the belongings, but she could at least take some food and keep her company. She could try to make her life worth living.

Irene knew that she was no longer a child. She was adamant that she would not allow fear and emotion to overrule her. Learning from her mother, her father and from Mrs Holden herself, she now understood that to get by in this world, sacrifices had to be made. As she walked home along the river after school, an idea formed in her mind. She would forge a plan that would bring an end to all their woes.

After sharing the cup of cocoa with his daughter, Mr Michael had fallen into a deep slumber beset by intense dreams. When he awoke, he had a realisation of what he could do to help Mrs Holden, clear and vivid in his mind, bringing a new sense of determination to his stride as he made his way to work. Though it had pained him to hear of his daughter's anxieties, he was glad she had sought comfort from him. It had never been his intention to involve his little girl in such a sad tale, yet he was grateful that he did not have to carry the burden on his own. Despite her sorry state, at least Mrs

Holden was not alone.

It was while carving a particularly ornate spindle in his workshop that Mr Michael finalised the details of his scheme. He would take on the task of tracking down the man who had robbed his friend, recovering as many of her possessions as possible before seeing that the culprit was sentenced to life imprisonment for his unforgivable crime. He imagined the villain to be a grim character, desperate and dangerous, skulking around the city's snickelways and hidden crevices, watching and waiting for his next victim. He could only hope that it would not be Mrs Holden and her letter opener.

Mr Michael knew that this was not a simple robbery. Such a vast quantity of items had been taken and each so distinctive that he was convinced there would have to be evidence somewhere. It was inconceivable that the likes of fishing nets and manacles, at least a dozen stained chamber pots, plus a ginormous oak bureau with ivory inlays could simply vanish without anyone having seen or heard a thing. Even with Mrs Holden losing her eyesight, there had been neighbours, customers, shop owners and a constant crowd of people filtering up and down the Shambles day after day. There had to be someone among them who knew something of relevance. And Mr Michael was going to be the man to find them and to bring justice to Mrs Holden.

Chapter Twelve

While at his workshop, Mr Michael would often remember the many figurines he had made for Agnes Dartton and the little boy all those years ago. He wished he had had a chance to know them both, to have visited more often and to have engaged in conversation. Perhaps then he would have formed his friendship with Mrs Holden earlier. He could have helped her through life's challenges. He could have learned what had happened to the infant all those years ago.

Though Mr Michael could not remember what the child had looked like, he would always imagine a cheerful grin and the sound of tinkling laughter. He must have been around the age of five when he disappeared, but Mr Michael had not heard anything from his family or neighbours at the time and had never dared to ask Mrs Holden. It had often crept into his mind during his visits only to be quickly concealed to the back of his thoughts. Somehow he knew it would be too painful for his friend. How terrible it must have been for the Darttons to have had such a happy household turned suddenly silent and sullen. He was sure Mrs Holden was haunted by the memory.

It seemed to be just one of many mysteries surrounding her life that he might never know the truth of, though there was one thing he did know for certain. After all that Mrs Holden had already been through, he would not stand by and see her suffer. As he carved, he made a mental list of all the locals he knew and the many more he had never met who could have walked past Holden's Haunt over the previous few weeks and potentially have seen something unusual. All those people, day and night, traversing along within inches of her front door; if they were keeping quiet to the police through fear or ignorance, then surely they would be happy to speak to a mere carpenter? There was only one way Mr Michael could know.

Just as the school bell began to sound, Irene raced for the door and sprinted towards the waterfront. The bitter wind whipped at her face, throwing her hair back across her shoulders and bringing a rosy glow to her elongated ears. She clutched her books tighter before collapsing down against her favourite clump of trees, catching her breath as she watched the familiar vessels transporting and loading goods along the river. From her pinafore she retrieved a piece of bread and chewed at one corner, deep in thought. The redcurrant bushes up ahead still had some of their berries remaining, so she plucked a handful and tucked them in her front pocket where the bread had once been. She would leave the fruits on Mrs Holden's window ledge to tempt the crow back home, for she was sure he could not have strayed far.

Wrapping the shawl tighter around her, Irene tucked her books under her arm and headed back into town, crossing the bridge and walking up Piccadilly before turning to enter the Shambles. Irene had never grown used to the raucous din of the street nor the constant flurry of shoppers. With hunched shoulders and one hand stretched out in front, she attempted to make her way as quickly as possible through the rabble, a miniature distance that still seemed to take an age. Eventually she sidled up to the desolate building of Holden's Haunt and inhaled deeply. There was now something unnerving about entering the shop that sent shivers down her spine, but she promptly reassured herself that there was nothing to fear. She had a duty, after all.

The door was ajar. Irene listened to the barely audible yet strangely comforting creak of its hinges as she pushed it fully open and walked through. She peered across the four walls, the bare floor, the grubby windows. It was empty just as before, just as Irene knew it would be, though somehow more eerily silent than usual. She could barely see Mrs Holden in her armchair, the last remaining piece of furniture in her home. The old woman seemed to be sleeping, slumped low and awkwardly, her dishevelled hair hanging across her face with her jaw wide open.

Irene reached to unlock one of the tiny windows, prising with all her might to unstick the frame. She scattered the redcurrants onto the sill wondering if the crow might be passing by overhead right at that moment. How wonderful it would be to watch it swoop down from the murky sky, greedily pecking its treats before returning to Mrs Holden's side. What a pleasing story she would be able to tell her father that evening if her wish came true! She sighed softly, wiping the berry juice along the length of her apron, leaving a pattern of red streaks. She returned her attention to the now illuminated room and the silent old woman.

As she looked, Irene's smile and calm countenance suddenly slipped. Her mouth became an open gape, her face blanched to a sickly pallor and her entire body began to shake. While at first glance Mrs Holden's face and upper body had appeared just as they should for a woman in slumber, from the waist down it was a sight from the most horrific of nightmares, an unimaginable vision. Thick crimson blood coated her lower arms, stomach and legs, saturating her clothes and spreading out across the floor, sticky and viscous like treacle. Her wrists rested on the sides of the chair, palms facing upwards as if mirroring a religious pose. The flesh was neatly sliced along the lengths from wrist to inner elbow exposing lumps of wet flesh and the glimpse of white bone within. The liquid had spilled and pooled around Mrs Holden's feet and the legs of the chair in a wide and nearly symmetrical sphere. It looked almost staged, as if it had been a carefully calculated ritual. It was the first time Irene had seen so much blood and the first time she had ever screamed her throat hoarse with absolute terror.

Once she could pry her hands away from her mouth, Irene shuffled tentatively towards the body, her eyes searching wildly as they tried to take in every detail, her mind still doubting the truth of the scene before her. She knew that soon someone would come to her rescue and take her away from this terrible scene, but before they did, she had to know one thing. Irene clenched her lips together and took another careful few steps towards the body, the tip of her shoe disrupting the edge of the red ring on the floor. She reached the fingertips of one hand down the side of the armchair, the dead body rigid against her palm, her skin becoming caked with blood.

A man appeared behind her quickly followed by another, then many more, all of them each crying out in horror, shouting out of the open window: 'Police! Murder! Help us!' Irene had already wiped her hand clean on the underside of her pinafore before they had entered. Now she just had to keep removing the tears that seemed to be falling in a constant stream from her eyes. She stepped back into the corner of the room and watched the whirlwind of bodies around her, each man eager to help yet repulsed by the sight and the stench, the women wailing and cowering, unable to take their eyes away, the children crying in shock and fright.

Eventually, Inspector Falmer arrived with several officers who attempted to clear the room of its shaken crowd. Irene found herself swathed by the comforting arms of a busty woman whom she did not know but who smelled like soap and fried onions. She allowed herself to be enveloped and hushed, burying her face in the soft fabric of the woman's blouse where she could weep unseen and unheard. The shouts and scuffles slowly faded around them as if she had slipped into a dream with only one thought prevailing. Mrs Holden was dead and the letter opener was gone.

Part Two

Chapter Thirteen

After cleaning and dressing the wound, Mr Michael sat by the open door of his workshop and listened to the din of the crowded street beyond. It was exceedingly rare that he sustained an injury while at work, but his mind had been elsewhere and the blade had suddenly slipped out from under his hand, slashing across the palm of the other. Thankfully, the wood had not been damaged or stained, though it would take some time before the wound would heal enough so that he could continue the commission to his usual standard.

His thoughts swam like the River Ouse when it flooded, thick murky water dragging up debris from the past, bobbing on the surface, pushed along by the current before being plunged underneath. He felt like he was drowning, unable to focus on one single idea alone, random questions and possible answers appearing then vanishing. He could no longer tell which were the accurate memories of his history with Mrs Holden and which were just impressions from the many stories he had listened to from neighbours, acquaintances, and even strangers he had happened to overhear on the streets.

Mr Michael had realised that each person he passed could be a potential suspect or else have some vital piece of information to help him discover the thief. He seemed unable to look at a face without wondering if they had been the one to have robbed his friend of every item she owned. Sometimes he would glance through the windows of households without realising, his eyes searching for the missing possessions, knowing how foolish he was yet unable to resist. The puzzle was becoming an obsession, clouding his mind by day and interrupting his sleep at night, but he knew there could be only one remedy. He had to find the criminal before anything else could happen to Mrs Holden.

Unable to return to his work with his damaged hand, Mr Michael put away his tools and tidied his workstation before locking up behind him. He had been the only one in that day and would have enjoyed the experience if it had not been for his overactive thoughts and clumsy error. He thought he would try to clear his head with one of his favourite distractions, watching the boats by the river, but as he headed in the direction of the water, he found his feet changing route in the opposite direction leading into the heart of the city.

Though ten times as wide as the Shambles, St Helen's Square was just as hectic and rowdy with a steady flow of human traffic nudging and shoving Mr Michael aside as he searched each of their unfamiliar faces. Suddenly filled with an uncharacteristic confidence, he found himself stopping any resident who made eye contact, eagerly questioning them about the friend he had only ever called by her surname. Had they known Mrs Holden in person? Did they ever venture into or procure anything from Holden's Haunt? What of the stolen items and the vacant bird? What stories had they heard? What could they tell him?

One after another, the queries tumbled from his lips as Mr Michael desperately sought even the smallest scrap of news, yet the more people he quizzed, the more hopeless it seemed. He now realised how deep the mystery had become. Everyone seemed well aware of the case but very few had information to offer other than a fading memory of an occasional purchase, the recollection always told with a glint in the eye and a wavering smile. Though they may only have stepped into the building for a few moments, Holden's Haunt had been a unique experience that many folks were only too happy to recall.

Once he had begun, Mr Michael found that people were willingly coming up to him to tell their own tales of Mrs Holden's many lives as a daughter, a wife, a mother, a neighbour and as a shopkeeper. Their descriptions ranged from her being a miserly, haggard, formidable old bat to a far more flattering thrifty, cunning and sharp proprietor, but they did not seem to mention her love of nature and wildlife. No one else had been privy to the comical recollection of her most memorable customers, nor did they know of her preference for oranges and walnuts, or how she liked the winter more than the summer on account of its reliability.

Most of the chatter consisted of fanciful fairy tales that Mr Michael had already heard time and again: the mystery of the crow, Dan Chelten's sock, the legend of Lanky Luke. Not one of the people he spoke to knew anything about Mrs Holden outside of Holden's Haunt. There was no mention of Agnes or the Dartton family, including the little boy. It was as if that part of her life had never existed. Their friendship had indeed been a rare thing, as Mr Michael seemed to be the only person alive who had known Mrs Holden as a person.

The light was changing rapidly as the night drew near and Mr Michael's thoughts turned to his ailing wife and his anxious daughter who would be at home awaiting his return. He followed the steady stream of people towards the market and made the decision to cut through the Shambles for a quick visit to see Mrs Holden. Despite the butchers cleaning their shammels and turning the signs on their doors, the street was still animated with all manner of folk heading home from work or their shopping, but as he approached the furthest end, the movement of bodies ceased.

A mass of gawking spectators crowded around Holden's Haunt, each watching wide-eyed as they whispered feverishly. Outside the front door stood a frightened-looking girl with sorrowful eyes and a trembling bottom lip. Like a startled rabbit, she suddenly came hurtling through the onlookers towards Mr Michael, throwing her arms around his waist. It was Irene. He clung to her as she wept into his shirt, his heart thumping against his chest as he wondered what had happened. Surely there was nothing more the thieves could have taken?

With one hand stroking his daughter's head in comfort, the other reached behind her to open the door. He peered into the gloom and spotted several identical men; police officers, six of them, with Inspector Falmer stood in pensive silence. It struck Mr Michael as an unusually busy scene for a robbery, particularly when the inspector had seemed so casual about his concerns a few weeks before. He wondered if they had come to inform Mrs Holden of a development in the investigation, or perhaps they had even caught the criminal, but he was promptly ushered aside. Two of the officers began shouting and waving their batons at the crowd who duly parted, except for father and daughter who remained clutching one another beside the entranceway.

Inspector Falmer appeared by their side, watching the bystanders reluctantly move on. "So sorry for your loss, Mr Michael," he muttered, the words well-rehearsed and void of emotion. Mr Michael held his breath, clinging his fingers to the fragile form quaking against him before Inspector Falmer encouraged them to one side. Still unable to fully comprehend the inspector's words, Mr Michael edged himself and his daughter against the exterior wall and watched as four of the officers came shuffling out of the doorway carrying a stretcher. It bore a domed shape covered by a thick beige cloth, the reek almost unbearable even with the stench of the street and smog.

Mr Michael thought his heart had plummeted to the soles of his feet. It was hard to believe that one of the most formidable women he had ever known was dead, departed, silenced forever. A handsome shire horse had somehow managed to make its way up to the property pulling a wagon, onto which the officers slid the body and secured the fastenings. The spectators had amassed once more, all eager for a glimpse of the deceased. Inspector Falmer wordlessly waved his truncheon at his officers, who were already attempting to part the pale-faced congregation to allow the cart to leave. With a whip crack, the horse's hooves began thudding down the street, every pair of eyes watching as the vehicle's wheels slipped and tripped down the cobbles under the weight of its load. The horse snuffled grimly as it tried to navigate the slimy stones, steam escaping its nostrils as the cargo bounced along behind. At least fifty people watched its progress, their mouths open but for once speechless.

Irene had ceased her tears but she still gripped onto her father as they listened to the clack and thump of the wheels fighting for traction. Mr Michael in turn pulled Irene close, as much for his own comfort as for hers. His disbelieving eyes stared into the distance where the body had disappeared around the bend, his dearest of friends gone. The idea still seemed somehow impossible, that a woman who had been through so much and appeared so strong could now be… dead. There was a soft cough at Mr Michael's side and a hand awkwardly cupped his shoulder.

"Rather a ghastly suicide, I'm afraid," the inspector sighed as the crowd began to disperse, their jaws already flapping with their own account of the incredible and horrific scene they had just apparently been witness to. "Looks like she used some kind of paper knife, right up each wrist. Too deep to be accidental. Death by blood loss. Doctor Pruce informed us of her suspected depression. Hardly surprising, really, with all's been going on."

The inspector's thick moustache continued to twitch

after he had finished speaking, his eyes darting across to each of his officers, they in turn dispersing to other duties with a single nod of his head. Mr Michael raised his eyebrows lightly in response but did not dare open his mouth for fear of the infuriated tirade he might unleash. The police seemed almost high-spirited in their response, but what good was it now? Where had they been when Mrs Holden needed them the most, to protect her against a criminal they should already have known was dangerous? Mr Michael was clenching his fists so tightly that the wound on his palm had split, fresh blood seeping into the bandage.

Having unwrapped her arms from around her father, Irene was also in a state of shock, but not from the scene she had witnessed. She too was dismayed at the nonchalant attitude of the inspector and the way he seemed neither surprised nor concerned by the dramatic turn of events. If she had learned anything from Mrs Holden and her predicament, it was the importance of speaking one's mind and telling the truth. She decided to test her lesson on Inspector Falmer.

"You're wrong, plain wrong!" Irene bellowed, her face a storm, "Mrs 'olden would never do such a thing! It's murder, can't you see? An' someone stole the letter opener too. She'd never let it go, not ever!"

The inspector and his officers all took a step back from the girl's unexpected outburst while Mr Michael wrapped his arm across her shoulders proudly. A few neighbours even began to clap in response to Irene's speech, chiming in with comments of approval as they too asked the inspector what he intended to do about the dreadful crime. They were now dealing with a murderer, after all, and Mrs Holden might only be the first victim of many. Facing finger jabs to his chest and sharp scowls from the encroaching crowd, Inspector Falmer visibly blanched, backing further and further against the wall while his officers took up their truncheons once more. Mr Michael took his opportunity to try to slip silently away from the scene holding Irene by the hand, but with his head bobbing well above the rest of the neighbours, the inspector easily made note of his hasty retreat.

"Don't be leaving the area, Mr Michael," he shouted above the rabble around him, a distinct note of warning to his words, "We'll need to question you."

Mr Michael quickened his pace, ignoring Irene's panicked enquiries as he gripped even tighter onto her hand. Of course, he should have realised. He had been the old woman's only companion, one of the few people who knew about the letter opener, and one of the most talented people with a blade in the city. Now he had been caught re-visiting the crime scene before sneaking away with a suspicious bloodied bandage. There was also his daughter to consider, who had been in the horrific position of having found the body, but who also might be a suspect herself. He had no doubt that he would be receiving a visit from Inspector Falmer soon.

There was another worrisome consideration plaguing his mind as he hurried down Fossgate with Irene at his heels. If his daughter had been right and it had not been suicide but murder, then the culprit must have been someone Mrs Holden knew. She had let them into her house and had not appeared to have put up a fight. The wounds were severe and apparently committed with a mere letter opener, so it must have taken someone with knowledge of how to use a blade to have delivered such precise and fatal cuts. Someone with strength, someone with anger.

He could hear the inspector's questions in his mind. Didn't you say your poor wife was infirm, Mr Michael? Thought you'd find yourself a new one, eh, Mr Michael? Maybe fancied a bigger house and a bit of wealth, Mr Michael? He fumbled with the key in the lock and quickly fled inside the safety of his house, watching as his daughter collapsed into tears once more in her chair beside the fireplace. As he locked the door behind him wondering how he could console her, he noticed that Irene's apron was stained with streaks of red.

Neither could eat supper and when they did retire to their bedrooms, they could not sleep nor even rest. Irene tossed and turned between fits of fury and weeping while Mr Michael wondered what he would say to the police when they did call him in for questioning. He had no alibi as there was no one who could confirm his location at the time Mrs Holden was murdered. He had awoken, eaten breakfast and spent the entire day in his workshop alone. Furthermore, his daughter had then been discovered at the murder scene. What if the police thought Irene an accomplice? Or that he had forced her to commit the terrible deed? What if they took his precious daughter from him? He did not know what to do.

Chapter Fourteen

Any noise within the Michael family home was drowned out by the incessant drumming of raindrops on the roof. Sheets of water cascaded down and pooled in the street outside as the residents tried to continue their morning routines regardless. Mr Michael sat in his kitchen trying to process the events of the previous day. The robbery alone had been brutal and heartless, but the murder was cruel beyond comprehension. The suggestion made by Inspector Falmer that it could have been suicide was ludicrous, though his misguided conclusion suggested that he had never seen any crime quite like this before.

Mr Michael knew without question that Mrs Holden had been killed with her own letter opener, which suggested that the offender had already been aware of its existence before they arrived at the shop. It seemed too coincidental that they would use it to fatally injure his friend without prior awareness. Living so close to Walmgate, Mr Michael was no stranger to a brutal brawl or petty theft, but on this occasion, it seemed they were dealing with someone far more sinister than the usual thieves and rogues that swarmed the city streets at night. He had never heard of a crime like this before in York nor in the county beyond. He feared that the police were completely out of their depth and that Mrs Holden's case would never be solved.

As he stared into the mug of tea growing cold before

him, Irene watched on with concern. Her father had not said a word all morning, though neither had she. For while she had somehow managed to recover from the distress of seeing the old woman and her violent injuries, she was now consumed by a new terror; the thought of her father being arrested for the crime. She knew he was innocent and could not identify a single soul in the neighbourhood who would ever think he could do such a hideous act, but the words of the inspector still haunted her.

A sudden banging on the front door cut through the noise of the storm and made both Mr Michael and Irene snap to attention. Their eyes met for the first time that morning, their faces frozen with the same look of alarm. They did not move a muscle. The bash of a fist against the worn wood sounded again with more force, followed by a voice calling only one name: Mr Michael. He rose from his seat slowly and opened the door with trepidation, anticipating the hardened stare of Inspector Falmer. Instead, he was greeted by two gentlemen he had never met before.

The first was dressed in a black waterproof cape with a peaked cap, under which his police uniform had turned black with damp. He promptly introduced himself as Officer Harding, the severity of his tone contradictory to the softness of his eyes and small smile as he grimaced against the deluge. The other gentleman quietly announced himself as Mr Roberts, his posture and smart attire giving him an even more authoritarian air than the officer. His red hair was scraped back and oiled, still retaining its shape despite the weather, and his lighter coloured beard was neatly trimmed around his pointed chin. He wore spectacles that were now fogged, forcing him to look over the top. Though a stranger, Mr Michael still recognised the man immediately; he was the city's coroner, and the two men had come to take Mr Michael to identify the body of his departed friend.

While the introductions were being made, Irene hid herself in the darkest corner of the kitchen where she could listen without being seen. She was relieved that it had not been the inspector, though she was still anxious about the possibility of her father's arrest. As he wrapped a coat around himself and left with the two gentlemen, he turned to give a small nod in her direction before locking the door behind him. She knew that he would want her to remain at home where she was safe. If Mrs Holden had been killed as some form of revenge, then she and her mother could also be potential victims.

Irene tried not to dwell on this thought and instead busied herself with cleaning the house and tending to Winifred. She wished that her mother were awake enough to be able to take all of this in, to listen to her daughter and offer the maternal advice and support Irene had so rarely received during her young life. Instead, the girl watched as Winifred's eyelids drifted open and shut, but once again no words were shared. Perhaps this was all that was needed; just to sit beside a person you loved and to know that they loved you back. Irene clung to her mother's cold and clammy hand and waited for her father's return.

At first, it had struck Mr Michael as somewhat comical

that he had felt so relieved on hearing he was to attend the morgue and not the police station, but his respite was brief. He was the only one who had known Mrs Holden personally and the only one who could identify her body with any confidence. He had not asked Irene about what she had seen, but he knew that it was something no person should ever have to experience, let alone a child. It was not merely the end of a life that Irene had witnessed nor the ruthless revenge of a cruel criminal. It had been their shared hopes of finding the thief and somehow managing to save Mrs Holden that had also died that day.

The rain had eased, though the pavements were still awash with excess water. Officer Harding talked ceaselessly to him as they walked through the deluge, his helmet perched under one arm while he smoothed back his hair with a moist hand, as if attempting to smarten his appearance next to the coroner. Mr Michael had not heard a word he had said. He had been watching the debris swimming between the cracks of the cobbles as they strode the long distance, though none among the party seemed to notice the passing time, their minds each distracted by the same concern. Mr Roberts had remained silent until the morgue came into view, at which point he paused and turned to Mr Michael, again peering over his spectacles. He said only two words but Mr Michael heard him clearly; 'prepare yourself'.

Once inside the building, both Mr Michael and the officer were stilled by the eerie atmosphere that immediately sent shivers up their spines. Apathetic to their anxieties, Mr Roberts led the way to a room where several bodies rested on wooden tables, each covered with a cloth. Officer Harding waited at a discrete distance while the coroner led Mr Michael to the furthest corner. It took no more than two minutes for him to look down on the face of Agnes Holden and to confirm that it was indeed his former friend. It was the first time he had heard another person use her first name and it had made him feel strangely relieved, as if Mr Roberts had confirmed that Mrs Holden had had a life before Holden's Haunt.

Mr Michael was also comforted by how serene and content she looked. Though he had not seen her injuries, he had vividly imagined them based on Inspector Falmer's brief description and from the many sordid comments he had been unfortunate enough to overhear in the street. Instead of a bloated bloodied mess, Mrs Holden had appeared quite at peace. Her usual soured expression had softened, her mouth softly curled up at its edges as if in a smile, while wisps of grey hair formed a gentle halo around her head. Was this what she had looked like when she was sleeping? It had been a long time, but Mr Michael now finally saw the girl he remembered. Here was Agnes Dartton, older but still quite beautiful in her own way. Mr Roberts offered him a few more minutes but there was nothing left to say. His friend had gone and no amount of grief, anger or regret would change that.

As they left the room, Officer Harding walked ahead eagerly, his pace quickening in anticipation of returning to the police station. He had looked tense and blanched ever since they had arrived at the morgue; perhaps he was not yet used to the peculiar smell nor the absence of sound in such a place. Once the officer had vanished from view, Mr Roberts stopped in his tracks, coughing into his fist lightly until Mr Michael paused and retraced his steps to meet him. The coroner had said next to nothing apart from the necessary procedural requirements, but now he looked at Mr Michael as if about to embark on a lengthy narrative, though he knew he would have to be brief.

"Mr Michael, I have some information which may be of significance. I believe it is best entrusted to you and not to the police at this point." Mr Roberts' words were hesitant but determined, carefully chosen and quickly calculated. "I have been informed that Mrs Holden had in her possession an unusual object. A letter opener with a unique pattern. I know this not because I have seen it for myself, but because I know of a man who has."

Suddenly, Mr Michael felt the hammering of his heart against his chest, apprehension merged with excitement, his eyes growing wide with expectation. He nodded softly, urging the coroner to continue.

"I am convinced the source is reliable, though I do not know how it may help. Perhaps if you speak to him first, before the police…" Mr Roberts trailed off, his eyes narrowing up the road as Officer Harding reappeared, waving his truncheon by way of encouragement.

"The name, please?" Mr Michael urged, nodding his head as he forced a smile back in the direction of the impatient officer up ahead.

"Keep it to yourself. Trust no one else," Mr Roberts

replied hastily. He turned and began walking back towards the morgue.

"I will, please just tell me," Mr Michael insisted, drawn between the two men. Over the noise of the busy street, the coroner was nearing the point at which Mr Michael would no longer be able to hear him. He watched Mr Roberts' face intently, his pace towards the officer as gradual as he could manage, his whole body tensed with anticipation. The coroner said something, a whisper, inaudible, swept away on the breeze, but Mr Michael had seen his lips move. The words were unmistakable. Mr Roberts had mouthed 'Dan Chelten'.

Chapter Fifteen

Though Mr Michael felt nervous arriving at the police station, he also felt unusually alert, fuelled with a determined energy to tell Inspector Falmer as much as he could remember in the hope that the police would begin to take the case more seriously. The only detail he would keep to himself would be the new knowledge regarding Dan Chelten, the name he was now positive the coroner had intended to share with him.

Why Mr Roberts had decided to tell him such information and for what purpose, Mr Michael did not know, but it was the only chance he currently had at coming closer to knowing who had robbed and murdered his friend. If he told the police what he knew now, they would simply arrest Dan and put the blame on him, just as Mr Michael feared they still might do to himself. It was as if Inspector Falmer did not want to admit that there was a violent criminal out there; perhaps he wanted to protect his reputation or was simply inexperienced in such matters.

Drunken scuffles and trivial muggings were one thing, but a case as unique and unusual as this one demanded something more. It needed an intelligence and expertise that the York police force did not at that moment possess. This was by and large a safe city with serious crimes a seldom occurrence, until now. Mr Michael hoped he would be proved wrong by Inspector

Falmer and his team, but he could not ignore the feeling in the pit of his stomach nor the compulsion to seek the truth. The police were making a mockery of Mrs Holden's death. He would tell them as much as he could and hope for the best before conducting his own private enquiries to see what emerged.

Above all, it was the three mystery men who had visited Holden's Haunt before the thefts began that concerned Mr Michael. Though he did not know their identities nor their connection to one another, they were one of the few recent memories that Mrs Holden had been able to share. The fact that their appearance coincided with the stolen objects and the money could not be a mere coincidence. As he sat in the police station waiting for Inspector Falmer to finish speaking with one of his officers, Mr Michael thought carefully about the descriptions of the men. He could recall being bemused by their odd imagery when Mrs Holden had told him, yet not one of them had given cause for concern. Now, with hindsight, they seemed so exaggerated as to be almost a joke. He began to wonder whether Inspector Falmer would even believe him, but it was the only lead he was willing to share in the hope that there was some truth in it. If the police could not find such unusual characters, then they certainly had no chance of solving a murder case.

Having finally finished his conversation, Inspector Falmer led Mr Michael to a narrow room with a square window so high and small that barely any light filtered through. There were two wooden chairs and between them a tatty table, names and shapes carved deeply into its surface. A stuttering gas lamp and two small cups sat to his left, both empty as if ornamental. Mr Michael surveyed the setup as he attempted to prepare himself, but his mind was a torrent of uncontrollable thoughts. He wrung his hands together, wishing he owned a watch. There was no indication of the time except for the slowly shifting light outside. He surveyed the window, silently praying for nightfall.

Even as he began, Inspector Falmer already suspected that questioning Mr Michael would reveal little of interest. The carpenter was well known for being honest and dedicated to his trade as well as to his family. Though he was growing increasingly frustrated at the lack of evidence in the case, the inspector knew he had not yet found the murderer nor the thief; far from it. If anything, Mr Michael and his daughter should have been rewarded as the only two people in the neighbourhood to have cared for Mrs Holden but, of course, he kept such thoughts to himself. It would not do to show sympathy when the body was still fresh and the crime so current.

Indeed, Mr Michael proved to be an exceptional interviewee and took barely any prompting to be able to recall the precise details of his relationship with and knowledge of the victim, along with thorough accounts of the information he had already been able to procure on his own. Mr Michael had been especially diligent with his recollection of the three men who Mrs Holden had described to him. The inspector had even scribbled a few choice words in his notebook for future reference.

There was almost a look of embarrassment on the man's face as he related the details, but at this point anything was better than nothing. Inspector Falmer was beginning to think that this case was too intricate and uncommon to be resolved.

There was the man with the gigantic moustache strapped across his face. It must have been fake, of course, and a sorry excuse for a disguise that even Mrs Holden should have been able to see through. The second man she had apparently described was the exact height and build as the former visitor. Brothers, he wrote down, or father and son? He left a trail of question marks in his notebook. Then finally, the one with the strange coat who had shuffled around in the wrong-sized boots. All highly suspicious. So why had Mrs Holden not questioned them?

Mr Michael did not have a response to the inspector's suggestion, though it was something he must have contemplated. What had the neighbours thought of such eccentrics? Did he himself not realise there was a pattern to the men? The inspector watched him closely as beads of sweat rolled down his face and into the collar of his grey frayed shirt. He noticed that the man kept coughing into his bandaged hand as if he had a permanent lump in his throat. He was also becoming increasingly tired and confused, repeating information two or three times. It was making the inspector himself weary, so much so that he ended up abandoning the effort of notetaking.

The light from the lamp had begun to flicker more forcefully as it neared the end of its supply of oil.

Inspector Falmer realised that they had been sitting for quite some time, the room having grown nearly fully dark and bitterly cold. He retrieved his pocket watch to check the hour and spun his head around toward the window for confirmation. It was now a tiny square of jet black. A growl from his stomach prompted him to cut Mr Michael off mid-sentence before excusing himself from the room. He wanted to give the man some time alone. The inspector closed the door behind him and watched through the bars as Mr Michael slumped onto the table with his head in his hands.

Ever since Mr Michael had reported the missing objects, the inspector and his team had followed standard protocol. They had questioned members of the local community, conducted a thorough search both within and around the property, and had even earwigged in bars and down alleyways for any whisper of useful gossip. There had been stories, descriptions, theories and even a mysterious clump of horsehair that had been found stuffed between the cracks in the brickwork outside Holden's Haunt, but there had been nothing in the way of conclusive evidence.

Most of the information Inspector Falmer had gathered sounded like children's fairy tales. Mystery men with bulging sacks slung over their shoulders, wheelbarrows filled with bedsheets apparently on their way to the washerwomen, even talk of Mrs Holden's crow being a shapeshifting witch that had been sent to spy on her by a criminal gang. He had been left with a bundle of notes that resembled a penny dreadful rather than a legitimate criminal investigation. He had hoped the post-mortem would reveal death by suicide, but this had not been the case. He was indisputably dealing with a murder.

The inspector had spoken to enough people now to realise that while the old woman had lived alone, she was not by any means hated. Fanciful as their stories were, the neighbours had painted a picture of an intelligent, perceptive and determined woman. She was not mad or depressed, they told him, just lonely. He had watched Mr Michael shake with fear as he had tried to defend himself, his daughter and his friend. This fierce loyalty moved the inspector in a way he did not expect. During the four hours they had spent in the cold cramped room at the police station, Mr Michael had left no detail untold, no thought or idea unsaid. He had talked of their childhood, their idle chatter, of the stories he had learned. He had looked into his pale palms as he spoke of the blame he felt for what had happened to his friend. Blame, the inspector had noted, but not guilt.

Once the interrogation had finally finished, Mr Michael was physically and mentally exhausted, his eyes bloodshot and barely open, the skin of his face translucent and damp. He had been wringing his hands together for so long that he had disturbed the scar from his accident at the workshop, the blood seeping out from the bandage and drying across his fingers. In comparison, Inspector Falmer felt unusually calmed by the experience. He was now thoroughly convinced that no member of the Michael family had anything to do with the robbery or the murder. They had indeed been Mrs Holden's only friends.

As the inspector called time on the interview and saw Mr Michael to the front door of the station, he pressed his palm gently to the man's back in a rare gesture of reassurance. It had not been the verbal battle the police so frequently fought with suspects. On the contrary, the inspector had had quite a pleasant time finding out more about Holden's Haunt and its history. On noticing the lack of light outside, Inspector Falmer bid Mr Michael a good evening and promised to let him know if there were any further developments in the case. He closed the door firmly, leaving a bewildered and dishevelled former suspect to make his way back home.

While he was glad to be a free man once more, Mr Michael was also dumbfounded at Inspector Falmer's casual attitude that had prevailed throughout the questioning, almost as if he were not to be believed. It had been like jumping into the icy waters of the Ouse on a winter's day, the shock and the pain so sharp and swift. Mr Michael's contributions had been carelessly cast aside, his revelations deemed useless. The culprit was still out there. Perhaps now they always would be.

As he shuffled home in the worsening drizzle, Mr Michael was consumed with shame. Not only had he been unable to prevent Mrs Holden's sorry demise, but he had put Irene in terrible danger too. He may have escaped arrest but he was by no means finished with this case. If the police would not seek justice for Mrs Holden, then it would be down to him.

The pubs were beginning to fill with their regulars,

bright lights shining invitingly with the stale smell of spilt ale, smoke, searing meat and urine wafting from the open doorways. He walked past his own front door but kept travelling onwards, watching the faces change and hearing the accents alter. Tired, hungry, but feeling the familiar throb of adrenalin deep inside, Mr Michael knew that it had to be him. He would find Dan Chelten and he would discover the truth. He would begin that very night.

Chapter Sixteen

The day had passed in a blur for Irene. After her father had left with the police officer and the unknown gentleman that morning, she had remained in the house trying to complete idle tasks while her mind raced with terrifying thoughts of what would happen to him. She had heard so many dreadful tales about suspects and what the bobbies did to make them talk, acts bad enough to be breaking the law themselves. Alone, accused, and confined to a cell with only the cold stone walls for company, she feared for her father's sanity as well as his safety.

The evening seemed to come suddenly, taking with it the light and her energy as she sat alone in the dark and empty kitchen, the fire nearly out and the supper long gone cold. Eventually Irene could bear it no more and decided to try to sleep, resting a gentle kiss on her mother's moist cheek before heading to her own bed. She lay listening to every single sound, waiting for her father to return home, wondering if he ever would. Somewhere out there, he was either locked in a cell awaiting his fate for a crime he did not commit, or else wandering the streets where there were criminals and convicts and the man who had killed Mrs Holden. Despite her silent prayers, she heard nothing all night. He did not return.

The following morning, Irene was trying to straighten

her unruly hair when her ears pricked to the sound of the latch on the kitchen door. She threw down the comb and ran, bolting down the stairs two at a time, racing to wrap her arms around her father. Mr Michael closed his eyes as the girl pressed her face into his chest, his arms holding her close even though his coat was still sodden from the downpour of the previous day. Despite his stature, he now slumped as if a great weight burdened his entire body, letting out a long low sigh into the top of his daughter's head. Irene noticed the faint smell of ale on his breath. She inched up her gaze and looked into his eyes, barely open and ringed with dark shadows as if bruised.

Irene prompted her father to wash and change while she made up the fire and prepared a hot drink and some toast to revive him. She did not need to ask where he had been. She had already imagined his every footstep as the minutes ticked by through the night. Her only concern now was that he was home. Together, they would somehow find a way to move on from this nightmare.

She watched her father readily tucking into his breakfast before taking the partially eaten toast from between his fingers and slathering it with jam, adding another two slices to his plate. For the first time in days, Irene heard him give a soft laugh under his breath, bringing warmth and reassurance to her work as she began chopping the vegetables for a comforting stew. She could not have known the secrets he was hiding, keeping quiet to spare her from further trauma.

Despite the steady thud of her knife against the board,

the kitchen still hung with an uncomfortable silence. Her father crunched his toast and sipped noisily at his tea, as if trying to add a sense of normality to a situation they both knew was anything but. He had come close to arrest and Irene had come close to losing him. Whether they liked it or not, they were both equally involved in the mystery and would need to see it through to its end together. At the same moment, Irene ceased her chopping and Mr Michael drained the last of his brew. They sat at the table opposite one another, the father rehearsing his words in his mind, the daughter silently praying once more that nothing bad would happen to them. Then Mr Michael began his story.

Irene sat with her hands steepled under her chin, completely engrossed by her father's words. Far from causing fear, she found herself stirred by his recollections. Mr Michael too seemed animated and almost excited by what had happened. The quiet calm of the morgue, the mysterious mouthed message of Mr Roberts, the endless hours recounting Mrs Holden's history to the inspector, followed by the immense frustration he had felt on leaving the station. The whole day tumbled out of his mouth with breathy relief, falling on the eager ears of his only child. He also revealed where he had been all night; out looking for clues. Descriptions, suspicions, impressions and opinions. Perhaps even the criminal himself.

It had not been easy. There had been malicious words and hurtful accusations spat at him, threats of violence and fists brandished in his face, but the very worst had been hearing the vicious lies about Mrs Holden.

Despite his best efforts, Mr Michael had to admit that he had not found out anything significant, but he felt he had had no choice. He kept replaying the movement of Mr Roberts' lips over in his mind, wondering if he could have been mistaken, searching for something he may have missed: a memory, a story, a suggestion he had overlooked. After the day he had had, trawling the streets had seemed a far better way to occupy his evening compared to spending a restless night at home consumed by guilt.

Irene nodded in understanding. It was in her father's nature to try to help, particularly if that person could not help themselves. Mrs Holden had always relied on him and he would remain loyal to her until the man who had betrayed her was found and justice sought. There was something in this final realisation that suddenly brought back a memory, an encounter she had pushed to the back of her mind. It had seemed irrelevant, but now that she remembered it, she wondered if it might not have been such a trivial meeting after all.

"Father, I've summat t'tell you," Irene began, her voice filled with worry as she shuffled in her chair, her finger tracing the age-old scuffs in its surface. She hastily wiped her sweating palms along the sides of her dress and swallowed the lump in her throat. Mr Michael watched her sudden change in countenance with concern.

"Speak, child. What is it that 'as you lookin' so frightful?"

"Papa, I 'ave a secret. A secret 'bout Mrs 'olden and me."

Chapter Seventeen

Irene's story began on a Saturday some two weeks previous. She had decided to go to see Mrs Holden as it had been a few days since she had last called to deliver some food and coal. She had taken with her a pair of shabby cotton smocks, a lightly stained pinafore and a crocheted shawl, all of which had been procured by Mr Michael from a neighbour who had just lost their mother. She had been an ample woman with arms set like tree trunks, her clothes specially made to suit her generous frame. The neighbour was glad to be rid of them, with Irene reassuring her father that they would be quite sufficient for his friend. She had washed and darned them to the best of her ability before neatly bundling them up to take to Holden's Haunt.

Despite Irene's hard work, Mrs Holden had been loath to accept the gifts. With some gentle persuasion, however, the young girl managed to relieve her load and even helped the old woman to replace her existing pinny with the freshly laundered replacement. Irene promised to take the rest of her garments so that she could clean and repair them at home. She knew her skills with a needle were not what they were with a knife, but it would have to do. Mrs Holden had to consider her health. The old woman nodded reluctantly, throwing the woollen wrap across her shoulders as she settled back into her armchair.

Though she always tried to stay for at least an hour, Irene no longer felt comfortable in Mrs Holden's barren shop. She had had far too many nightmares about vicious crimes and cunning criminals since the belongings had been stolen, and she was now worried that her thoughts could well be premonitions rather than her imagination. As she watched Mrs Holden's eyelids flutter open and shut, she tried to remove such concerns and instead made herself useful. She retrieved some fresh water and washed the borrowed implements from the Michaels' own kitchen: two small cups, a wooden spoon and a chipped plate, which was currently piled with what looked to be the wrinkled skin of an orange. Irene did not remember having ever brought her such a thing, but perhaps it had been a gift from a kind neighbour or even her father. At least it was a sign that she had eaten something.

Irene then emptied the basket she had brought with her, placing the coal in the second-hand bucket, the food in a small wooden box her father had made, and the bottle of ginger ale on the floor. She had discovered the drink stashed away in a kitchen cupboard at home where it had been covered by an even layer of dust. Irene could not recall ever tasting it, and her father so seldom used the kitchen that she was fairly certain he would not notice its absence. It had been taken on a whim, a rare flurry of rebellion fluttering inside her, but she was certain that Mrs Holden could be trusted to keep her secret. Besides, they both deserved a treat.

Though she could not see, Mrs Holden still seemed to have perfect hearing, her head tilting this way and that as she followed the echo of the girl's footsteps around the house. At the sound of the cork popping and the dull fizz of the contents, the old woman twitched her nose and pursed her lips, almost anticipating the brew. Irene seated herself on the floor in front of Mrs Holden and poured a little into each of the cups. She carefully handed one to the old woman, helping her take it in both hands. The satisfied smack of her lips as she took the first sip reassured Irene that she had made the right decision in taking the bottle that morning.

Once they had both relaxed a little, Irene asked Mrs Holden about the three strange men her father had mentioned to her the previous evening. They had sounded most suspicious, yet he had not seemed overly concerned. Mrs Holden gave no word of response to the enquiry, so Irene had proceeded to tell her about Mr Michael's anxiety instead. He was gravely worried about the thefts and could not sleep properly for fear that the villain would come back. Irene paused but still there was no reply. She then told the old woman how everyone on the street and in the neighbourhood and perhaps even the whole city were all so very afraid for her safety and wanted nothing more than to help. Still, the old woman was silent.

Irene's face was flushed, her eyes beginning to well up against her will as she clutched tightly onto her cup. She grabbed the bottle and poured herself another serving of ginger ale, hoping to quell her emotions as she downed the contents. As she finished the last drop, Mrs Holden stirred. She tucked her empty cup between her thigh and the armrest, then did something she had not done in an exceptionally long while. She held out her hands, reaching with her arms until they were extended at full length, the weak muscles quaking as she struggled to keep them aloft. Her empty eyes scanned the room searching for the girl, begging her to come forward.

Burping under her breath, Irene wiped the sleeve of her dress across her mouth before slowly shuffling on her knees closer to Mrs Holden. She folded her fingers around the hands that reached towards her, feeling the old woman gently squeezing back, her flesh surprisingly warm despite the cracked and crusted skin. Mrs Holden held her for a few moments, her milky gaze focused straight ahead.

"Listen to me," she whispered, her voice calm and consoling. Irene felt a tension release from her shoulders, her eyes firmly fixed on the face before her. This was the moment she had anticipated. Finally, she would receive the answers to her many questions and have some kind of conclusion to take home to her father and resolve his concerns.

"You've a rare thing," Mrs Holden continued, holding onto the girl's hands with determination, "You're an innocent, you've a good 'eart. But you'll soon find 'em folk who 'ant. Some people keep their problems t'themselves. Years o' suffering, all in 'ere." She released a hand and tapped the fingertips to her chest. "And it ne'er goes away. Year an' year they live with it, gettin' angrier an' bitterer 'til they can't stand it n'more. They find a way." She let go of Irene and clenched both hands to her breast, clinging to the ragged pinafore as her bosom heaved up and down with weighted breath. Her hollow eyes began to look lost, even scared.

Irene did not understand what was going on or how this had anything to do with her father. Maybe the old woman had lost her mind after all, just like the neighbours had said.

"Mrs 'olden, please," she implored, resting her clammy hands on the woman's knees, searching her face in desperation for any sign of sanity.

The snowy globes of Mrs Holden's eyes rolled around in their sockets and watered as she returned her hands to her lap. She paused then reached down the side of her armchair and produced the letter opener, caressing the blade with her fingers, her breathing returning to normal like a child being hushed by its soother. She seemed to forget the girl's presence entirely after that, even though Irene pleaded for her to continue. But there was nothing she could do. Feeling mounting frustration growing once more, she picked up the laundry, her basket and the empty bottle, muttering a curt farewell as she headed for the door.

Just as Irene reached the corridor, she heard Mrs Holden shout.

"Your father'll be fine… but my days are numbered." Irene paused but did not respond. She headed home, determined to forget the meeting had ever taken place. From that day on, she had focused on caring for her parents, putting her faith in the only hope that they and Mrs Holden had left: the police. It did not take long for her to forget the exchange had ever happened.

Chapter Eighteen

Irene slowly rose from her seat at the kitchen table and returned to the pile of vegetables she had been slicing. She was thankful to have an excuse to turn her back, knowing her father would not be pleased that she had kept such a story hidden for so long. She felt as if she had failed both him and Mrs Holden, but Mr Michael did not see it that way.

"You were good t'tell me," he replied, waiting until Irene met his gaze before giving her a kindly smile and gentle nod. He did not look angry or upset as she had expected. Indeed, his eyes were surprisingly bright and alert.

"I don't believe Mrs 'olden were going mad," he reasoned, "It's a clue."

Clapping his hands together with a short sharp snap, Mr Michael promptly retrieved his boots from beside the front door and began fastening them with haste. He pulled on his coat, fumbling to do up the buttons with a look of determination growing on his face. Irene replaced her knife and watched her father with confusion. She did not understand his sudden energy. What had he heard in the story that she herself had missed? Mr Michael answered as if he could read her thoughts.

"Mrs 'olden knew he were gonna come back, Irene. She were waiting fer 'im."

Realising the truth of his words and the implication they held, she replied, "But father, doesn't that mean she knew who the killer were?"

"Exactly!" he almost shouted, a tone of triumph to his voice as he drew his daughter into a rough hug. Mr Michael kissed her forehead as if she had just created a light where there had long been only darkness. Then he left the house once more, Irene watching out of the window as he strode swiftly down the street.

As he walked, Mr Michael considered the possible identity of the felon. He was unquestionably smart and would not have sold anything just yet for fear of being discovered. He would also need a fairly sizable house or perhaps an outbuilding in which to hide the items before selling them, no doubt to other rogues on the black market. That meant that he was likely to remain close and that perhaps he would even have stayed in the city.

There was one man whose name continued to thrum round and round Mr Michael's mind. No matter how much he had doubted the possibility, there now seemed no other character that fit the bill. A notorious trickster whose business as a blacksmith was almost entirely founded on his ability to manipulate others: Dan Chelten. Yet despite his reputation, Mr Michael could not believe him to be the criminal. Instead, he was sure the man had some insider knowledge that would prove vital to the case.

Parliament Square was pulsing with activity as the crowds clustered for the Saturday morning market, the sights, smells and sounds causing a cacophony of sensations as Mr Michael attempted to scan the scene. He extended his long neck out to peer over and across the hordes of shoppers filling every available space between the stalls. He was looking for one man only. If Mr Roberts was right and Dan Chelten had indeed known about the letter opener, then it was entirely possible that he had seen it in the hands of the murderer but did not know it. All he had to do was to find him and ask him before the police knew anything about it.

Shuffling as fast as he could manage through the ebb and flow, Mr Michael completed lap after lap of the market looking for Dan but could see no sign of him. The air was thick with smoke, soot, sweat and steam, choking his throat and stinging his eyes. Perhaps it was already too late. After the eighth or ninth attempt, Mr Michael conceded, suddenly overwhelmed with exhaustion, the sleepless nights and constant worry weighing him down like a packhorse. He could smell the enticing food stalls and reasoned that a reviving snack might help. The seafood stand usually had a queue of at least a baker's dozen, but today there was no one in line and the display still looked fresh and plentiful.

Resigning himself to his lost cause, Mr Michael surveyed the display and ordered his favourite, cradling his chosen pickings with both hands as he walked round to the low wall of Whip-Ma-Whop-Ma-Gate and slumped himself down. He watched the animated throng mill pass as he stabbed his wooden pin into the moist and salty whelks and ate them one by one, indulging in the many happy memories that resurfaced.

Childhood visits to the market with his mother, the occasional jaunt to the coast for a commission at work, the time he had brought a bagful of seafood home so that his then four-year-old daughter could fall in love with whelks too, which she had.

As he chewed the slippery flesh, Mr Michael began to muse on Mrs Holden in her final days, sitting in that empty room in her decrepit armchair with just the items she was wearing and a useless letter opener for company. All her own precious family experiences, all those years of history kept within each and every object scattered around her, until they had all disappeared. Not just vanished but stolen, forcibly taken against her will. Had she known that the same man was robbing her, she would never have allowed him to get away with it. Mr Michael was sure of that.

Though he had not been a witness to Mrs Holden's death, he had formed several theories regarding her demise and the unusual posture in which she had been discovered, which Inspector Falmer had gone into great detail describing during his long interrogation. Perhaps the letter opener had been kept as a weapon and she had died trying to defend herself, but there was something unsettling about the pose. Her arms were open, almost comfortable, as if she had not resisted the attacker. So it was entirely probable that she had known them, with Irene's story seeming to provide proof of the fact.

Mr Michael drained the briny liquid from the paper cup before forming it into a small ball with his good hand and tucking it into his coat pocket. He was about to give the market one last check for Dan Chelten when an old man approached, limping and leaning heavily on a walking stick with an ornate owl carved on the top. The stranger smiled as Mr Michael watched him then shuffled himself onto the wall with the help of his stick. He smelled of peat and damp straw, his thick and dusty clothes swamping his frame. There were coarse black hairs growing from his nostrils and his ears, and when he smiled, his tongue protruded from between two missing front teeth.

"You the man lookin' fer tales 'bout our Mrs 'olden, then?" the stranger began with a thick Yorkshire accent and a faint hiss on account of his absent dentures.

"Aye. Name's Mr Michael, sir. She were a dear friend o' mine but sadly she…"

"I know, I know, I 'eard from them down there." The man waved his stick across his shoulder in the direction of the Shambles behind them.

Mr Michael could not take his eyes off the owl atop of the walking stick. He was sure it had come from Holden's Haunt. The man noticed his stare and began stroking the bird's head with a finger.

"Beauty, ain't she? Just one o' many things I bought from that nice lady. Paid enough fer it like, but I knows good quality when I sees it. Now, on t'business, Michaels." He waved a hand to prevent the other man's interruption.

Stuart Ainsley Junior, the man Mr Michael was now speaking to, had been one of the few people to have known the Dartton family when Agnes was a girl. His father, Stuart Ainsley, had run a successful grocer's in the centre of town where the Dartton family always visited for their fruit and vegetables, usually sending young Agnes on the errand as her mother was so often unwell. Stuart had worked in the shop ever since he was a boy and had watched Agnes grow from a little girl into a polite and pretty young woman. He enjoyed helping her pick out the choicest examples from the displays and she always seemed grateful for his assistance. Matthew Holden had also been a familiar face and had been particularly vocal about his newfound admiration for the Darttons' daughter. He had even taken one of the kittens that Stuart's brother had found in the back yard, saying it would make a perfect present for Agnes.

Mr Ainsley could not remember precisely when Agnes had abruptly stopped her visits to the shop. He and his father had waited as days became weeks and weeks turned into months, but still their loyal customer did not return. Fearing that something was amiss, Stuart the younger walked to the Dartton family home to check. There he saw Agnes in the garden rocking a baby boy in her arms, her face a picture of contentment. She seemed shocked and even upset to see him but eventually agreed to let Stuart bring her some groceries every week, making him promise to never tell a living soul about the child.

"Ne'er knew what t'fuss were about meself," the old man shrugged as he reflected on the start of his story, gazing off into the distance as if he could picture it.

Mr Michael was enthralled. It was the first time he had ever heard anyone talk about Agnes, the Darttons, or the new addition to the family.

"What 'appened to the bairn?" he asked eagerly.

"Dunno. Funny one, that," Mr Ainsley mused, wriggling his shoulders before scratching a hairy lughole with his little finger, "Ne'er saw much of 'im, seemed to 'ave disappeared when he were a nipper."

Mr Michael could still recall having seen the boy on the rare visits he made with his wooden carvings, but he had never given much thought as to what had happened to the youngster. It was unfortunate that Mrs Holden had never mentioned him, though her silence suggested that the boy's disappearance had been a source of further distress. His thoughts were cut short as Mr Ainsley continued.

"Now then, our friend Matthew 'olden, I do know a little bit more 'bout that there story." The old man retracted the finger from his ear and wiped it along the fabric of his trousers before shuffling himself into a more comfortable position on the wall. Resting his hands in his lap, Mr Ainsley began to share what he knew of Mrs Holden's husband.

Chapter Nineteen

Agnes Holden had spent more of her childhood among the local wildlife than with people and considered her upbringing and temperament all the more serene for it. She had been brought up in an unusually quiet area of the city just outside of its ancient walls. Near the river and a small woodland, she would spend hours exploring the plants, flowers and animals along the banks and beneath the trees.

Sometimes Agnes wished she could have kept birds and mice and fish as pets, but they were so much more beautiful in the wild. She had, however, seen other children put things in jars or tie wool around their necks, which had filled her with sadness and anger. Her neighbour would often boast of her latest find and shake the container with such force that Agnes nicknamed her 'creature killer'. When given the opportunity, she would sneak into the girl's garden to rescue the prisoners and release them back into nature. Though an honest and demure young lady, she also possessed strong morals and could not bear to see another living soul suffer. She would remind herself that the risk of being caught and punished was far outweighed by the benefit of sparing an innocent life.

While the Dartton family were no longer in regular attendance at church, they still considered themselves to be followers of God. Agnes' parents had belonged to the same congregation since they were children and it was there that they had fallen in love, their eyes meeting across the pews every Sunday. With his growing experience as an apprentice carpenter and her respectful background as the daughter of a successful tradesman, their families were quick to approve of the match and the couple moved into their family home before either of them had turned the age of twenty. As their only child and having been raised in a quiet suburban area, Agnes grew used to her own company and came to prefer it. She was naturally shy and had been brought up to believe that children should be seen and not heard, which made her even more reluctant to converse with strangers or to try and make friends.

As she matured, Agnes' mother would increasingly reference her daughter's prospects for marriage, talking across the kitchen table with her husband over dinner as if the girl were not there. Agnes would listen with mixed emotions. She knew that marriage could be a wonderful blessing, as her parents' own example proved, but she also feared that she was still far too young and that she would never be able to find a man that would understand her. Though she had had few children to compare herself with, Agnes sensed inside herself that she was different; her nature, her feelings, the private passions that swelled in her mind as she lay on her back in the grass watching the clouds roll by. Who would understand her independence? What man would allow her to simply be herself?

Her mother already had a few suitors in mind, sons of local merchants who would likely inherit a good trade and be able to provide a secure life for Agnes and her aging parents. Mr Dartton would never pass comment, instead preferring his mealtimes to be silent, as did Agnes. Neither would speak as Mrs Dartton continued on and on, with Agnes frequently excusing herself from the table as her head filled with ever more frightening thoughts. She was beginning to wonder if it would be a matter of years, months or even days before her mother packed up her only daughter's belongings and waved her goodbye with the promise to visit her after the wedding.

As if having overheard their evening conversations whistling through the chimney, a young man called Matthew appeared at the Dartton's door one late September afternoon with a bunch of wildflowers and an eager smile. Mrs Dartton called after her daughter, eventually finding her at the entrance to her father's workshop where she was watching him and his young apprentice at work. Mrs Dartton introduced Matthew and encouraged the pair to sit and talk on the garden wall at the front of the house. She observed them like a magpie from the kitchen window, silently hoping that his family were wealthy and well bred.

Agnes was embarrassed and confused. She had seen this boy often enough but he had always called for her neighbour, not for her. Now it seemed his affections had shifted. After their first meeting, he returned almost daily with colourful posies that she had no choice but to meekly accept. On her mother's insistence, she took her place on the wall and bashfully averted her eyes as Matthew told her how pretty and charming she was. Her silence seemed only to encourage him, with his visits continuing into the winter and on through the spring. Eventually Agnes grew used to his company and even began to look forward to him calling. She now realised that she was no longer a child and she would need to find a husband soon.

Matthew brought more impressive presents with each visit. Mrs Dartton gave them pride of place on the dresser in the kitchen, assuring her daughter that they were not only love tokens but evidence of his growing success in his profession as a stonemason. Each gift escalated in luxury as he grew ever more enamoured with this quiet and unassuming girl, whom he had already decided would be his future wife. The wildflowers were replaced with lovely bouquets and single red roses, punnets of blood-coloured cherries and cones of roasted nuts, and countless paper parcels of violet lozenges, coltsfoot rock and twists of barley sugar. Matthew would never touch the sweet treats himself, preferring instead to slip them one by one between Agnes' tight lips as he watched.

On Agnes' birthday, Matthew appeared carrying a wooden crate. Inside was a tiny mewing kitten as black as tar with two yellow eyes that searched her face helplessly. Agnes longed to set the poor creature free in the woods, but she knew it would only perish from either cold or something far worse. Instead, she and Matthew took the box to her father's workshop and constructed a little pen complete with a saucer of water and some curls of sawdust for the kitten to play with. As they watched it chase a flake across the floor, the neighbour's daughter appeared at the doorway carrying her own cat writhing in her steadfast arms. She did not say anything but looked in turn at Agnes, Matthew and the kitten with a glare of pure hatred. She gave her cat a sharp shake before departing from the workshop.

The following day, Agnes hurried downstairs to visit her new companion but when she reached the pen and looked inside, she was met by a horrific scene. A fluffy ball lay in a pool of blood on the saucer, the severed body lifeless beside it. She cried into her mother's arms all morning while her father cleared up the mess. While she had no proof, Agnes could sense in her heart that the girl next door had been to blame, though she could never understand why she had acted so cruelly.

Agnes did not mention the kitten to Matthew, fearing that he would think her a bad person and maybe even a terrible mother. She had never known pain nor guilt quite like it, but eventually she would come to know far worse in her lifetime. Matthew assumed that the pet had simply escaped and attempted to console his beloved with stories of the kitten having found a new home somewhere else in the city, ignoring the constant stares of the young neighbour as she watched the couple in conversation, her face contorted with jealousy.

Though the brutality of the girl's actions and her subsequent spying had unnerved Agnes, it had also served to convince her of Matthew's goodness and the promise of a better life that he had repeatedly sworn to her. Whenever the proposal arrived, she could now feel content in her acceptance, but it would be another five years before Agnes and Matthew would wed. A sudden and serious private matter arose requiring the Dartton family to stay at home, withdrawing from society, neighbours, friends and, most especially, from casual suitors. Matthew's visits went from routine to sporadic as Agnes and her parents made their mumbled excuses, avoiding his eyes before slamming their front door shut.

Stuart Ainsley Junior gave a hearty chuckle at the end of his speech as if he had been reciting a famous fable. Mr Michael, on the other hand, was most disturbed by the story and the impression he now had of Matthew Holden.

"Agnes were a good gal," the old man nodded, gripping the carved owl of his walking stick as he eased himself off the wall, "I be sorry to 'ear the sad news." He bowed his head politely in goodbye and ambled off in the opposite direction towards the market, one hand on his stick while the other hastily brought up his breeches before they slid down any further. Mr Michael watched the former shopkeeper leave, wondering how many more people had known Agnes in her prime and whether he might still have the chance to find them. With his stomach full and his head spinning, Mr Michael made his way home.

Chapter Twenty

Mr Michael pottered around his kitchen attempting to make some tea. Still spinning from Mr Ainsley's story, he needed to keep his hands busy as his mind repeated the new information he had gleaned. He set the pan of water to boil before searching the sideboard for a scrap of something to eat. Finding only a wrinkled apple and half a turnip, he turned to survey the empty kitchen and realised that something was wrong. The coals in the fire were glowing softly as if they had been smouldering for some time. There was a pan on the kitchen table with an inch of cold water in the bottom and beside it a wooden chopping board scattered with onion and carrot peelings. A small knife rested idle on top, the one Irene usually carried in her pocket. The scene was a half-finished still life, its most vital element missing. His daughter.

Mr Michael called out for her but received no response, not even a cough nor the creak of a footstep. Abandoning his tea, he made his way swiftly through the small house until he finally found Irene by Winifred's bedside. The girl was knelt pressing a damp cloth to her mother's head, gently humming a song he did not recognise. The window was open though no air seemed to circulate. Instead, it hung with the sickly smell of animal innards after slaughter. Mr Michael noticed the chamber pot at the end of the bed full of what looked like bile with flies buzzing across the surface. On the side table was a small bowl with sprigs of rosemary floating on top. Irene dipped the cloth in, wrung out the excess water, and replaced it over her mother's head.

"She is ill," the girl whispered, her words barely audible above the din of the street below. There was an edge to Irene's voice as she held back her tears.

Mr Michael hovered in the doorway watching his daughter, frozen by a new sensation of fear as he watched her sponging Winifred's forehead with great care. His wife's eyes rolled around in their sockets under the film of her closed lids as if in a nightmare, her lips clenched tightly together and her body rigid under the single sheet. Irene did not turn to look at her father, not wanting to see the look of worry on his face. It had been his only expression for the past few months and she was not sure how much longer she could bear witness to it without going mad.

Leaving his dutiful daughter to his wife's care, Mr Michael raced from the room and through the city to the home of Doctor Pruce. A kindly butler led the way through the prestigious property to the dining room, where the doctor along with his wife and son were just about to begin tucking into a roast pork joint. Mr Michael apologised profusely as he explained his predicament, but thankfully the doctor and his family were used to such disturbances and allowed the man of the house to leave and see to the emergency. Doctor Pruce knew Mr Michael well enough to know that he would only dare ask for help if the woman was genuinely suffering. She had been through so much already and he had been the only physician to attend to her, witnessing every lost infant, failed remedy, and screaming fit of agony.

On arriving at the Michaels' residence, the doctor immediately inspected the patient but could only declare that, once again, there was nothing that could be done. Winifred was lucky to have survived this long, he sighed, not fully recognising the weight of his words. He commended Irene on her help and left Mr Michael with the promise that he would visit again the next day if he could spare the time. Father and daughter could do little more than to continue to watch their loved one and try to provide comfort in the cramped and airless room. Irene took to her vigil once more, tucking the threadbare sheet around her mother before repeating the herbal water ritual. The house fell into a heavy silence save for the few mumbled words of enquiry passing from Mr Michael to Irene, her response always a solemn nod. He made tea and brought bread with jam to his daughter, but she would not take it. No one ate nor slept that night.

The following morning, Winifred had not improved. Her temperature had increased and her eyes, now open, roamed around wildly. As it was a Sunday, Mr Michael did not expect Doctor Pruce to return despite his promise, yet still he peered out of the window at the faintest hint of footsteps, hoping the doctor had returned. It was only as night fell once more that he realised he would not. Irene stayed by her mother's side hour after hour and waited, whispering prayers to a God she now feared, watching for any sign of improvement.

Even though Mr Michael and his daughter were

used to living a life without their loved one, the painful uncertainty of Winifred's future brought an even darker cloud over their troubled home. Irene was already used to balancing her schoolwork and house chores, but in her desire to prove herself mature and capable, she had now added extra responsibilities to her list that kept her moving like a spinning top from dawn to dusk. Physically and emotionally exhausted at the end of each day, she would collapse on the thin mattress that she had dragged into her mother's room and stay awake listening to the rasp of her breathing, hoping for a miracle.

Irene's father, meanwhile, escaped to his workshop for as long as he could each day, though she was never sure whether he was able to concentrate on his work there. He often seemed to stare into an unknown distance during their silent suppers together, as if he were still hunched over his workbench sanding the same piece of wood over and over. Though she was afraid to leave her mother's side, Irene knew how much her father was relying on her to continue as normal. It had not been the first time Winifred had been ill, and the only way they had coped in the past had been to remain as they were. Her feelings of isolation, desperation and depression were now all so familiar that Irene barely noticed them, bravely bearing their weight as she focused her efforts on her family.

While deeply concerned about his wife's deteriorating illness, Mr Michael was also heavily distracted by the unsolved mystery of Mrs Holden's murder. He was wary that his knowledge about Dan Chelten would not remain a secret for long; the man was too convenient a scapegoat for the police, which would leave the real criminal still out there. Even though it would mean less time spent at home with his wife and daughter, Mr Michael nevertheless felt compelled to continue his own enquiries as a matter of honour and duty. What kind of an example would he be setting for Irene if he allowed an innocent man to be arrested and a murderer to remain free?

One morning, having noticed the melody of church bells, Mr Michael had decided to visit Holy Trinity Church and speak with the vicar for any information on Mrs Holden and her past. The soothing sound of the familiar chimes had reminded him of the faint humming of Agnes Dartton, her slim fingers curling around the door of the workshop as they had both watched her father, the sound of her voice only just audible above the slicing and chipping of the blade against wood. After checking once more on his wife and daughter, Mr Michael left the house and followed his accustomed route up Fossgate, then Colliergate, and along to the square.

Despite the imploring smiles of the parishioners, Mr Michael was not persuaded to attend the service that day, though he did say a prayer for his wife while he waited in the churchyard. He ambled around the gravestones listening to the haunting hymns from the united chorus within, their sound both soothing and sorry. He paused opposite a stone bearing a familiar name; Matthew Holden and Alice Holden, father and daughter buried together, though they had not known one another in life. He realised at that moment that Mrs Holden had probably arranged both funerals herself, and that there was now no soul remaining to arrange her own. Yet again, he was made aware of his singular importance in his friend's life – and, it seemed, in her death.

Seating himself on the low wall opposite the gravestone, Mr Michael traced the carved letters with his eyes. He wondered what little Alice would have been like, what kind of a girl she could have become, whether she and Irene would have been friends. Maybe his life too would have been different had Mrs Holden had children. Maybe he would have become reacquainted with her sooner and perhaps she would have been happier, more welcoming and talkative. He might even have had the opportunity to discover more about her past instead of trying to find out about her from strangers after her death. It did not seem right.

Lost in thought, Mr Michael did not realise the passing time nor notice the lull from inside the church followed by the murmur of voices and the hollow thud of footsteps. Dressed almost entirely in black, as was the latest fashion, he observed the congregation filing one by one out of the open door and ambling along the path towards him. He noticed how every person paused to thank the vicar before walking down the path and onto the street to join the existing crowd, where they would each make their way home and enjoy good food and drink, conversation and company, their hearths warm and their hearts pure.

The vicar said goodbye to the last family and

followed them until he reached Mr Michael. He was a short and slight older man who seemed to glide rather than walk, his round rosy face serene with crinkled lips pulled into a kindly smile. He stood beside him facing the Holden family gravestones, arms crossed in front, his hands hidden by billowing white sleeves. He looked incredibly calm, even comfortable, despite being surrounded by death. Perhaps it was something one grew used to, thought Mr Michael, though he could not understand how. Memories of his own lost children began to resurface, fading again as the vicar spoke.

"I don't believe we've had the pleasure of meeting. I'm Reverend Gannet."

"Name's Mr Michael, sir." He nodded his head politely, realising how long it had been since he had last attended church, he too having worn black with a frail and grieving Winifred by his side. Noticing the furrowed brow of his companion, the vicar paused to view the sky above as if in awe of its rare clarity.

"The funeral has been arranged," he began, assuming the reason behind the stranger's visit. Mr Michael's head snapped from the gravestone to the gleaming eyes of the man beside him, his cheeks glowing all the brighter in the crisp morning air.

"But how? By whom?" Mr Michael was confused and intrigued. Mrs Holden had no family and no will had been found. How was it possible a service had been arranged, and so soon? Reverend Gannet looked amused at his puzzled expression.

"Why, Mrs Holden herself. She came to see me a few weeks ago." He turned his attention from the sky to the graveyard ahead while Mr Michael took his time to absorb this information. It seemed typical of his friend to have saved him the burden of organising such an occasion, as well as the cost of paying for it, yet the revelation proved once again that she had been expecting to die. How could she have known such a thing? Could it have been suicide after all? The vicar did not move so Mr Michael took the opportunity to ask him a question.

"What d'you know of the 'olden family, Father?"

"Reverend, if you please," he replied with an almost girlish coyness, "Three of them were buried here after the accident. It was a sad day when the bridge collapsed, for all of us. They were good men."

"Aye, sad indeed. An' the child, o'course. An innocent. Days old, I 'eard." Mr Michael traced his eyes back across the girl's name on the stone.

"Always a tragedy, yes. A loss no parent should have to endure." At the reverend's words, the memory of burying his own stillborn children returned along with a sharp stab of guilt in his stomach. For someone who had lost so many young lives, why had he not found the strength to attend church and pray for their tiny souls? Mr Michael had no answer, no excuse to offer this man of God.

"Matthew was a strong boy, ambitious, determined," the reverend continued, "I regret that I did not come to know more of Mrs Holden until recently, though young Matthew often reassured me of her goodness." Reverend Gannet pursed his lips in thought. "Whatever her position on religion, I do remain in admiration of the Holdens' commitment to their marriage. A most happy union, by all accounts, despite their unfortunate loss. The death of a child can never quite be forgotten. It is a sorry tale."

The vicar turned and made his way back down the path towards the church, pausing halfway to wait for Mr Michael, his fluffy grey eyebrows high on his forehead in expectation.

"Come, let us take a turn around the pews and I will tell you what I know about the Holden family." Reverend Gannet led the way inside with Mr Michael at his heels.

Chapter Twenty-One

Matthew Holden was lucky. He had inherited a fine property on the famous Shambles in the centre of town where he could easily reach the stonemason's and still come home for lunch. Once belonging to his uncle, the house was furnished as if for a family of twenty. Perhaps compensating for the loss of his loved ones, the old man had become a compulsive hoarder. When Mrs Holden's parents had passed away, the couple took on even more belongings to form a messy yet beloved amalgamation of the many different lives, tastes, travels and treasures of their combined pasts. They had enjoyed purchasing new items too, unable to resist the allure of a rag and bone man or the local pawnbroker's once payday arrived. Soon enough, they could barely see one another across the dinner table or when sat in opposite corners of the front room, obscured by all sorts of furniture, fixtures, objects and curiosities.

When Agnes discovered she was pregnant, the impulse shopping stopped to allow for more practical purchases. The promise of a second chance had come true, just as her mother had suggested, and Agnes began to come back to life again. While she had stopped going to church and kept to herself whenever she had to leave the house for provisions, she was comfortable in Matthew's company and began to enjoy his return from work and their evenings together. They would talk about the remarkable changes happening in the city, of events and celebrations taking place and being planned, of the noble queen and her glorious reign, or of the latest household innovations lining the shop shelves and adorning advertisements.

As the baby grew, Agnes could feel the sharp sting of loss within the pit of her stomach begin to subside, the memories of her former life becoming friendly ghosts rather than haunting spectres. As she pressed her hand on the warm curvature of her stomach, she imagined she could feel the new baby's heartbeat, the same steady thud that she had listened to night after night when sleeping beside Benjamin. She could now hold the letter opener without it causing her to weep, though she still kept it hidden from her husband.

Alas, Agnes had hoped for too much, had allowed herself to feel joy all too soon. She awoke at a late hour on a bitter winter's morning shaking from the cold as newly fallen snow drifted onto the cobbles outside, the ident of her husband's form still visible in the sheets beside her. She tried to rise to pull the fallen blanket up off the floor but was prevented by an agonising stabbing sensation in her lower abdomen. She peeled back the covers and saw a pool of blood. Her legs were dark crimson and something strange was heaped on the mattress. She could not prevent the scream that leapt from her throat.

On hearing the commotion, a local neighbour arrived and called for a doctor. The physician examined Agnes and gave her a cup of warm water into which he had dissolved some medicine and a little sugar. She sipped, silent tears streaming down her face, already knowing the words he was being so careful to share with her. When Matthew returned from work and heard the news, he too began crying, but Agnes would not let him near her. She stayed in the bedroom alone for three weeks, sleeping, weeping and reluctantly sipping on a small bowl of soup at the doctor's insistence. Matthew slept downstairs surrounded by the possessions new and old that they had so painstakingly collected together.

On the Monday of the fourth week, Agnes left her bed. She got washed and dressed, had breakfast, then scrubbed the entire house, carefully moving each object to remove the layers of dirt and debris that caked every surface. She lifted, shuffled, reached and edged her way through all the rooms, wiping away the bitterness she had held inside her, the blame and the humiliation, watching the dirty water flow away with her feelings. Once she had finished and with her husband away at work, she sat down in the old armchair that had been beside the fireplace long before she had even arrived at the house. She picked at the shabby discoloured fabric, tracing its curve until her fingers reached the deep crease of the cushion edge. She removed the letter opener from her pinafore pocket and tucked it down the side. Her secret. Her memories. The one remaining symbol of hope she had left.

Matthew Holden, meanwhile, had found God. Following the death of his daughter, he attended church almost every day when he was not either at work or drowning his sorrows at the Eagle and Child Inn. It was a comfort to know that in his time of need he could reach both the Lord and the good stuff a short walk from his front door. Agnes had even seen him late at night in the front room praying on his knees for a son. It had been one o'clock on a Sunday morning and she had tiptoed barefoot downstairs to find him pleading by candlelight. She wished his prayer would be answered but she knew it would not. Her life as a mother was gone and so too was any hope she had left of future happiness.

During his numerous drinking sessions, Matthew had befriended a particularly devout older gentleman who had shared with him all kinds of incredible stories from the Bible. It had made Matthew realise that miracles were indeed real and that they could happen in the most ordinary places, even in a city like York. But it had also reminded him that God giveth and God taketh away. Despite his attempts to bury the thoughts to the back of his mind, Matthew Holden had a secret that he had never revealed to another living soul. He had caused pain and suffering to an innocent. Now, it seemed, he was receiving his punishment.

Caught between guilt and hope, Matthew prayed at every available opportunity, at church or at home, by day or by night. He even began forgoing his evenings with Agnes to pursue his determination that God would provide. When his prayers remained unanswered, he numbed his growing anger with nectar and banter at any inn with its doors still open, often spending consecutive nights wandering the streets in search of succour. Agnes would sit in silence in her armchair listening for his return. She forgave her husband for every night he did not come home. There was no right or wrong way to grieve, she reasoned, and she was only too glad to have him alive and well when she had lost so many of her loved ones.

The couple continued to live a life of relative comfort and contentment, though there would be no more children. As if confirming her marital rather than motherly status, Matthew took to calling his wife Mrs Holden, and she in turn referred to him merely as Husband. After her miscarriage, Mrs Holden had been informed by the doctor that the damage she had suffered would make it extremely unlikely that she could conceive again. Ten years of tried and failed attempts confirmed that the diagnosis was correct, no matter how much she and her husband wished it were otherwise.

Mr Holden tried to show his wife kindness and patience as they took to their bed together once or twice a week and waited with hope for the telling signs. But as the years went on, their unions stopped without a word spoken. Mr Holden sought solace in his work while Mrs Holden took to her armchair to while away the hours simply sitting in solitude surrounded by their countless belongings. She reached a place of disconnection from the real world. The heartache had grown into a dull pain like a chronic illness and she began to think less and less of the future. There was only the present to concern her now – her home, her husband, and she, his aging wife. Mute, sullen, barren. Neither could have known that there would be more heartbreak to come.

Chapter Twenty-Two

Following his conversation with the Reverend Gannet, Mr Michael had remained seated in a pew inside the church silently considering the figure hanging above the altar. It was a wooden carving of Christ on the cross, the oak weathered into a dull hue with curls of brown, yellow and red paint across his hair, loincloth and wounds. The expression was not one of pain or anger but of quiet contemplation. Mr Michael stared at its still features for a long while, his thoughts chasing one another, but this time, he did not stop them. His wife and Mrs Holden had both endured a loss that only a mother could understand, and perhaps neither had fully recovered from it. While Winifred was still suffering the physical effects of her departed children, Mrs Holden had been fighting the emotional impact of never being able to raise a family. He regretted that he could not have done more for either of them. For the first time in many years, he knelt and prayed to the Lord's Son.

For the remainder of the day, Mr Michael was absorbed by his thoughts and reflections on his meeting with the vicar. It seemed that every step he took towards helping Mrs Holden only served to emphasise how little he had truly known her. It was now the story of her husband that intrigued him, particularly his death. He had been well aware of the accident that Reverend

Gannet had referred to. For months it was all anyone could talk about and the mournful event still continued to serve as a warning for construction workers across the city. He was sure there would have been some form of memorial erected at the site.

The following day after finishing his nine hours at the workshop, Mr Michael decided to detour from his usual route home to pass across the famed structure that had cost the life of Matthew Holden. Despite its initial problems, Lendal Bridge had opened in 1863 and for the past decade had served as the main thoroughfare between the city centre and the railway station. As usual for a late afternoon, it was heaving with horses, traps, carts and commuters. All competed with one another for priority of the road, each moving to its own rhythm, a cacophony of sounds merging with the dust clouds and heavy smog to create something that struck Mr Michael as faintly biblical in its drama.

To look on it now, one would never know that the bridge had claimed lives and left others broken-hearted. It seemed so familiar to the cityscape that one could easily have believed it to have simply grown from the earth itself. Mr Michael turned his attention from the traffic to the river, watching wearily as a couple of boats passed in opposite directions at a gentle pace compared to the vehicles above, the water softly rolling at either side and engulfing the already muddy embankments. He followed the cobbled pathway down and noticed a round sign against one of the balustrades: 'This plaque was erected in commemoration of the lives lost on 27 September 1861. May their souls rest in peace'.

Mr Michael muttered an amen as he finished reading and felt glad that there was at least some evidence of the event other than Mr Holden's tomb. It was through the tragedy of others that one could learn to appreciate life, he thought, and here was a reminder. He traced the date with the tips of his fingers, wondering if Mrs Holden had known of the plaque's existence, though he doubted she would ever have ventured this far out from the shop. Perhaps it would only have served to remind her of her grief.

As he removed his hand, Mr Michael heard a soft cough from behind him. A man with hunched shoulders and a lopsided smile was watching him with kind wide eyes. He was about the same age as Mr Michael though dressed in much finer attire, and wore round spectacles pushed right up to the top of his nose. His entire face was deeply pockmarked and he kept coughing into a handkerchief, his face contorting with pain before calming again.

"Didn't know anyone else came down 'ere," he croaked, his eyes scanning the letters of the sign with fondness as he tucked the dampened square of cloth back into the top pocket of his tweed waistcoat.

"Name's Anderson." He held out a hand for Mr Michael to shake.

"I'm Mr Michael. First time I seen it meself. Sorry story, weren't it."

"Aye, that it were. Lost me brother. Good lad he were." Mr Anderson suddenly began coughing again, though this time he did not have the chance to remove his hankie. Instead, he turned away, bending double before righting himself again. His face was flushed and his eyes slightly bloodshot.

"I'm sorry fer y'loss," Mr Michael replied once Mr Anderson had recovered, "Did y'know the others?"

"Aye, we were down t'pub often enough. Charlie, Alf, Matthew, Henry an' meself."

"Would that 'ave been… Mr Matthew 'olden?" Though he had tried to sound casual in his questioning, Mr Michael had piqued the interest of the other man. It was not often he talked of his brother and it had been even longer since he had thought about their mutual friend, Matthew. Mr Anderson bounced softly on his feet as if considering his next action. He looked Mr Michael up and down before replying.

"Time fer a swift 'alf?" he asked, miming the action of drinking a pint. It did not take Mr Michael much thought. He nodded before following the other man across the bridge and towards Blossom Street.

The pair passed by the train station, an assortment of travellers, traders and workmen moving in and out of its mouth along with thick plumes of fragrant smoke and a barrage of noise from the roaring engines within. They managed to edge their way through the crowd, Mr Michael eyeing every single face as had become his habit. Eventually, they emerged from the hubbub and were soon in the solace of The Windmill pub, one of the oldest and most well known in the city.

Though he had never been inside, Mr Michael had instantly recognised the building's distinct black and white exterior, which he had seen often enough from the window of his workshop on the opposite street. The pub squatted in the shadow of Micklegate Bar, one of the many city gateways, with its historic portcullis and stone watchmen that still managed to fascinate and unease him whenever he paused to look upwards. The attractive timepiece behind the pub's bar informed the two men that it was just gone five o'clock, with the pub already half full of locals enjoying what was left of their weekly wages and sharing stories from their working day. A roaring fire emitted a comforting scent from the corner and several curiosities hung from the walls and the beams much like they had in Holden's Haunt.

The two men found themselves a secluded nook beside a window and settled down with two pints. Mr Anderson hastily stuffed a large clay pipe with tobacco as soon as they had taken their seats. He lit it with a match, took a deep inhale, then began to cough violently into his already sodden handkerchief. Mr Michael leaned back, grateful that he had never taken to smoking having tried it once or twice in his youth. As soon as the coughing subsided, Mr Anderson took another puff and began the whole process again, taking a steady sip of his drink when he could.

Growing impatient and a little uncomfortable at the passing time and his companion's health, Mr Michael finally mustered the courage to ask the other man about his history and what he could remember of the accident involving Mr Holden. Luckily, Mr Anderson seemed only too happy to oblige, having now recovered his breathing once more in favour of finishing his drink and enjoying the atmosphere. He even replaced his pipe on the table so that he could settle his clenched hands underneath his chin before beginning with his story. Mr Michael edged a little closer, eager to learn more.

Mr Anderson's brother Charlie had been friends with Matthew for many years before they had both begun working together on the building of the bridge. During that time, they would often visit The Windmill for a refreshing beverage along with two other colleagues, Alf and Henry, plus Mr Anderson himself. The accident had taken the lives of all four men, leaving wives, children, parents and siblings behind. He did not know much of the accident itself, only what was reported in the papers. Mr Michael expressed his condolences as he watched the man's eyes fall to the table, his shoulders hunching even further. Despite his evident sorrow, Mr Anderson took another deep sup of his pint and prepared himself to reveal what else he knew about Matthew Holden.

Chapter Twenty-Three

Ten years following the death of their firstborn, Mr and Mrs Holden had become used to their quiet childless household. Mrs Holden tended daily to the constant upkeep of their crowded collection while Mr Holden worked hard to earn both higher wages and a solid reputation in his trade. Business was booming thanks to the railways, with York being one of the main cities in the country to have developed and improved its service, which had in turn led to the swift growth of other industries.

The city skyline had gradually transformed with taller and broader factories appearing along with numerous smoking towers that bellowed out great tufts of cloud that never seemed to shift. There were even special housing areas being built for the chocolate factory workers with sprawling parks, a variety of shops and resurfaced roads, all for the benefit of the expanding and demanding population. It was a fine time to be alive with the likes of young couples such as the Holdens reaping the advantages the changes to the city brought.

Along with the development of the station plus the radical improvements to the central streets to allow for the safer passage of vehicles, there were also new bridges being commissioned to accommodate the growing traffic. The structure on Lendal was among them and Mr Holden had been able to secure a lucrative job working on its construction. With increased competition for such positions, he considered himself extremely fortunate to have been selected and made it his mission to work to the best of his ability in the hope of decent pay and better prospects.

Mr Holden had decided that he and his wife deserved some good fortune having now lost all their older family members as well as their stillborn daughter. He needed to restore not only their dwindling finances but also his dignity and pride. Thankfully the work continued, the wages trickled in, and the dull sense of doom in the pit of Mr Holden's stomach began to subside. Little did he know of the tragedy that was to come.

One dull September morning, the sky gloomy with smog and rain clouds, Mr Holden was working alongside two other men to secure a large stone boulder that had not been positioned precisely enough and was threatening to cause a serious constructional defect if ignored. The men heaved and strained, pulled and pushed, trying to remove the stone so that they could replace it. Suddenly, the air around them seemed to reverberate. The three men looked at one another, their ears alert to a peculiar and loudening sound. The sky seemed almost to be weighing down on them, then Mr Holden felt it. The drop in his stomach. There was a shout and then another, followed by a sudden tumultuous rumbling before everything went black.

Having been crushed by falling stone, it was feared Mr Holden was worse on the inside than he looked on the outside, but he did not seem to be in severe pain. On the contrary, he appeared quite calm, cheerful even, to be warm and dry in a comfortable bed on the quiet hospital ward. He was well tended to by the doctor and two nurses, who treated him as if he had performed some heroic deed, but then that was what these new structures had become to the city: symbols of success. Though aching and fatigued, Mr Holden felt a glow of pride at their praise, reflecting that perhaps life had not been so unkind to him after all.

As night drew near, the matron brought each patient a cup of cocoa. Mr Holden had never tasted cocoa in his life before, but he had heard all about the famous factories and had watched in amusement as the strange folk with their flyers and placards tried to promote it as an alternative to alcohol. He himself could not imagine replacing his favourite ale or a good whisky with something so foreign, but at that moment he was quite glad to receive a cup of anything so long as it helped him to sleep. He took the mug in both hands and savoured the aroma, heavy and peculiar, though not unpleasant.

Taking a generous mouthful, he could feel the silky liquid warming his throat and then his insides, like being hugged by a loved one or standing close to a fire. He swiftly downed the rest of the contents, hoping the matron would be generous enough to provide a refill. The peace was broken by the man in the opposite bed, who had begun shouting and pointing at the other patient. A nurse rushed over to Mr Holden, followed by another and then the matron. There were raised voices, cries for a doctor, and a woman's scream. Mr Holden had dropped the empty cup onto the floor where it had rolled under his bed, drawing dust into its sticky interior. He would never taste cocoa again.

When Mrs Holden learned of her husband's death, she experienced a new kind of grief. It did not bring up memories of the other times, which already felt like distant dreams belonging to another person, but instead the pain was compounded by dread, a sudden realisation that she was now entirely alone. She did not mourn. She decayed. There were no tears or anguished cries, no hollow stomach or shortness of breath, no headaches or hot flushes or panics of anxiety. She simply sat in her chair staring at the same possessions crammed into the room, each growing thick with layers of dust, droppings and mould, the light slowly fading as the windows became ever more opaque.

The widow quickly fell into a routine of sitting, eating, shopping and sleeping that ran like the rotations of clockwork, barely aware of her motions. She did not see or speak to anyone, keeping her door locked and allowing the two tiny windows at the front of the property to become thick with black grease. The items outside rattled and rocked in the wind, abandoned and forgotten. She accepted the parcels of food left on her doorstep by neighbours, replacing them with small clusters of coins in cloth bags, though her funds were quickly declining. She lit the fire and the gas lamp only when she needed to, which was not often. She grew accustomed to the dark, to the silence, and to life alone.

Though the graveyard of Holy Trinity Church was literally a stone's throw from her house, Mrs Holden never visited the resting places of her daughter and husband. She had arranged and paid for both funerals from the inheritance her parents had left but did not attend herself and did not invite anyone else to do so. She had already had the experience of watching her parents being buried a few years previous and that had been traumatic enough. Both had died within weeks of each other; first her mother from a wasting disease, followed by her father from a heart attack, though the doctor had said he had been in a fit state of health before her mother died.

Even though Mrs Holden had lost her parents, her daughter and her husband, their deaths combined still did not match the anguish she had felt when she was Agnes Dartton the day she had held her darling boy in her arms and had visibly seen his life slip away. Benjamin had died and there had been nothing she could have done to save him. She had failed him; she had let him go. Her parents would not tell her where the body was buried, so she had never had the chance to say goodbye. The pain and the memories of her many years of sorrow began to consume her day by day, eating away at her, body and soul.

Three pints later, Mr Anderson completed his tale with a sorry shake of his head and another hearty coughing fit. As they watched the ebb and flow of drinkers moving to and from the bar, it occurred to both men that perhaps the real victim had always been Mrs Holden. While his death was indeed tragic, Matthew had died doing what he loved, with the notoriety and respect he had earned still etched in the plaque on Lendal Bridge. His wife, on the other hand, had suffered heartbreak repeatedly and had finally been left completely alone with not a single soul for comfort or support. Saddened by his renewed regret, Mr Michael excused himself and made his way home, where he hoped his own loved ones would be safe and soundly sleeping.

Chapter Twenty-Four

On hearing the stories of both Mrs Holden's only child and the traumatic incident her husband had suffered, Mr Michael had decided to create a commemorative token from a charming piece of mahogany he had left over from a previous commission. He had chosen a design that featured a small cross on a mound, perhaps inspired by his recent visit to the church, which he thought he would embellish further with a flock of tiny doves either side of the base. As there were no engravings save the names and dates on the tombstones, he felt it would be comforting to see something sacred and symbolic there once Mrs Holden had joined her loved ones in their resting place.

Mr Michael began to spend the few precious hours of daylight the season permitted working on his regular commissions before filling the twilight with carefully carving the model. With his wife still spending most of her days and nights in fitful sleep and his daughter dutifully caring for her under Doctor Pruce's orders, the carpenter was even more grateful for the sanctuary of his workshop. It had always been the place where he felt most at home, his introverted personality only able to concentrate when it was just him, his tools and a simple piece of wood. Whenever he focused fully on the task, he could feel everything else drift away. His mind cleared, his muscles relaxed, and for a few hours he could be himself. It had always been a comfort but had in recent weeks become a soothing balm against his ever-growing concerns regarding Mrs Holden and the unsolved murder case.

He completed the carving the day before the funeral. While he was always glad to finish a commission, Mr Michael felt particularly proud of this piece. It was bold and celebratory yet dignified and personal, quite different from the furniture and fittings he was used to making. It had not been a happy experience, having brought up so many difficult memories and regrets, but as he looked at the finished object and ran it between his fingers, just as Mrs Holden had done with his previous carvings, he felt calmed. Though he always worked with diligence and care, the completion of the small memorial had been a therapeutic process and its subsequent worth beyond value. He had put not only his time and skill into its creation but his soul too. He hoped Mrs Holden and her family would have approved.

With every nick and chip of its surface, Mr Michael thought about his friend's funeral that she had herself arranged. Could she have found some form of faith in her later years? Perhaps she had silently prayed to the saints like her husband had, the chimes from the church ringing down the chimney and through her partially opened door. After all, she had felt it necessary to visit the vicar herself and arrange a proper funeral prior to her death. Could this have been a sign of salvation, a welcoming of religion and its relief at a time when she had needed it the most? Mr Michael would never know and now felt he could no longer be sure of anything related to Mrs Holden. He had known so little about her, though he remained grateful that he had had the opportunity to expand his knowledge and admiration through the tales told by so many people. She may not have had many friends, but Mrs Holden would by no means be forgotten.

While he was putting the finishing touches to the model in the dim light from the flickering lamp by his side, Mr Michael's daughter was at their home in the kitchen preparing one of her famous pies. Earlier that afternoon, Irene had been tending to her silently sleeping mother and reflecting on the stories of Mrs Holden that her father had recalled to her most recently. She could not quite believe they would soon be watching her body in a box being lowered into the earth. It somehow did not seem possible. There was still a doubt in Irene's mind that she had even seen Mrs Holden that evening, arms sprawled out, her head lolling, the metallic tang of blood in the air. When the vision returned as she slept, it was as if she were watching a street performance, a comical masquerade in which the actors all rose to their feet at the end and the audience clapped and laughed. It was only on waking that she knew the death had been real. No clapping, no laughter, just loss and misery.

Making a pie seemed trivial but Irene did not know what else she could do for such a sad occasion. If anything, she needed the distraction and the sense of purpose. Perhaps a comforting slice would be just the thing her father needed too, for she knew attending the funeral would not be easy for him. At least they would be able to eat and drink away their sorrows at the wake afterwards. She had decided to make the largest pie she could fit into their small and well-worn stove, enough for the three or four people she thought might accompany her and her father back to the house after the service. Irene did not know who precisely might arrive, but she secretly hoped that there would at least be someone who had held a fondness for her father's friend and wished to pay their respects.

Welcoming the opportunity to become lost in her work, Irene also made a platter of fruit, meats and cheeses on a large wooden board and placed fresh herbs and orange slices in a pewter jug of iced water as an accompaniment. How strange, she thought, to be organising a party for the city's most notorious recluse. She wondered if Mrs Holden would enjoy the spectacle from Heaven. When she asked her father the question after he returned from the workshop later that evening, he had smiled at her with a quivering lower lip and moist eyes.

On the morning of October 20th, 1872, Mr Michael and his daughter woke early to prepare themselves for the long day ahead. The air was cool and still as they left the house, the sun forming an eerily glowing orb behind a thick layer of silver cloud. Dressed head to toe in their smartest and darkest clothes, father and daughter walked arm in arm to say their goodbyes to Mrs Agnes Holden. As they made their way from their home to Holy Trinity Church, they could hear the bells ringing solemnly, their steps falling into its rhythm as they prepared their wearied minds for the sombre occasion.

Winifred had barely been awake in the past few days, giving some reassurance to Irene that her attention would not be missed for a few hours. She had tucked extra blankets above and hot stones below her mother's bed, leaving a jug of fresh water and some bread on the small table beside her. Though she was loath to leave her, she knew that it was her father who now needed her support. White as snow and just as soundless, he had seemed a million miles away all morning.

Before they had left the house, Mr Michael had silently helped his daughter to arrange the food she had prepared the previous night across the kitchen table. It looked like quite the banquet, though they both doubted there would be anyone to admire it other than themselves. As time had proven again and again, they seemed to be the only two people in the city who had cared for Mrs Holden. They could not think of any other soul alive who would want to attend the funeral nor the wake. Little did they know that Reverend Gannet had taken care of every aspect of the event, including its attendees.

Mr Michael and Irene stood beside the vicar at the front of the church watching the growing number of unexpected guests bow their heads and take to their seats. There were a few shady characters who had turned up merely for the drama, looking around like hungry gulls for any sights or stories that would make for enticing gossip, but their kind were thankfully few. Instead, most of the pews were filled with locals who had come to express their genuine sympathy, each holding their own fond memories of Mrs Holden. There were her neighbours from the Shambles who had enjoyed seeing the house blossom into a shop, along with former customers who came proudly wearing or carrying the treasures they had procured. Some of those seated were rival businessowners who had secretly admired the old woman's venture, while others had come simply out of kindness. Lingering at the back, his sun-bleached hair clearly visible above the crowd, was none other than Lanky Luke.

A mere boy when he had made that very first purchase, the now prosperous fisherman had heard of Mrs Holden's death all the way out in Staithes and had decided to make the long trip to pay his respects. The nets had proven not only useful but also surprisingly lucky, frequently earning him prize catches and grand sums of money. Yet not even the memory of his greatest hoard could feel as vivid as his recollection of that day in York. He was only too sorry to be saying goodbye to Mrs Holden. It was a sentiment shared by nearly every person seated.

As the well-wishers continued to pile into the already busy church, Irene spotted another familiar but unexpected arrival. She locked her gaze with a set of attentive eyes peering down between the branches of the old weeping willow tree in the graveyard. A silky black crow was sat silently watching the long line of mourners shuffling along in their drab clothes dotted with flowers. While she had loved taking seeds and berries to the bird when it had been at Holden's Haunt, Irene was now struck by fright at the sight of it. It seemed impossible that a wild creature who had vanished months before should be here in this place and on this day. She had never believed in coincidence or miracles, but she could not explain its presence when she had not seen a single other bird like it for so long.

As she stared, Irene tried to spot the tell-tale sign of its chipped beak, but it was too well hidden behind the foliage. She tugged at her father's sleeve wordlessly. He paused briefly in his humble greetings to see what had made his daughter's face so pallid. Mr Michael spotted the crow and watched it for a few moments before taking Irene's hand and leading her into the church to take their seats at the front. She tried to speak but his stern expression quickly reduced her to silence. Filled with unease, he wiped his sweating palms against his trousers, wishing he had never seen the creature. He did not want his mind clouded by superstition.

While they waited for the vicar to begin, Mr Michael could already hear a cluster of voices behind him mentioning the crow, each trying to recall the many fictions that had once held such fascination citywide. Inhaling deeply, he tried to cast the bird from his thoughts and focus instead on the sorry wooden coffin under the cross. The voices faded as a myriad of emotions flooded his mind, memories of the past both ancient and recent tinged with sadness but also with hope. He had become trapped in the story, he realised, the murder mystery that could not be resolved, leaving him infuriated yet completely compelled. Irene pulled again on his sleeve, restoring his awareness and encouraging him to his feet. They began to sing, though his voice was not quite his own, as together they remembered Mrs Holden.

Chapter Twenty-Five

Both the church service and the burial passed Mr Michael by in a blur. It was almost as if he was not fully present, as if his spirit had somehow wandered up into the clouds and was watching the whole event from above, separate and indifferent. Irene too felt numb until a stranger began shovelling dirt on top of Mrs Holden's coffin in the ground. Like a sharp stab with a poker, she suddenly realised just what was happening. Tears welled in her eyes, thick and heavy, swiftly rolling down her cheeks and soaking into the neck of her dress. She had bowed her head so that her hair fell over her face, covering her expression from her father.

By the time the ground had been completely filled, Irene's face had dried and the numbness had returned. She stood next to her father and helped him to quietly thank the visitors gathered around the grave, the tombstone now adjusted to list the name of Agnes Holden alongside her husband and child. Even though there were many faces Mr Michael and Irene did not recognise, every person seemed to know the talented carpenter and his helpful daughter by name and expressed their condolences with care and compassion.

When they were eventually left with no more hands to shake or smiles to fake, Mr Michael seized the quiet moment to remove the small wooden carving from his pocket, unwrapping the handkerchief from around it before placing it against the tombstone. He stood with his head bowed and his hands clasped as he recited a prayer of his own making, Irene identically positioned in his shadow, repeating amen and crossing herself as she had seen some of the women do in the church. She did not know what it meant but it felt respectful and brought her a rare moment of peace. It also made her father smile softly for the first time that day.

Mr Michael and Irene held hands as they walked home after the funeral, a small gathering following them in the hope of sustenance and a warming fire. As he looked over his shoulder into each sombre face, he noticed with some surprise that Stuart Ainsley Junior was one of the number, his walking stick clicking against the cobbles as he tried to keep up with the group's striding pace. Mr Ainsley had worn a dark corduroy jacket with a carnation in his lapel for the occasion and a flat cap with wisps of fraying fabric around the edge so that it formed a sort of crown above his wide flat face. He slipped it off and tucked it inside his trouser pocket as Irene welcomed the guests into the Michaels' home before tending to the fire.

Mr Michael brought through more chairs and helped his daughter to serve thin slices of cold pie on their mismatched collection of chipped and cracked crockery. The kitchen was an eclectic assortment of neighbours and acquaintances, each humble but amiable as they quietly befriended and conversed with one another. Mr Michael could not remember the last time they had had other people in the house save for Doctor Pruce's visits to Winifred. It felt strange though not disagreeable. The subtle hum of voices and the movements of furniture and food gave the kitchen a vibrant ambience quite different from the times when it was just him and Irene.

Stealing a few minutes to himself, Mr Michael took a plate of food and tiptoed upstairs to check on his wife. Cautiously creeping into the room, the air humid and noiseless, he noticed Winifred was in the same position she had been in for days. Curled into a ball with only her head visible, her cheeks were flushed and her lips emitted a soft rattling sound as she slept. He set the plate down and called to her gently, but she would not wake. It was perhaps for the best, he thought, hoping the congregation downstairs would not cause a disturbance. As he watched his beloved resting, he realised he had not thought about her once during the funeral. He had not wished her by his side, holding his hand, admiring the cross he had made. He was a bad husband, a bad father, a bad friend. Mr Michael was a sinner.

On returning to the kitchen, his head hanging, his face a weary grey wash, Mr Michael's attention was caught by Mr Ainsley beckoning him over to a vacant seat in a quiet corner. Mr Michael helped the old man to sit down and propped the owl-topped walking stick by his side. He watched as the older gentleman snuck a hand into his jacket and retrieved a half-full bottle of scotch from an inside pocket, pouring them both a generous tot into two tumblers. Mr Michael downed the contents in one and helped himself to another as his throat burned and his insides pulsed.

"D'you 'ave another story t'share?" he wondered aloud, his tongue already loosened by the alcohol, "Is there summat else to know 'bout Mrs 'olden?" He could not waste any more time, he realised. If he wanted to prove himself a faithful friend, a dutiful husband and a decent father, then he would need to find out what had happened to Mrs Holden and put the past where it belonged – behind him.

"O'course there's more, lad!" Mr Ainsley nodded, "You'd be surprised!"

"D'you know anythin' else 'bout the boy? Or the letter opener?"

"Oh ho! We do know more than we're lettin' on, don't we? Aye, I know a little." Just as Mr Ainsley was tapping his nose, Irene brought over two slices of pie for the pair before returning to the fireside to talk with Lanky Luke about his coastal adventures. She could happily have listened to him all evening, with his tales of fish the size of shire horses and the fierce waves he had seen consume whole houses.

The two men watched the girl giggle playfully while they themselves wolfed down their food and took a few more gulps of scotch. Mr Michael ignored the dizzying effects, blinking his eyes in the hope of being able to focus fully on the old man's narrative, which his quivering lips indicated he was about to reveal.

Agnes awoke to a blue and cloudless sky, the dull haze of the early morning sunlight bathing her sheets in warmth. Even though she was now a young lady of fourteen, these idle moments to herself made her feel like a child again. With no thoughts of the future or regrets of the past, she was free to watch the birds swoop and soar outside her window and enjoy their morning song as if they were calling just to her. She imagined she could speak their language and whistled her own happy tune as they in turn wished her a beautiful day with their sing-song chirps.

The chorus was punctuated by faint thuds and hushed voices from elsewhere in the house; her parents in the kitchen preparing breakfast in her absence. She felt a numb ache of guilt inside her ribcage, knowing she should have been up earlier to help, especially with her mother in such a condition. It would only be a matter of days before her new sibling arrived and she was giddy with excitement to be a big sister. She had so much to teach the new child about all the wonders of nature. For now though, she would enjoy just two more minutes to herself.

Eventually peeling back the covers and rising from her bed, Agnes opened the window to enjoy the cool breeze and to peer into the garden with the woodland and river beyond. They were her favourite places to explore. She had lived in the house all her life but had spent most of her waking hours outdoors. It was there that she felt like her true self, continually delighted and inspired by the flora and fauna she discovered. She could not imagine being anywhere else and vowed to live in this house forever, hoping to never have to set foot into the big city with its choking smoke, its littered streets, and its raucous residents. One day she would marry and have children of her own, living happily in her childhood home with the trees and the water just a few footsteps away. It would be the perfect place to raise a family and her offspring would grow up just as she had, revelling in the joys of nature.

Agnes cleaned and dressed herself, choosing a loose summer shift even though the air was still crisp. She softly treaded into the kitchen and cast an earnest smile for her parents, who were both absorbed in consuming their bread and tea, their actions heavy and forced. They did not speak nor even raise their heads to look at their daughter in her pretty floating dress with her bare feet already sooty. Sensing something amiss, Agnes sat silently at the table and helped herself to the crusted end of the loaf and a glass of fresh water. She inched a soft golden lump of butter across the stale slice as quietly as she could, looking from one parent to the other and back again. She noticed that her mother in particular did not look well. Her face was even paler than usual, her hands shaking as she picked at her plate, her eyes two hollow shells staring into an unknown distance. She appeared to be on the edge of tears, but though her eyes watered, her cheeks remained dry.

Agnes wanted to ask what was wrong but she already knew. There was the faint smell of blood and bodily fluids in the room, just like before. She knew that she would not have a baby brother or sister to play with just yet. She remained an only child, trying desperately to be enough for her parents. Suddenly, she felt ashamed of her choice of dress; it was frivolous and naive. She should have been there to help earlier, to have supported her mother through the agony and heartbreak. It must have happened during the night, she thought. She had slept through death once more.

After breakfast, Agnes assisted her father with burning the soiled clothes and bed linen in the garden. He did not need the help but she felt useless otherwise. Her mother had returned to bed after finishing half a mug of tea. She had eaten a piece of bread then vomited it back up minutes later. Agnes thought that perhaps she could go with her father down to the river and try to catch a fish for their supper. It had always been her mother's favourite meal and she hoped it might help to bring back her strength. Her father did not say anything in reply to the suggestion. Instead, he went back inside the house and sat in the kitchen, stoking the fire with a poker as he stared morosely into the embers.

Would there be another burial service? Agnes wondered, pulling a shawl around her as she paced the garden watching the branches above gently swaying in the swelling wind. It would be the fifth time her mother had lost a child since she herself had been born. She did not know how many more had gone before. Her parents sometimes called her a miracle baby, but she did not feel special. On the contrary, she felt like a burden and a constant reminder of their loss, like the ghost of every child they had ever loved. Why had she lived? What made her so different? The happiness she had experienced on waking that morning suddenly felt like a pitiful fantasy, a childish wish ignorant of the truth. Life was not joyous. Life was cruel and futile.

She walked beyond the garden to the trees where they thickened to create a permanently dark canopy, the plants beneath dense and varied after the recent rains, the faint snaps, whines and buzzes suggesting the many animals hidden within. Agnes felt as cold and hollow as a spectre and just as unseen. She found her favourite nook in the partially hollowed trunk of an ancient oak and nestled her lithe body inside, feeling the fabric snag on the rough bark. Safe at last. Peace, solitude.

When Agnes returned to the house an hour later, it was as if she had wandered into a different world. There was her father by the sink, gutting and scaling a fish fresh from the Ouse. It was a decent size, enough for two meals at least, and he hummed with satisfaction as he worked. The table was already arranged for dinner but there was extra bread and butter along with a glass jar filled with lavender stems. She longed to reach over and inhale their musty scent, but she was too distracted by the woman in front of the fireplace. It looked and sounded like her mother, cooing softly and swinging gently from side to side, but in her arms was a bundle of taupe cloth, a tiny pink face with two eyes as wide and round as buttons peering across the room. It was her own mother, she was sure, but that was not her child.

It could not be the baby, Agnes reasoned, slowly walking round the table to take a closer look. She had seen for herself the creature her mother had produced during the night, the bits of blood and flesh barely resembling a lifeform at all, so swiftly reduced to ashes in the smothering flames that morning. Her mother turned to look at her, her face somehow fuller and younger, her gaze bright and alight with what could only be love. Agnes could not remember having seen her mother like this before. She turned her attention to the babbling noise coming from the weight in her arms.

Her mother was holding the child as if her limbs were made of wood, sturdy and strong, like they had been carved for this very purpose. Agnes bowed her head over the baby and stared into its eyes, two tiny pebbles searching her face as it gurgled in contentment.

Mr Dartton came over and rested an arm across his wife's shoulders, gently prodding a finger into one of the dimples in the infant's cheek. Both mother and father wore expressions of utter happiness which were so rare as to make Agnes feel like she had entered a stranger's house. Neither parent seemed to acknowledge her presence and there were too many impossible questions to ask, so Agnes retreated to the kitchen table and sat watching the scene as if in a dream.

Beside the jug was a neatly folded crocheted blanket that she did not recognise. She stroked her hand over the pattern, noticing the comforting bump of its weave beneath her fingertips, the material so soft that it must have been new. As she continued to caress its surface, she felt something underneath. Agnes opened the blanket up to find a strange-looking object, a blade with a curious symbol on the pale handle. It was a letter opener, she realised, and an expensive one at that. With her parents still absorbed by the infant, she tucked the item into the pocket of her apron and headed out into the garden to be with her thoughts.

Chapter Twenty-Six

Despite their initial joy, the Dartton household did not find it easy to adjust to life with a new-born. It seemed such a long time ago since Agnes had been a baby that her mother had quite forgotten the daily demands of caring for a child so young. The emotional and physical strain of losing so many infants had affected Mrs Dartton more than she had realised. As much as she was relieved to finally have the son she had always wanted, the new mother found herself becoming more and more distant and ignorant of his needs, relying increasingly on her daughter to provide the relentless attention he required.

After only a few months of familial harmony, Agnes' mother developed a severe infection and could no longer care for the boy. Her milk dried up within days and she did not have the strength to rise from her bed, let alone to attend to the needs of a child. As the man of the house, Agnes' father had paid little attention to the new-born in terms of his wellbeing, instead retreating into his role as the provider, working harder than ever in his carpentry workshop at the side of the house. He took on more commissions than his two hands could realistically handle, grafting through the night to complete them and barely seeing his wife or children.

It quickly fell upon Agnes to perform the roles of sister, mother and housewife. Though young in years, she welcomed the added responsibility and was able to manage her time equally between daily housework, caring for her parents, and doting on her little brother. It was Agnes who had chosen his name a few days after his arrival; in a matter of weeks, she and Benjamin Arthur Dartton were inseparable. With his mop of dark hair, lithe limbs and curiously red lips, the boy did not resemble any member of their immediate family, but his distinction only made him all the more beloved by Agnes.

While she occasionally feared for her mother and pined for her father, she was otherwise overwhelmed by a permanent sense of gladness and peace. She welcomed each dawn as if she were a wild bird released from a cage, relishing every opportunity she had to spend with Benjamin, delighting in watching him grow and his personality blossom. She did not care that she also had to tend to the house, the cooking, the cleaning, emptying her mother's chamber pot or taking food out to her father, who would not even sit down to share a meal with her. Life no longer held any unease for Agnes, not with her little boy by her side.

Benjamin's infant years passed by happily, though far too quickly for his older sister; soon enough, he was attempting to speak and crawl and copy everything that Agnes taught him. While she had had no formal schooling, Agnes had always been a clever and inquisitive girl, routinely asking questions of her parents when she was permitted to speak at the dinner table. The woodland and the river in particular had always held a fascination, and she loved to hear her father talk of tickling trout and swooping swallows, or for her mother to mention the changing seasons or which seeds and berries were safe to eat.

Agnes had enjoyed finding various leaves, flowers, saplings and stones to bring home, stuffing them into countless jars and bottles as she quietly queried her mother for their names and uses as they prepared supper together. When she was seven, her father had bought her a second-hand picture book which contained illustrations of different natural specimens and their Latin titles. From the moment the book fell into her hands, she had spent hours poring over its contents, carefully peeling back the already well-thumbed pages in wide-eyed wonder before returning outside to hunt for her own examples.

All of this had been a solitary indulgence until Benjamin arrived. Once he was old enough to shuffle after her and make inquisitive squeaks, Agnes delighted in showing him all the marvels she had come to adore in the outside world. As the boy grew older, they began frolicking under the shady branches of the boughs in the back garden, fishing out tadpoles with their hands in the river, and making miniature men from sand, mud or snow depending on the season.

Like Agnes, the boy was remarkably bright and easily picked up details with only a few repetitions from his sister. She had proven to be the perfect teacher, encouraging her pupil's keen mind with her own bespoke lessons, tutoring him on everything from cooking and basic carpentry to reading, numbers and writing. Though she dreaded the day when she would have to take him to school, she felt proud to have given him a head start in life, an opportunity to learn and discover that she herself had had to experience alone.

Benjamin came to define her existence, becoming not only her brother but also her son, her student and her best friend. He was the reason she woke up every day and the only person she prayed for when she fell asleep. When he passed away on his fifth birthday, Agnes was sure that she could feel her heart physically break. His loss was irreplaceable and irreparable. Everything after that day seemed to happen as a mirage, a faded image, as if she were not really a part of the world but merely an observer, an apparition or a shadow. She was not so much living as existing, but for what and whom, she no longer knew.

Five years after Agnes had rejected his attentions, Matthew Holden returned to the Dartton residence a changed person. Little did he know that the family too would be much altered. As he sat sipping tea with them at the kitchen table, he tried to discern the nature of the transformation. The house and its inhabitants looked the same but the atmosphere felt both charged and empty, his former acquaintances seeming withdrawn and nervous as if they had befallen a tragedy of some kind. Despite his polite enquiries, the family remained allusive in their responses but welcomed him back to their home nonetheless.

While the Darttons appeared as they had done five years ago, Matthew in contrast had grown into a brusque block of a man with an uncanny resemblance to a bull. His forehead and jaw appeared even wider, his shoulders muscular and stocky while a rotund stomach poked out from under his waistcoat. His hair and eyes both seemed even darker, while his nose now slanted to one side as if it had been broken and had not healed properly. Agnes was pleased to see that Matthew had not grown any facial hair like she had seen on the other young men who occasionally passed by the house, their mutton chops and wiry beards making their expressions harsh and unkind. He had dressed smartly too, his clothes made from decent cloth and in demure colours that complemented his complexion. She was suddenly made aware of her own appearance and for the first time in many months, Agnes wished she had worn the pretty yellow dress with the frilled collar.

Since his last visit, Matthew had worked diligently to build up his experience and reputation as a stonemason before being offered work with one of the city's most notable construction companies. In addition to his changed exterior, the young man had grown more mature in character too, and now possessed an almost ruthless determination to attain the life he had so often described to his childhood sweetheart. He had never met anyone quite like Agnes and, despite her former rejection, he had convinced himself that she would be his future wife. While Agnes lowered her head, abashed at such an admission, her parents simultaneously released a sigh of relief. With Mrs Dartton physically recovered from her illness and Mr Dartton having decreased his busy schedule, they were now keen to see their only child married and moved on to better prospects; the chance of a normal life.

A mere two days later, Matthew marched back up to the house with a bundle of blossoms in one arm and the finest marzipan money could buy in the other. When Agnes finally answered his persistent knocks, he swiftly placed the gifts at her feet before enveloping her in a determined embrace, his thick arms wrapping around her like ivy. Having deeply inhaled the smell of her hair, he released his grip and dropped to his knees amid the flowers and confectionary, taking her cold lithe hands in his own as he stared up starry-eyed. There he promised with a look of absolute sincerity to keep Agnes safe and comfortable for as long as they both lived.

Mr and Mrs Dartton hovered behind the door listening to the proposal, feeling a rare sense of calm releasing them from their former purgatory. To have lost one son but to be gaining another felt like a blessing after all they had been through.

As Agnes gazed down at the figure before her, a pair of piercing eyes narrowed in her direction from the open window of the house next door. Hidden from view, the young woman glared with mounting envy at the ritual, angered and amazed in equal measure that Matthew Holden would dare to want someone like Agnes Dartton as his bride. She muttered curses under her breath, the couple oblivious in their courtship.

With the determined man and his gifts at her feet, Agnes realised that this was her chance. She was finally being offered the opportunity to leave home and her painful memories, to be taken care of and provided for, to live a life not of grief and regret but of happiness and love. She nodded bashfully to her suitor and felt herself once again swept up and off her feet by Matthew's embrace.

One week later, Agnes' parents waved their first-born off to her new life with a sense of relief rather than heartache. They reassured Agnes that it was the right thing to do. After losing the boy, she could now look forward to a new life. She took with her a few clothes, the picture book, some wooden toys that a young apprentice had once made her, and the secret letter opener. As she said goodbye to her parents and closed the door of her family home, she swore to herself that her husband would never know about Benjamin nor the blade. They would be hers and hers alone.

It was long gone nightfall by the time Mr Ainsley had finished his tale. The old man was visibly worn and weary from recalling what he could remember of the Dartton family and Matthew Holden. Fuelled by liquor and pie, his imagination had aptly completed the gaps in the narrative with astute conclusions, while Mr Michael himself amended his own chosen details using what little he knew of his friend and her character. As he watched the former shopkeeper totter back down the street, his walking stick firmly in his grasp, Mr Michael sifted over the story again and again, trying to find the vital clue he knew he was sorely missing. Still, the truth of Mrs Holden's murder alluded him.

Closing the door on the old man and the dusky street, he turned intending to recount the conversation to his daughter only to find her fast asleep in a chair beside the fireplace. It had been a long time since he had seen her looking so peaceful. He crept across to tuck the shawl tighter across her shoulders then placed a few more coals in the fire before heading up to his own bed. Listening to the steady hiss of his wife's breathing on the opposite side of the wall, Mr Michael somehow managed to still his thoughts and fell quickly into a deep and restful sleep.

Part Three

Chapter Twenty-Seven

It had only been a week since Mrs Holden's funeral, but for Mr Michael and Irene, the world had somehow irrevocably shifted. What had formerly been a private matter between themselves and Mrs Holden was now the talk of every townsfolk. The newspapers had gone wild with the release of the post-mortem report confirming that Mrs Holden had been the victim of a murderer. Inspector Falmer had had both the press and a frantic public banging on his home and office doors at all hours of the day demanding justice. Despite his apathetic efforts to conduct an enquiry, he was acutely aware that the villain was still out there, hiding in the snickelways by day and stalking the streets by night. Mothers called their children inside off the streets well before dusk, men went to work with kitchen knives in their pockets, while the old and the infirm screamed out during the night in fits of fright.

The inspector had attempted to demonstrate his vigilance and authority by commanding his men to conduct yet more searches and interrogate all possible suspects from the city and beyond. Nevertheless, the gossip grew more macabre and extreme as the thirst for information was satiated by lurid lies. With every sorry story he had the displeasure of overhearing, Mr Michael became more agitated in his frustration. His only source of comfort was Irene, though she too had had to endure the countless cruel chants being shared across the playground, a number involving her discovery of Mrs Holden's body; 'Tell-tale Tilly, she was silly, went into the shop unseen. Found a body, battered 'n' bloody, 'cause that lady were so mean.'

When she told her father the song, he shook his head in dismay, assuring her that she would not have to return to school and face such bullies, but Irene was determined not to let them win. Despite her father's concerns, she returned day after day and grew used to ignoring their rhymes, shoves and kicks. Knowing she could come home and spend the evenings with her father, listening to one another talk about anything or nothing over a platter of meats or a baked potato, somehow made life bearable for Irene. Each of them now knew that they could cope with anything so long as they had each other. Sharing their stories seemed to halve their pain.

Of course, Mr Michael had told every last detail of the tales he had heard to his daughter, including what Stuart Ainsley Junior had recalled at the wake. While fascinating to imagine, the story had provided just as many problems as possibilities. Each time the pair scrutinised the information together across the kitchen table, they found themselves creating knots that they could not unravel. Despite their best efforts, they were no closer to discovering who had robbed and killed Mrs Holden.

Above everything, Winifred had remained in a delicate state confined to her room. Despite attending school, cleaning the house, doing the laundry, making the daily meals, and the countless other tasks she had to perform, Irene still spent every spare moment by her mother's bedside. She had slept night after night on the crude mattress on the floor, somehow managing to wake herself several times to check on her mother's condition. Mr Michael was heartened by his daughter's care, realising what a difference she must have made to Mrs Holden's life too. This brave young girl was now his only source of happiness.

Sundays provided a rare opportunity for father and daughter to rest, even if only for an hour or two. Mr Michael would often invent excuses to visit his workshop while Irene would inevitably have some form of cleaning to attend to, but come the afternoon, they would always reconvene in the kitchen to enjoy a leisurely late lunch with one another. As the weather grew increasingly bitter, Irene had taken to preparing rich meat stews using whatever cheap cuts she could procure at the local butcher's. Buoyed by his daughter's determination to lead a normal family life, Mr Michael had made a point of buying a fresh loaf of bread every Saturday on his way back from his workshop to accompany the Sunday meal. It was always a sorry form of compensation for his routine absence from the family home, but he knew his daughter appreciated the thought.

It was an unseasonably clear Saturday, the smog having been dampened into submission by an early deluge of rain that had subsided by mid-morning. Mr Michael turned his face to the rare sunlight as he departed from his workshop, having finished early in order to take a gentle walk home through the centre of the city and along to the market. Having bought his bread, he was perusing the rest of the stalls when he spotted five helmets bobbing above the crowd. Inspector Falmer was at the head of them, an unsettling expression of victory clearly visible despite his heavy moustache. Mr Michael knew that there must have been a development in the case. He forgot his shopping and quickened his steps to meet the officers.

"What is it? What's 'appened? 'ave y'found 'im?" he asked urgently, wishing he could feel reassured by their happy countenances rather than concerned.

"Good day, Mr Michael," Inspector Falmer replied, taking a step forward ahead of his men, "Yes, you'll be pleased to hear the culprit has been found and is now locked behind bars awaiting questioning, though we don't think it'll take long. He's already admitted he was at the residence on the night of the murder."

Mr Michael was incredulous. How had they discovered the truth so soon? Was it something he had said during questioning? Or had they finally discovered who the mystery man was, or perhaps even found his hidden lair and the objects within it?

"Who? Who were it?" Mr Michael pleaded, almost bouncing on his toes with anticipation. The inspector and the other officers looked at one another with small smirks creeping across their faces, as if Mr Michael had made a joke.

"Now, now, Mr Michael," the inspector replied, his moustache quivering as he tried to control his smile, "It's been a difficult time for you. I understand. You get some rest and leave the criminal to us. We'll see he gets what's coming to him."

Inspector Falmer went to rest a hand on Mr Michael's shoulder, but it was a long way to reach. Instead, he settled it awkwardly on the loaf of bread tucked under his arm. The five men nodded their helmeted heads in unison and bade Mr Michael goodbye as he stood speechless in the middle of the street. After the many people he had spoken to, how had he not been able to find the man for himself? What additional information had the police received to help them? Just who was the man they had arrested? Perhaps the coroner had spoken to the police after all.

As the officers made to walk away, Mr Michael replied in haste, "Did y'speak to Dan Chelten? What did 'e tell yeh?"

The inspector shook his head almost in pity, exhaling slowly to ease his growing frustration.

"Mr Michael, it was Dan Chelten," he frowned, as if it were obvious, "He was there in the house with Mrs Holden. He knew about the letter opener. And no doubt soon we'll find out where he's hidden the loot. So that's that. Now, go home. You look like death yourself."

The four officers around him each gave another titter, their eyes twinkling. They all looked far too pleased with themselves. Mr Michael gripped the loaf with mounting anger. He shook his head, astounded at their naivety. An innocent man had been imprisoned and the real villain was still out there. How could they have been so rash, so reckless? He watched them walk away, the bread reduced to a messy wedge as he grasped it ever tighter. Mr Michael knew that he could no longer rely on the police to help. It was now down to him to bring justice to Mrs Holden.

Chapter Twenty-Eight

Following his meeting with Inspector Falmer and the officers, Mr Michael stormed home in a fierce rage and almost pulled his front door from its hinges as he entered the kitchen, bashing his head on a beam in his haste. Feeling foolish, he threw the battered loaf onto the side and splashed his face with cold water, wiping it against his shirt as he tried to steady his breathing. He knew the police were wrong. Dan Chelten may have been devious, but he was no murderer. It would only be a matter of time before the police discovered this for themselves, but while they wasted their energy on a wild goose chase, the real criminal would still be out there.

Mr Michael had hoped his previous information would have been enough to prompt the inspector to pursue the stranger with his mystery disguises, the man they really should have been hunting. Yet it now seemed like those four hours of so-called questioning had all been for nought. It appeared that Inspector Falmer was not concerned with justice after all, and it was brazenly obvious why Dan Chelten had been blamed. It had been too good an opportunity for the police. His nosy nature and taste for trouble had seen Dan at the centre of suspicious activities far too often, and now here was the ideal excuse to end his meddlesome ways once and for all. How could the inspector resist? The chance to catch a murderer and solve a mystery. He would be admired and respected, praised by the people for making the city safe again. It would be the perfect outcome for the police, but not for Mr Michael.

During dinner, Irene attempted to engage her father in conversation, but his mind was once again elsewhere. She had been only too sorry to hear of Dan's arrest, especially when they both knew the punishment. For all its positive progress, the judicial system remained ashamedly in the past and bordered on barbaric. They had both heard the stories. They had both seen a policeman or two striking out against someone on the street. They could only imagine what it must be like in a prison cell or being led to the rope. Irene ladled another serving of stew into their dishes, but Mr Michael pushed his aside. He needed to clear his head.

The weather had turned in a matter of days. Gone were the soft showers and scattered glimpses of sunshine that gave autumn its picturesque skies and pleasant ease. The golden leaves had turned to rust then fallen, the gentle sway of the river replaced by a ferocious haste, the residents hunching ever further forward under thick cloaks and extra woollen wares as the cold set in. Mr Michael turned up his collar against the evening gust, his feet pounding the moist cobbles as he headed down Fossgate and onto the Shambles, slipping into The Shoulder of Mutton almost instinctively.

He ordered the first beverage to catch his eye and remained at the bar as he sipped the amber liquid. There was a dull hum of chatter interspersed with the high notes of an accordion playing somewhere in a back room. Singing and laughter followed, the shared chorus of a familiar tune. He remembered when he and Winifred used to listen to music and even dance, all those years ago. The young courting couple discovering the city's nightlife together, finding nooks and staircases that led to parties and promises of better times ahead. He could recall them toasting the young monarch in this very pub – a depiction of the coronation still hung from a blackened beam in its ornate golden frame. Winifred used to spend the few coins he gave her each week on new dresses and elegant hats, the latest fashions that made her look like royalty. Just as magnificent as Her Majesty, he would jest.

Somewhere between learning the skills of carpentry with Mr Dartton and finding himself the sole carer of a little girl with his wife in permanent discomfort, Mr Michael had forgotten his life between the two. There had been days that were so carefree and idyllic as to seem narrated from a novel. Indeed, Winifred used to be an avid reader and would often recite passages aloud to him, wondering whether their own romance would one day make the pages of a popular tome. 'Life is just a story,' she would always say, 'and we narrate our own destiny.' How could she have known that such grief would be waiting for her, poised to chip away at her wholesome soul and optimistic outlook, reducing her to a shell? Mr Michael missed Winifred the way she once was. He missed the life they used to have.

He nodded to the barman for another drink, barely waiting for the foam to settle before taking a hearty swig. He noticed that his body was swaying softly, his thoughts now so tangled that images and ideas were floating around independent of his will. His wife, his friend, their shared pasts and alternative futures. There were endless questions, yet he could find no answers. He wanted desperately to help but he had nothing to give. No information, no assistance, not even a few well-chosen words of comfort. He had let them all down. Just like his father before him. When his mother and brother had died of the consumption when he was sixteen, he had not experienced grief because he had believed his father would know what to do. His old man would have a solution, a way for them to survive and thrive. Instead, he had taken his own life. As much as Mr Michael had told himself it was an accident, deep down he had long ago realised the truth. He had been abandoned. Forgotten. There had been no resolution. If he was meant to write his own story as Winifred had said, then he had run out of words.

He suddenly felt overwhelmed with fatigue, wanting nothing more than to be at home resting his head in a darkened room, to sleep with his mind and body stilled and silent. His eyelids lowered as the thought alone lulled him into slumber, only to be abruptly awakened by the pub landlord giving his arm a sharp shove. With a start, Mr Michael righted himself and wiped the drool from his mouth with his hand. The landlord grinned and shook his head.

"Don't worry, y'not the first," he shrugged, mopping up where Mr Michael had left a little pool on the counter. The landlord threw the filthy cloth over one shoulder and observed his customer with a reassuring smile.

"Friend o' Mrs 'olden's, aren't yeh?" he grinned, his eyes narrowed in thought, "Funny woman she were, but what a cracking shop, eh? Bought meself quite a few bits from there over t'years."

His speech made Mr Michael's ears pound with every stressed syllable, but anyone with a tale to tell about his friend was worth the effort of listening to. He blinked sharply and tried to focus on the voice.

"We 'ad a chap in 'ere t'other day on about a nice painting 'e'd bought, lovely view o'the sea out b'Whitby or some such. Waves an' cliffs an' that. Anyways, I says, 'oh, it's from 'olden's 'aunt then?', 'cause I were sure I'd seen it in there, but the bloke says, 'no, got it out Helmsley way, grand shop they got with all sorts'. Well, I raised me eyebrows at 'im an' said n'more." The landlord sniffed and wiped a hand over his nose, flicking the rag from off his shoulder to continue his cleaning.

"Funny that, ain't it? Some shop in Helmsley just like Mrs 'olden's!" He chuckled as he walked away to see to another patron, the night still young and the pub now heaving with regulars.

Mr Michael steadied himself and shuffled out of the door into the pitch-black night, the cobbles lightly frosted and shimmering in the dull glow from the pub windows. His head throbbing and his mouth as arid as straw, he managed to find his way home again, throwing himself face-down onto the bed still with his coat and shoes on. He slipped into an effortless sleep, the many days of anxious thoughts followed by sleepless nights finally catching up with him.

Chapter Twenty-Nine

Several weeks later and the weather had worsened still. The banks of the river had swelled with the combination of heavy rainfall and melting snow, the first few flurries leaving the streets with a dusting of white that soon disappeared under the footfall. With the festive season on the way, folk were occupied with their early preparations, scouring the streets for the choicest gifts, foods, decorations and clothes to take their minds off an otherwise humdrum existence. With Winifred remaining unwell, Dan Chelten still imprisoned, and Mrs Holden's murder no closer to being resolved, there seemed little for Mr Michael and Irene to celebrate.

After a particularly arduous day in his workshop, Mr Michael trudged home through the revolting combination of seasonal slush and thickening refuse swelling up from the overflowing gutters. Heading straight home where he intended to warm his bones before the fireplace, he found the kitchen vacant and the coals unlit. There was an empty pan on the table and the ingredients for his evening meal lay half prepared on the chopping board beside it, much as they had appeared the day Winifred was taken ill the previous month. Cautiously he headed upstairs, muttering a silent prayer for the safety of his wife and child. As he opened the door of Winifred's room, he immediately sensed that the atmosphere had changed.

Gone were the stenches and stale air, replaced instead by the scent of soap and a thin cool breeze wafting through the window along with a few flakes of freshly falling snow. He watched as Irene draped a shawl around her mother's shoulders as she sat up in her bed before feeding her oats soaked in water with what looked like honey or syrup. There was now a gentle flush of colour to Winifred's cheeks and her eyes, though weary, were calm and focused. Irene told him that they had spent much of the afternoon talking about the weather, her schoolwork, and which type of pie they should bake at the weekend.

It was as if life had been restored, not only to Winifred but to the whole family. While her skin was still pale and clammy, her hair lank and her wrists as thin as twigs, his wife was otherwise exceptionally well, healthy and happy under her daughter's care. Irene too was convinced that her mother was no longer in danger. She replaced the empty bowl and spoon and rose to hug her father, her long arms almost wrapping double around his skinny hips. How she had grown, Mr Michael thought as he gazed between his two women, the two anchors of his world.

Though she was by no means fully recovered, Winifred gradually regained enough of her former strength to be able to sleep without fitting and eat twice a day without heaving it back up. Mr Michael was able to focus fully on his work again and Irene tried her best to catch up on the schooling she had missed while trying to defend herself from the other children. As soon as the bell chimed, she would bundle her books up and run home to prepare supper, creating feasts with new herbs and strange-looking vegetables she had taken a chance on at the weekend markets. Once her father returned from his workshop, they would take their plates up to Winifred's room and sit by her bedside discussing the day.

Even though Winifred was by now aware of Mrs Holden's stolen possessions and gruesome death, it was never discussed openly in the family. Instead, there was an unspoken agreement to continue as if life were perfectly pleasant and normal, commenting on the darkening days or the absence of birdsong, which fruits were the juiciest or what flower smelled the sweetest. Winifred knew her husband and daughter were protecting her, sparing her ears from the horrors they had had to face over the past few months. She swore to herself that one day when she was well enough, she would repay their kindness with boundless love.

Life began to assume a steady routine. Neighbours commented on how well both Mr Michael and Irene looked now that the heathen Dan Chelten had been locked away and poor Mrs Holden had been put to rest. It was true that Mr Michael had found his appetite again, his muscles growing stronger from the ample food and his renewed enthusiasm at work, but knowing Dan had been wrongly arrested had played no part in his improvement. On the contrary, it still caused him much distress to think of the man in prison, and he asked after his condition whenever he saw Inspector Falmer or one of his officers in the street.

Irene meanwhile was finally able to form new

friendships at school. Now that her mother was almost fully recovered and she did not have to worry about her father, she could go outside or down to the river to play, making snowmen or buying roast chestnuts with the few pennies her father slipped her as a treat. It was as if she were rediscovering her childhood again. Winifred remained in her room, but she was often awake and bright enough to enjoy short conversations with her daughter, who she was relieved to see growing happier as well as prettier by the day.

It was all too easy to pretend. As he helped himself to a third serving of stew or brought home a currant bun for his daughter, Mr Michael fought against the guilt, the memories, and the burning anger that continued to simmer in the pit of his belly. His dreams were haunted by the vision of approaching helmets, smirks stifled behind quivering moustaches, the strangled cries of their scapegoat travelling all the way from the cells to his bed. He tried to remain rational and calm, telling himself that it was not his fault, that it was a matter for the police, that he should focus on his carpentry and his wife and daughter, but it was no good. Wherever he walked, Mr Michael could not help himself stopping a vaguely familiar passer-by and quizzing them about Holden's Haunt or the little boy who had vanished decades ago. Every response was either a mumbled apology or a story he had already heard. Despite his determination to solve the case and bring peace to Mrs Holden's memory, he was slowly starting to believe that the culprit was too cunning and would never be caught.

It was nearing five o'clock one afternoon when Mr

Michael heard the unmistakable sound of his daughter's feet running towards his workshop. He downed his tools and headed for the door just as the girl swung around the corner and straight into him. Her hair had blown into a messy screen across her face and her shoes and legs were covered in all manner of gunge and debris. Irene panted as she tried to catch her breath, dragging her coat back up to sit on her shoulders. Mr Michael felt fear rising as he looked at her wide eyes, wild and startled like a rabbit's. Still clutching her chest, Irene managed to pant out the only two words her father needed to hear: 'Dan's free'.

Chapter Thirty

After locking up his workshop, Mr Michael instructed his daughter to return home and check on her mother while he went to find Dan. Even though she was just as eager to hear what he had to say as Mr Michael, Irene obliged and shuffled off down the street while her father made his way briskly towards the police station. Just as he turned the corner, he spotted a man ambling up ahead who resembled the former blacksmith, limping along the cobbles. Mr Michael followed him like a bloodhound, turning this way and that before he saw the shape staggering into the dark depths of the Eagle and Child Inn. Looking around the dim interior of the pub, Mr Michael spotted a hunched and dishevelled form at the bar – Dan Chelten, a free man, but now a shadow of his former self.

"It's on me," he said as he approached, slipping some coins onto the counter as he nodded to the barman. Mr Michael tried to keep his expression neutral as he surveyed Dan's face. It was gaunt and pallid, mottled with bruises and speckled with sores. His eyes were swollen, his lip split top and bottom, his posture hunched as if in permanent pain. Mr Michael took a heavy sip of ale, but it could not remove the lump that had formed in his throat.

The men took their drinks to a far corner and slid uneasily into the booth, the fabric sticky against their clothes. They each took a long and slow mouthful of drink, absorbed in their thoughts and appreciative of the relative silence their concealed nook provided. Each knew why the other had come, and that there was only one thing they had to talk about. Dan nodded his head in the direction of the bar and smiled softly, raising his glass in a toast. Mr Michael followed Dan's gaze and saw what looked to be an old sock dangling from the ceiling beam, a single nail piercing its centre. He already knew the story, of course – it was a local legend – but he was surprised to hear Dan confess that he had tried to return the sock to Mrs Holden on the very day that she had been killed.

As he listened, Mr Michael knew that he was talking to a changed man. Doing time had reduced Dan's former swagger and confidence so that he now spoke meekly and cautiously, as if measuring the value of every word. Mr Michael could only guess at the methods of interrogation Inspector Falmer had permitted. He tried to resist the dreadful imagery that began to creep into his mind as he focused on Dan's story.

Though he already knew that the man was no murderer, he was still surprised he had felt sorry enough to have tried to show Mrs Holden some small kindness in her time of need. He listened intently as Dan described how he had entered Holden's Haunt through the open door and spotted the old woman stroking her beloved letter opener. At first, he thought she had not heard him, so he had stood there watching in silence before taking a few tentative steps forward to try and get a closer look at the unusual emblem on the blade she held. Dan had never seen anything quite like it. It had an almost mysterious power that drew him to its beauty against his will, making him crave its touch, to hold it, to have it in his possession. He did not believe in witchcraft, but the thought had crossed his mind at that moment, so enthralled was he by the object. Perhaps some of his drinking buddies had been right; maybe Mrs Holden practised the dark arts after all.

As if hearing his thoughts, the old woman had snapped her head up in his direction, two puddles for eyes scanning helplessly around the room. She had called out, quietly at first, then louder, panic etched in her words despite her attempts to conceal it. Dan had watched as Mrs Holden turned the knife in his direction and held it with both hands firmly in front of her. He had decided at that moment that he would not try to take it. Instead, he announced himself and explained the real reason for his visit; to return the sock. On recognising his voice, Mrs Holden's face had softened. She placed the letter opener back in her lap then shook her head, a strange sound gurgling in her throat – laughter, a forgotten reflex now returning.

The old woman gave a phlegmy cough and told her former customer that he could keep the sock. He had paid a fair price for it after all, and she still had the two socks left on her feet. What could she do with a third? Dan gave a small chuckle before looking around at the barren space. He tucked the sock into his pocket and turned to leave, but as he did so, Mrs Holden called after him.

"D'you 'ave time fer a story? I can't sell yeh this

here beauty, but I can tell yer how it came t'be in me possession. It'll not tek long." She waved the letter opener briefly in the air and Dan was once again hooked by its enchantment.

He seated himself on the cold and dusty floor in anticipation of Mrs Holden's tale and the opportunity to know more about the intriguing object.

Reflecting on his memory, Dan did not know why Mrs Holden had chosen him of all people to reveal this secret history to, but he was glad that he could now share the story with Mr Michael. The police had heard it too, of course, but it had been of no use to their investigation. They had accused Dan of wasting valuable police time and concealing the truth. Perhaps the information would have a different meaning to Mr Michael though, Dan had thought. It could even help him to find the real murderer. The men ordered two more ales before Dan shared what Mrs Holden had told him on the night of her death.

The Dartton family celebrated Benjamin's fifth birthday with a garden party – just the four of them, as always. Rising with the sun's first rays, Agnes arranged a large rug just beyond the house in the partial shade of the trees with a comfortable chair covered in cushions for her mother. She left the little boy dozing on the mattress next to her own bed, the dappled light from the window painting patterns on his mass of black hair splayed out on the pillow. She helped her mother to bathe and dress in a cream linen frock with a high-necked collar. Agnes herself chose a pale yellow shift with tiny navy spots and decided to wear her hair loose around her shoulders with a wide navy ribbon across her head.

She skipped into the garden and made a chain of daisies to tie around her bare ankle before waking her brother and fitting him with a smart pair of corduroy trousers, a deep crimson shirt, and a green waistcoat with shiny silver-coloured buttons that she had made herself. With his new shoes and hair combed to one side, he looked like a miniature version of their father. The little boy held a pencil up to his nostrils like a moustache and they both fell onto the unmade mattress with laughter. On descending to the kitchen together, they saw Mr Dartton in a similar combination of corduroys, shirt and a waistcoat, but in shades of tan and ochre, with Mrs Dartton lovingly stroking his collar as she admired his appearance.

Agnes had spent the previous two days in the kitchen making and baking all of Benjamin's favourite treats. Though a slight child, he was always hungry and loved to try any new foods. Agnes had made a cake and a pie, some biscuits and egg tarts, chopped vegetables into sticks and fruit into slices, mounded nuts and berries along with shellfish and cheeses, and added two bottles of her own homemade lemonade, which she served in sugar-rimmed glasses. It was all amassed on the kitchen table, every inch taken up by either edibles or decorations: leaves, flowers, stones and even a few shells from her collection. Benjamin was open-mouthed and wide-eyed when he caught sight of the bounty. He rounded the table again and again, picking parts off each plate in turn until Agnes had to pull him away so they could all sit outside, the whole family together.

Despite the occasional unseasonal downpour earlier that week, the day was blissfully warm with tufts of thick white cloud forming shapes in the sky above them. Agnes and Benjamin lay with their heads side by side on the rug, both pointing up and tracing the outlines of pirate ships, fairground rides, and exotic animals with their fingertips. Though she had slowly gained in strength since the boy's arrival, Mrs Dartton was still weak in body and spirit, and spent most of the day slumbering fitfully in her chair despite her efforts to remain awake.

Mr Dartton sat opposite his wife, sipping lemonade and watching his children. He had rarely spent any time with the pair as they had grown up, though often presented them with giant curls of sawdust to play with or the odd wooden toy that had been accidentally damaged as he had worked on it. Today, however, he had made a surprise especially for Benjamin; a small fort constructed from oak and complete with a working drawbridge. The boy was delighted with his gift and ran around the garden in circles squealing his gratitude. Mr Dartton patted his son's head before taking his wife indoors, leaving the children to their games and feasting.

After their celebratory lunch it was time for Benjamin's second treat, a special present just from Agnes. She took him by the hand into the woods behind the house where there was a small box waiting. Inside was a tiny black lump shaking and chirping, its beak snapping open and shut hungrily. Agnes took out a handful of seeds from her apron pocket and scattered them in the bottom of the box, giggling as the hatchling crow pecked away. Benjamin was enraptured, gasping at the creature's every move before Agnes encouraged him to stroke its head with a single finger. He reached in slowly then snapped his hand back with a shriek of laughter as the little bird attempted to peck at its intruder.

Though she was sure that Benjamin would have loved a proper pet, after the unfortunate incident with the kitten, Agnes could not bring herself to have an animal in the house. When she had found the little crow on its own, desperate but still clinging on to life, she had welcomed the opportunity to take care of the creature and to gift it to her brother, who loved wildlife just as much as she did. They would be able to rear it together, and once it was big enough to fly, they would release it into the woods. She had imagined every precise detail of the event in her mind.

Thrilled with his friend, Benjamin plucked the bird from the box and gave it a new home in his fort. He had decided to simply call it Crow and began telling him all about his wonderful birthday, while Agnes tiptoed into the kitchen to clean away what remained of the banquet. An hour later, Benjamin ran past the room and stomped his way upstairs. Agnes dried her hands and followed, finding him sat on the mattress with the letter opener in his lap.

"Be careful there, Benjamin, 'tis very special an' fragile," she warned softly.

Sliding the blade from his hands, she held the

handle towards him so he could run his fingers over the emblem: his favourite ritual. He would trace the same shape in the mud with a stick or dip his finger into a jar of jam to smear the outline on his empty plate at breakfast. Agnes had even caught him trying to carve it into a tree with a stubby kitchen knife. Hearing the story of the letter opener was one of Benjamin's most loved bedtime tales, with Agnes inventing a multitude of myths about its previous owners and what adventures they had enjoyed. In truth, she knew very little about the object and its fascinating symbol. She had discovered it on the day that Benjamin had arrived and, in a moment of spontaneous decision, had appointed herself the letter opener's custodian until the boy was old enough to look after it himself. Her parents had not said a word, so Agnes had assumed them to be ignorant of its existence. It had become a cherished secret between her and Benjamin.

The birthday boy leapt to his feet and took Agnes by the hand, leading her and the blade back outside to the fort where Crow was huddled in a corner, chirping continuously. Benjamin wondered if the miniature sword, as the letter opener had now become, was magical enough to make Crow into a big bird so that he could fly. Agnes stroked her chin in exaggerated thought and nodded slowly, the boy staring up at her bright-eyed with awe.

"There were a witch long, long ago who med the magical sword full o'wishes. She said y'touch the tip o'the sword to any door an' who's inside will be fit an' strong after." She watched the child with amusement as he hopped from one foot to the other before carefully resting the tip of letter opener to the wooden toy. He scrunched his eyes closed and whispered his own invented incantation.

As the pair waited for the spell to materialise, there was a sudden silence, a shift in the air followed by the tiniest of noises that made Agnes glance over her shoulder. It was so small and had moved so quickly, she could not really be sure of what she had seen, but she had sensed the slip of a shadow disappearing behind a bush next to the house. She watched and waited, but nothing happened.

As she turned her attention back to Benjamin, she felt a chill tingle across the length of her arms despite the pleasantness of the day. Agnes did not know why she suddenly felt so wary, her ears and attention heightened for potential dangers. Perhaps it was simply a mother's way, for that was what she had come to think of herself, her bond with Benjamin having grown far beyond that of a sister. He was her darling, her hero, now nearly a fully-grown boy; the time had slipped by like the current of a river. Agnes shook off her agitation and returned to the game, settling herself on the grass as she helped him repeat his enchantment to Crow, the charmed letter opener tap-tapping against the fort.

As the spell proved fruitless, Benjamin began using the blade to dig for worms instead, taking great pleasure in mashing and feeding them to the hungry bird tweeting wildly in the fort. With the boy entertained by his toy and his pet, Agnes subtly retrieved the blade, wiping it through a handkerchief before sliding it into the pocket of her apron. She rose to her feet, ruffling a hand through Benjamin's already dishevelled locks before heading back indoors to tend to the kitchen.

As she walked, Agnes felt the letter opener bounce against the top of her legs and the same uneasy tension she had experienced earlier returned. While she had always considered the object to belong to Benjamin and him alone, she was cautious about leaving it in his care while he was still so young. She was often plagued with vivid nightmares about the boy being injured or lost, or even just hearing him cry. The pain in her heart she had felt on waking was severe enough to make her worry constantly for his wellbeing. She did not know what she would do if anything bad happened to him.

Even though she was sure he could come to no harm in the garden, Agnes still opened every window of the house so that she could hear Benjamin's happy chatter. Soon enough, she was lost in her own thoughts as she cleaned, dried and stacked the dishes at the sink, humming gently. It took her several moments to realise that all was quiet. Too quiet. No words, no laughter, not a single sound caught on the light breeze. Agnes paused in her duties and held her breath, her whole body alert. Still, she could hear nothing.

Trying to remain calm and rational, she wiped her damp hands down the length of her apron before making her way outside, calling Benjamin's name. There was no reply, but as she entered the garden, she could hear a gasping and whining noise. She saw the boy crouched on the lawn, one hand clutching at his throat while the other gripped a cup, his knuckles white with tension.

Agnes knew it was her dearest but everything about him looked wrong. His face was blue, his eyes bulged from their sockets, the skin on his arms pale and patterned with red mesh. In place of his dainty laughter came a pained and pitiful wheeze.

Agnes ran towards him, dropping to her knees just as he fell forward, both hands now around his neck, the cup sent rolling across the grass. She tried to reach two fingers into his mouth in the hope of alleviating an obstruction, but the boy's tongue had swollen to the size of a saucer and his lips were bloated with blood. His eyes were feral and frantic, pleading for help. She grabbed his tiny frame and threw him face-down across her lap, smacking the base of her palm between his shoulder blades, but he only coughed and squealed louder. She pushed her fingers into his mouth again, then repeated the blows, until eventually she could no longer hear him. She turned Benjamin over. His eyes were empty.

They did not know how long Agnes had been out there. It was nightfall when Mr Dartton found her still hugging the infant's dead body, which had to be prised from her grasp. She did not cry nor speak despite all her father's questions; she could barely even walk. He helped his daughter to her feet and took her upstairs, where she would not take to her own bed but instead curled into a ball on the boy's mattress, tears finally, silently, rolling down her cheeks.

During that sleepless night, Agnes remembered the strange cup she had found next to Benjamin's body. It had been empty, though some brown substance coated the bottom. While she was certain she had never seen it in her family home before, her thoughts were so confused that she could not be certain. The object faded from her mind, replaced instead by the dying moments of her dear little boy.

The following morning, Mr Dartton found his daughter covered with a blanket and her eyes closed, though she was not sleeping. He left a plate of food by her bedside and placed the toy fort by the window, its walls and turrets bowing slightly with damp from spending the night in the garden. Agnes waited for the door to close shut again before she looked inside the wooden structure. The bird had gone.

Mr Dartton then went to check on his wife, having left her to a deep sleep before sharing the sorry news. At his few mumbled words, her anguished scream rang out through the house, penetrating the walls, crushing what little spirit remained in Mr Dartton and his daughter. Stricken with misery, Mrs Dartton refused to see both the boy's body and her remaining child, letting only her husband enter the room to bring tea and bread that she would barely touch.

Eventually, Agnes found a way to sleep a few hours each night, eating a little more every time she received a meal, until eventually she could resume some of her daily duties. She never saw her mother and spoke only to pass pleasantries with her father, forming a near silent and automated routine to occupy her waking hours without the need to think or feel. That part of her soul, she believed, was now gone. She never knew what her father had done with Benjamin's body. There would be no funeral and she was still prohibited from mentioning him. Sometimes she thought she could hear the little boy's voice floating through the open windows and would run outside to greet him, only to find that the noise was coming from her neighbour, weeping and wailing with her own unknown grief.

As she grew up and started a new life, Agnes often wondered if she had dreamed the entire story. Was it possible for a child to arrive only to disappear again five years later? Over the course of a few weeks, every trace of his being vanished from the house. Clothes and toys, books and blankets – even the cup that she had found on that fateful afternoon was removed and disposed of by her father. The house became as it was when she was a child: functional, sparse, the domain of adults. For Agnes, the air still hung with Benjamin's laughter. She knew that she was not mistaken in her memories. After all, she still possessed the letter opener, the only proof of his existence, and the only evidence of her enduring love.

Chapter Thirty-One

After Dan had finished the tale, Mr Michael spent several moments silently nursing his empty glass, tracing his fingers across its smudged surface. The pub had filled with patrons and yet he did not notice the din, the crowd, the smell nor the heat. Instead, he felt numb in thought and in feeling, overwhelmed by one single day of Mrs Holden's former life, a life that until quite recently had been a complete mystery to all but the woman herself. It took a few seconds before Mr Michael realised that Dan had begun speaking again. As he focused on the words, he realised that they mirrored his own contemplations.

"I'll say it now as I said to 'er back then – Mrs 'olden, you did not kill that young lad," Dan repeated in a low voice, his eyes skirting the crowd as he drank steadily from another pint, two more having appeared at the table without Mr Michael even noticing.

"Can't 'ave been 'er, not a chance," he sighed in agreement, though there was an unintended tone to his voice that caused both he and Dan to look at one another, their eyebrows furrowed and lips twisted.

It could not be true, they each told themselves silently. Yet if these were Mrs Holden's last words, uttered on the day of her death, then could it really be possible? Was this the last admission of a murderer? Was this why she had herself been killed? Or could it in fact have been suicide after all?

"Even if s'true, who'd be out for revenge?" Dan pondered aloud, echoing Mr Michael's mind.

How many countless hours had he already spent running through lists of possible suspects, slumped by his fireplace, his poor daughter trying desperately to help? For even though Mr Michael had found several neighbours who had not especially warmed to Mrs Holden, there was not a soul he had spoken to nor whom he could think of that would go to the extent of robbing and killing her. He was back at the beginning once more, clueless yet compelled to discover the real story.

Benjamin had been part of a happy and loving home for five years. However hard the family had tried to keep him a secret, Mr Michael – and possibly Mrs Holden herself – knew that there must have been others who had seen the little boy. If Stuart Ainsley Junior and now Dan Chelten knew of his existence, then surely there would be more? Perhaps one of them had been witness to that terrible event and come to the wrong conclusion? Mr Michael felt torn between believing in the goodness of his friend and reading between the lines of her final words. Why had she shared the tale with Dan if not to confess her guilt?

"How were she? When she told yeh the story?" he asked, suddenly wondering why it had not been him to hear the truth but Dan Chelten, of all people.

"Oh, y'know… quiet. Distant. Like 'er body were there but 'er mind were somewhere else, y'see? Those eyes o'hers were like snowballs, but I could tell she were sad an' sorry. Broken 'earted, even."

Dan himself looked quite taken with emotion as he brought his pint up to his lips again before mopping his brow with the back of his sleeve cuff. His eyes stared at the sock hanging above the bar. Much to his own surprise as well as those around him, Dan had formed a fondness for Mrs Holden. She seemed to have that effect on people; once met, never forgotten.

"An' the letter opener, o'course," Mr Michael replied, wondering if it was the object and not the boy that had been the real reason for the attack on Mrs Holden.

Dan shrugged as he scratched his chin, taking one final gulp of his drink. Despite the much-needed refreshment and his comfortable surroundings, he still looked weary and woeful, tired of talk and of thought. He was carrying a burden which did not belong to him, and its weight had drained his mental and physical energy ever since that fateful visit to Holden's Haunt. He blinked heavily with sore shadowed eyes.

"Yer a good man, Mr Michael, an' I'm sorry 'bout what 'appened. I d'know why she chose me t'tell 'er story to, but s'only me an' thee that know it. I've not said a word t'police nor t'folk round 'ere. We know she's innocent, but someone out there ain't. Find 'em, Mr Michael, wherever they are."

With that, Dan swiftly slid from his seat and took off from the pub, vanishing into the night before Mr Michael could even open his mouth to reply. He stared after the absent man, grateful for his courage and his honesty, but above all for providing Mrs Holden with the one thing she had needed the night she knew she would die – someone to talk to.

As he took his time to finish his pint, Mr Michael was struck by the last few words he had heard Dan utter: 'Wherever they are'. Like a match to a wick, the flame of an idea suddenly ignited within his mind. Helmsley. The Shoulder of Mutton's landlord might already have provided the answer he so desperately needed.

Somewhere between leaving the pub and collapsing on his bed, Mr Michael had mused on Dan's final parting words and had come up with an idea. While it had not been forged in the clearest frame of mind, it was the only course of action he could think of following. He now realised that his chance conversation with the pub proprietor had imparted some information of significance. He would have to make the journey to Helmsley and find out for himself if there really was a shop that looked just like Holden's Haunt. It could not be a mere coincidence, nor was it the sort of story someone could invent – especially not this particular landlord, who was famed for his exceptional honesty.

Though he had visited Helmsley many years ago, Mr Michael could not remember a shop that even remotely resembled Holden's Haunt, but he knew that even the most rural of towns could change a great deal within a decade. He had already seen how Mrs Holden had managed to build up a business within the space of a few months, so it was not altogether impossible that another entrepreneurial homeowner had achieved the same. As for the painting the landlord had mentioned, seascapes were still vastly popular with the county having such a close connection to its coastline, so this too could quite easily be a coincidence.

As his slumped on his bed and felt his body drift into slumber, Mr Michael's inebriated mind swayed constantly between believing and discrediting the account, but his intention was set. He would go to Helmsley and discover the truth. The longer he lay staring at the ceiling of his tiny room, the more his confidence and determination grew.

Just as the sky began to shrug off its dark canopy, Mr Michael hauled himself up, washing and changing as quietly as he could before creeping into the kitchen to make himself a strong cup of sugary tea. He peered out of the window into the street beyond, only a few surfaces and shapes visible in the dim light, the faint clamour of his neighbours audible as they began their working days. An icy breeze drifted down the chimney disturbing the ashes below, kicking up a faint smell of smoke and charred meat that reminded him of simpler times.

As he sipped his brew, Mr Michael tried to recall every precise detail of Dan's recollection the previous evening, which had cast light on yet another part of Mrs Holden's heart-breaking past. He could not help but feel an immense shame that he had known so little about his friend. All those wasted hours talking about the weather and the market and the price of oysters when he should have been helping her to overcome the loss, to find a way to cope with the memories both happy and sad. In his heart, though, he knew that his friend would have wanted her past to remain a mystery.

Though they had known one another when they were both young, their friendship had only been formed within the previous ten years. It had not been the past that connected them but the present – their mutual interest in the power of objects, the items that he carved and the treasures that she sold. Now it seemed that their relationship had changed once again. Mr Michael was the only person who could find out what had really happened to Mrs Holden and her shop. The decision had already been made. It was time for him to go to Helmsley.

Swilling and downing the last remnants of his tea, Mr Michael retrieved a piece of cloth from the kitchen cupboard and packed it with some bread, cheese, fruit and nuts. He placed a small number of coins in a drawstring leather bag, which he tucked carefully inside the waistband of his trousers. He checked to make sure that there was enough money in the secret salt jar by the basin so that Irene could buy groceries for the next few days. He hoped to return that same evening, but if he was delayed, at least his daughter could be trusted to take care of the house and Winifred in his absence. She had done as much for many months already. His carpentry commissions could wait; he was already ahead with his orders and he knew that the workshop would be well looked after by the other men. He even had a friend with one of the newly popularised velocipedes that he might be able to borrow. There was nothing stopping him, and he knew it could be his very last opportunity to finally find the real culprit.

Ducking to peer out of the kitchen window again,

Mr Michael could now see the detail of the houses on the other side of the street as night had given way to day. There was no snow nor rain; even the air seemed still, providing the perfect conditions for travel. With his supplies slung over his shoulder and the rest of the house still in slumber, Mr Michael closed the door silently behind him, quickly side-stepping to avoid the dirty bucket of water being hurled by his neighbour. She gave a curt nod in his direction before he hastily informed her of his plans. If anyone were to come looking for him, at least someone would know. He turned up the collar of his coat against the cool air and headed along the cobbles towards Walmgate Bar.

An hour following Mr Michael's departure, Irene woke to find the kitchen empty. She had not heard her father return to the house that night, but she knew he could take care of himself. There were two rolls, three apples and half the cheddar missing, so he must have packed himself a hearty breakfast and headed off to work early. It was not uncommon and she was glad he had at least returned home. He would be at work now, she imagined, absorbed in some intricate carving, bent close to the blade, working the wood with his deft hands and precise eye. The thought filled her with comfort. Normality was returning.

The girl busied herself with whatever she could chop into small pieces for her mother's breakfast and took it up with a cup of steaming milky tea. Winifred was still sleeping so she left the tray by the bed and opened the tiny window to try to encourage some air in. Her mother had not deteriorated but neither had she fully recovered. Irene tried to remain hopeful about her condition and instead set her thoughts on the day ahead; a few hours at school, then a walk in the park with her new friend Simon, followed by one of her famous meat and vegetable pies.

As she left the house, the woman who lived opposite heaved up her skirts and crept her way across the cobbles. She did not know the woman well but she had always been friendly enough, having frequently enquired after Winifred's health over the years. Irene remembered that she had once offered a few lumps of coal when she had been on her way to Mrs Holden's, sending her sympathies following the old shopkeeper's robbery. The neighbour always seemed to have a disgruntled look to her expression despite the goodness of her heart. Today her brow was furrowed so sternly as to make her appear in pain. She grabbed Irene by both arms and brought her face in close, the two almost the same height.

The woman explained that Mr Michael was 'gone away t'nother village' and that he had planned to borrow a contraption from 'tha' bloke down t'road' so he could try to find 'them wot dunnit'. Irene nodded, not in understanding but merely in the hope of the neighbour releasing her grip. She thankfully did so, giving the girl's tender cheek a quick squeeze before asking to send her love to her 'poorly mam' and tottering off across the street again to where her twin boys were wailing at an open doorway. Irene smiled as sweetly as she could as the woman closed her door before hurrying off in the direction of the market.

There would be no school, no walk and possibly not even supper that day. Irene's mind was firmly fixed on one intent. She marched on through the city, up past Holy Trinity Church and on towards Goodramgate, her shoes squelching in all sorts of sodden muck as she hurriedly sped ahead without watching where she was going. Her socks slid down to her ankles and she kept having to haul her shawl back over her shoulders, but she could not stop. Finally, she reached the police station and bashed against the door with her fist. An officer appeared, seemingly still half asleep with crumbs in the corners of his mouth. He led her to see the inspector.

Inspector Falmer listened patiently to Irene, pulling his mouth into the same smile he had perfected over years of working with the general public. He patted the girl on her shoulder and ushered her towards the door with a sigh of apology. She may have been right about Mrs Holden's murder, but now she needed to leave matters to the police. If her father had decided to depart the city and look for the criminal himself then that was his choice. It was foolish and potentially dangerous but not in itself a crime. If he found the man then the inspector would gladly send his officers to assist, but in all likelihood, it would prove to be a wasted journey for Mr Michael. He suggested that Irene stay at home with her mother and wait for her father to return, unsuccessful though perhaps a little rejuvenated from his travels. A few days away to himself might do him the world of good, the inspector had concluded. Irene thought the exact opposite, but her concerns had fallen on deaf ears.

She stood outside the door of the police station as it slammed shut behind her, a surge of emotion suddenly swelling to fill every inch of her body. She wanted to scream and throw her tatty old shawl in the gutter, to cry and claw at her own flesh with frustration, to swear and shout with all the unfair and unkind deeds that had been done to her and her family and to that poor old woman in her shop all alone. Instead, Irene took a deep breath of the dirty city air and returned to the market to purchase the ingredients for supper, having already missed most of her lesson and no longer feeling cheerful enough to meet with her friend.

Walking home with her bundle, she was further disheartened that the meat was not the freshest and the carrots were spotted with bruises, but she would nevertheless try to have a delicious meal ready for when her father returned home, whenever that might be. Irene decided that she would just have to trust him, exactly as he had counted on her to attend to Mrs Holden and to her mother. Her father was honest and gentle and kind; he would never leave his wife and child without good reason. Maybe he would even find the criminal and be a hero in the city, then they could go back to family life as normal.

Irene tried to find that place inside her that brought reassurance and warmth, that had made her believe all those fairy stories when she was a little girl. She tried to remember and to have faith, but something had changed. She was not the same girl she had been and she could no longer stand back and watch her father grow weaker in heart and mind. She owed it to him, to her mother, to Mrs Holden, and to herself to help in any way that she could.

On returning home, Irene began preparing the vegetables in the gloomy light from the window. She gazed out onto the bustling street beyond, her fingers deftly following the moves they had performed a thousand times before. In her mind she had begun forming a plan which, though she did not yet know it, was uncannily like her father's. There were secrets out there in the city just waiting to be discovered, she reasoned, their owners eager for a pretty face and an attentive ear. She would start her own search for the culprit, her intentions masked by a veneer of girlhood innocence. Together she and her father would solve the mystery. If Irene had learnt anything from Mrs Holden, it was that the women of this world were able to wield more power than society gave them credit for. They just had to know how to use it, and Irene was now determined to learn.

Chapter Thirty-Two

Mr Michael pounded the cobbles oblivious to the increasing ruckus around him as the city gradually awoke. While he knew that his journey to Helmsley was fuelled by a sombre purpose, he could not help feeling a quiver of excitement on having the opportunity to be visiting the town again. It had been so long since he was last there and his memory of that time was a happy one thanks to his daughter's company.

Irene had been only young, approaching her sixth birthday, but she possessed the height and confidence of a child twice her age. With her inquisitive mind and docile nature, Mr Michael had felt comfortable taking her to work and on occasional excursions out of town while Winifred was confined to her bed. Irene would gladly sit and play in the corner of his workshop, joining her father for a short while to enjoy lunch beside the river where they would share stories and savour meat sandwiches with fresh milk.

As soon as she could walk and talk, Irene had been desperate to follow in her father's footsteps and loved any opportunity to explore the world by his side. As a baby she would toddle around after him in the house, following him to the privy or even down the street if he had not locked the front door. When left with neighbours, she would wait by a window and watch her father disappear, remaining in the exact same position until he returned. It did not take long before he was glad to have her with him instead, their bond becoming even closer.

Irene had inherited her father's deftness and quickly found herself happiest in the family kitchen where she could learn useful skills and become absorbed by their repetition. When her mother was well, they would work together preparing the daily meals. Irene became proficient with a blade, slicing away at vegetables, fruit and meat with the same precision Mr Michael applied in his workshop. By the time her mother was bedbound, Irene could skin rabbits and fillet fish, reduce mounds of potatoes to thin slices in minutes, and even shuck oysters with the speed of an experienced fishmonger. But it was the preparation of her famous pie that she relished the most.

Irene had first learned how to make a pie during a visit to Helmsley with her father. She had been young in years but full of spirit, elated to be riding with him in the trap with the commissioned vanity table between them. They had both shared the memory on many occasions since: the thrill of the journey, Irene waving her handkerchief to her mother as they rode through the city and out of Walmgate Bar, the cart rocking merrily over the uneven road, the pony tossing up its nose and shaking its mane as they hurried along.

The town itself had seemed like another world with its pretty cottages, bubbling stream and quaint market. Mr Michael had watched as Irene's head snapped one way and then the other, taking in as much detail as she could. It all seemed so vastly different from home. They had pulled up to a grand stone building flanked by two imposing pillars. Mr Michael had taken his daughter by the hand to the front door, pausing on the way to let her stroke a black cat that had sauntered towards them, the thick fur tickling her ankles and fingertips.

As Mr Michael talked to the man of the house, Irene had been told to wait in the kitchen where the cook was busy preparing lunch. The young girl had been fascinated by the process and could not resist helping to knead the dough when the chance was offered. The kindly woman demonstrated just the right way to mould and turn it before helping Irene to roll it out on the floured surface. She was spellbound. Mr Michael had had to apologise profusely to the cook as he whisked his daughter away, though later on the ride home he would tell her of his pride in watching her learning a new skill.

The pride had returned with every mouthful of pie Mr Michael had enjoyed ever since, lovingly prepared by Irene at least once a fortnight. She would usually make one on a Sunday so they could linger over its crumbling pastry and rich filling, helping themselves to a second or third portion though they tried to resist. He allowed the memories to absorb his mind as he neared the home of his friend on the outskirts of York, grateful for the distraction from the expedition's true purpose.

After arriving at the house of his acquaintance, Mr Michael agreed to share one quick drink in gratitude of being able to borrow the 'boneshaker' bicycle. Bobby had only purchased it two months ago and had kept it in a fine condition, constantly tinkering with the mechanism to improve it. As they sipped, Mr Michael asked him what he knew of Mrs Holden, but all of Bobby's stories were frustratingly familiar – the mass of mysterious objects, their strange and sudden disappearance, the crow with the crooked beak. He reeled off the tales as if they were centuries old, removed from reality and stripped of their emotional impact.

Having finished their drinks, Mr Michael bid his friend farewell and began walking with the bicycle to the end of the road. Looking around for any traffic, he spotted the unmistakable silhouette and bald head of Doctor Pruce emerging from the doorway of a cottage on the corner. They greeted one another amicably and continued walking together, the doctor to his next appointment and Mr Michael towards the outskirts of the city with the bicycle by his side. Having already spent much of the morning reflecting on his daughter's childhood and the missed opportunity of young Benjamin, Mr Michael could not help himself asking the doctor about the little boy's death that Dan Chelten had related to him.

Fearing for his friend's reputation, he did not mention Mrs Holden or Benjamin by name and introduced the story as merely hearsay from a neighbour. A child around the age of five had been found choking, Mr Michael explained, with a blue face and large tongue, along with strange patterns on the skin. A mother would naturally slap the child on the back, but this had not worked, nor had the attempt to remove an obstruction from the mouth as there seemed to be nothing there. The child had died, but was it murder?

Doctor Pruce had paused in his motion, a gloved hand readjusting his spectacles as he stared at the ground. Eventually he raised his gaze, his eyes faintly shining as if a series of thoughts had just aligned themselves harmoniously in his mind.

"I have heard such a description before, exactly as you have related, though not a child," he replied, his stare made all the more intense by his lenses.

"An' what were the cause?" Mr Michael replied.

"I believe the term being used is anaphylactic shock. Fascinating chap on the continent has done some intriguing research," the doctor continued, though his enthusiasm was lost on his listener, "It's an extreme allergic reaction."

"A reaction?" Mr Michael wondered aloud, "But t'who or what?"

Doctor Pruce started on his route again, his arms crossed behind his back, his eyes looking beyond the end of the street as he plucked the key points from his memory and attempted to rephrase them for his companion.

"Most certainly a 'what', and it could be any commonplace item. It is not precisely known why such conditions develop. Many are simply born with them, discovering their catastrophic consequence only when it is too late. It is possibly hereditary."

Mr Michael nodded with limited understanding, his free hand rising to his own chin as he mulled over the possible scenario, the two wheels beside him quietly clicking as they rolled along the uneven surface of the path. He did not fully comprehend what he had been told, but any information seemed better than none at all when it came to the mystery of Mrs Holden's vanished child. The pair soon reached the front door of the next patient. Mr Michael thanked Doctor Pruce for his time and company before mounting the bicycle and heading on his way; it was already nearing noon and he had not even left the city. He crouched low on the handlebars and began pumping at the pedals, quickly gaining speed along the dusty road.

As he trundled along, the icy wind whipping against his protruding ears, Mr Michael reflected on his luck in life. His loving daughter, with whom he had already shared so many adventures, was now growing into a strong and capable young woman able to take care of a home and a family, not to mention attending school. He could not imagine feeling prouder. Yet it could all have been so different. As he edged ever nearer to his destination, Mr Michael's mind inevitably strayed to Mrs Holden and Benjamin, the little boy of whom she had never spoken.

Though he did not doubt that Mrs Holden had cherished the five years she had shared with him, Mr Michael could not help but feel sorry that the boy's life had been cut short so soon. Perhaps he could have learned how to make a pie or have visited Helmsley on a bicycle too, maybe even have formed a friendship with his own daughter. All these things and so much more had been denied to poor Benjamin and in turn to Agnes. While Mr Michael strongly believed that his friend had been trying to rescue her son, he needed some form of proof. It was the only way he would be able to save her memory when he had failed so terribly at saving her life. He owed her this at the very least.

Keeping well to the edge of the road, Mr Michael pedalled over bridges and past factories, the noise and smoke of industry choking him briefly before finally the congestion gave way to open pastures and a clear band of grey sky beyond. He could not remember the last time he had been able to breath without feeling a pinch in his throat. He pumped his feet harder and firmer, revelling in the thrill of the speed, the vibration of the bicycle beneath him, the clouds of dust following in his wake. He felt young again and free. How he wished he could have done this years ago.

After some hours, a familiar church spire came into view along with a small mound of rock on which several small letters had been studded black on white. Mr Michael slowed his pace just in time to be able to make out the word 'Helmsley'. He had arrived. He ambled over the bridge and followed the road as it curved round to his left, cycling past the entrance to the estate and beside the bubbling brook as it ran along the gardens of cottages. He took a deep intake of breath and felt his whole body become invigorated by the clean air, a stark contrast to the soot and smog of the city. He let the bicycle roll to a stop and dismounted. Now all he had to do was to find the shop.

Chapter Thirty-Three

With the pie in the oven, the kitchen cleaned and mopped, and her mother soundly asleep in her room, Irene was free to leave the house and to try to find her own answers to the mystery of Holden's Haunt. Though she had heard plenty of stories about clever detectives and their extravagant escapades catching criminals, such adventures had never appealed to her. Like Mrs Holden, she was a lover of nature, of the creatures that lived deep in the woods, or at the bottom of the river, or in unknown lands. Animals that could hide from humans and lead their own lives free from noise and commotion, sewage and smoke; all the things Irene loathed about the city from which she wished to escape.

As she left the house and walked up past the church towards Coney Street, Irene imagined her father having arrived in Helmsley many miles away. She regretted that she could not remember anything of the town itself save for the feel of her fingers working through the dough when she had learned how to make it smooth and supple alongside the cook. She had frequently asked her father to describe that day along with some of the other places he had visited alone. They all sounded so peaceful, safe and comfortable in comparison to the streets she had grown up on.

It was not that Irene thought York a terrible place to live. She did love their little house and her school, the river and the market. It was just that she had never felt quite at home. Perhaps she was an outsider by nature, like Mrs Holden had been. Nevertheless, she would much preferred to have gone with her father to Helmsley and enjoyed the pretty cottages and the little silver stream rather than to be wandering the cold and familiar streets of her home city on her own.

When the neighbour had first told her about her father's absence, she had felt sorry that he had not wanted her with him. On reflection, however, she had imagined that there might be some danger involved in his quest, particularly if it led to finding the murderer. What he would think of Irene conducting her own investigation, she did not want to consider. He had never been mad or angry at her; far worse was when he was disappointed. She was sure he would look at her with the same furrowed eyebrows and downturned mouth if he could see her now. But she had no time for such concerns and could not afford to linger over regrets. She had her plan and she would follow it through, starting with a visit to Stuart Ainsley Junior.

The Ainsley Grocery Store was located halfway down Coney Street with its back to the river, where they still received supplies by boat. The shop front was smart and proud with its navy wooden boards and white curled lettering, the windows filled with an array of fresh, packaged, tinned and dried goods carefully aligned. Behind them an assortment of colourful advertisements recommended everything from butter and baking powder to soap and boot polish.

Irene stood along with several smaller children

peering in, their grubby fingers leaving smears on the glass as they pointed at the range of treats inside, wishing they could afford even one. It was no Holden's Haunt, but it was mesmerising in its own way. Drawing her attention away from the display, Irene entered the shop and waited in line for her turn at the counter. Once the burly lady in front of her had shuffled out of the way with an almighty basket of produce, Irene was greeted by a young woman with brown curly hair held back by a yellow ribbon.

The lady was pleasant and welcoming, calling into the rear of the shop with a heavily accented holler to bring Stuart Ainsley Junior hobbling to the front. He came slowly, his huffs becoming more forceful as he struggled to catch his breath before pausing to lean on his walking stick, a beautifully carved owl on its top. Irene had not expected the man to be so old and felt sorry to have removed him from the comfort of the back room. She explained that she was Mr Michael's daughter and had come to speak with him in private. Despite his shortness of breath, Mr Ainsley nodded happily before promptly ushering Irene to follow him.

He led the way into a little sitting room and brought up a stool with a floral cushion for Irene, waiting for her to sit down before offering a plate of biscuits. Irene took the biggest she could see; a thick pale sphere dusted with sugar. She closed her eyes and inhaled, relishing the scents of sugar and vanilla and wet dog, a friendly spaniel whipping its tail as it watched her from the comfort of the hearthside rug.

The biscuit crumbled down her front as she bit into

it. Not wanting to waste a morsel, Irene licked a finger to retrieve every piece before the dog could get there first. Mr Ainsley dipped his confection inside the rim of his cup and pulled it out again quickly, just in time to ram the soggy square into his mouth in one go. What a wonderful place to work, Irene thought. Far nicer than the dusty old workshop her father had to spend his days in.

After the plate had been emptied, Irene asked about the Dartton family and Mr Ainsley's visits when Agnes had been a girl. He seemed quite content to recount his few experiences of delivering groceries to the family and could remember each time in vivid detail, much to Irene's delight. He even knew who lived in the house now, just out past Peasholme Green following the river. A couple called Johnson with three very pretty girls, each a year apart in age and all now grown and married with their own families. Irene leaned in further as Mr Ainsley beckoned with his finger. He took up the empty plate and began making shapes against its surface; he was drawing a map, showing the route from his shop to the Johnson's house, a simple set of directions that instantly etched themselves in his visitor's mind.

Lost in the old man's careful musings, Irene had not been aware of the time. When she noticed how much the light had dimmed outside, she hastily thanked Mr Ainsley and fled from the shop, running as fast as she could back home. She darted down Coney Street and up towards Fossgate, launching herself through the door of her kitchen just in time to find the pie perfectly crisp and golden in the oven. She placed it on top of the stove and covered it with a teatowel, pausing to rest in the chair by the fire as she tried to catch her breath.

Once recovered, Irene slipped upstairs to check on her mother. She was still sleeping but had been awake long enough to finish the plate of apple slices Irene had left that morning. She took the empty dish back to the kitchen, wondering if her father would return that evening so that they could enjoy the pie together. With still a few hours remaining before nightfall, Irene pondered her options, the tales of Mr Ainsley swimming in and out of her thoughts. The property he had described seemed only a short walk away, his map still clear in her memory. The weather remained calm and clear, and she could always enjoy a little lunch on her walk. Stuffing a piece of bread and cheese into her apron pocket, Irene left the house once more.

On reaching the end of the third and final street, Irene was surprised and relieved by how easy it had been to follow the old man's route. In what had seemed only a few minutes, she had found herself outside of the city walls and standing in front of a small but cosy-looking cottage, the river flowing off behind the garden and the tall trees of a woodland visible beyond. Brushing down her hair and skirts, Irene tentatively knocked on the front door using a rusted but charming metal handle in the shape of a bell, the worn wood thudding softly underneath.

A middle-aged woman appeared at the entrance, her face weathered but welcoming and her auburn hair tied into a pretty braid that fell over one shoulder. She smiled at the stranger and wiped her hands down her apron, coating the thick fabric with streaks of red. Animal blood, Irene realised, the same colour and texture as had so often stained her own hands. From the space between the door she could smell some sort of delicious stew, similar to her own but far richer. She inhaled the pleasant aroma and introduced herself with a grin, not worrying when the woman reluctantly held her sticky palm outwards. Irene shook it gladly before stepping inside.

The woman addressed herself as Mrs Johnson, the very person whom Mr Ainsley had spoken of earlier that day. She welcomed the young girl into her home and Irene nodded in bashful thanks as she looked around the kitchen in wonder. Her mind raced with images of Agnes Dartton and her parents, here in this very space. She could imagine them at the table eating breakfast, by the fire warming their hands and feet, doing the dishes at the sink overlooking the lane. The air positively hummed with their long-forgotten conversations.

The room was simply furnished with a few sparse and worn items, the walls dark and the windows small, the only painting hanging lopsided above the fireplace. Yet to Irene it still seemed a most loving and comfortable house. She could feel it in the air, within the walls, radiating from the flames of the hearth that had been lit a thousand times before. There had been life here for many years; memories, love and laughter. She could not help but feel that her own home was somewhat cold and barren in comparison.

Mrs Johnson made them both tea and spooned some jam onto two pieces of bread. She told Irene that it was homemade using fruit she had collected from the garden earlier that year; enormous blackberries that she had left overnight in a pail of water to force out the maggots. Though Irene had identified herself as the daughter of Tobias Michael, the woman had not shown any response to the name. It was understandable, considering how far out from the centre the house was. It almost felt like another village all on its own. Irene could easily imagine Mrs Holden having felt safe here in its isolation, alone with her parents and Benjamin.

Mrs Johnson swiftly emptied her cup of scalding hot tea and consumed the bread in one bite as if she feared being caught eating it. Irene, feeling suddenly awkward, attempted to do the same but ended up burning her tongue on the drink and choking on the food. She was handed a cloth serviette to mop her chin. Anxious that she was about to be thrown from the premises for bad manners, Irene passed on the pleasantries and explained to Mrs Johnson the real reason behind her visit.

"I 'eard that the Dartton family were 'ere, the parents an' the girl an'… a young lad," she began, reluctant to give too much information away or to make herself even more unwelcome. Mrs Johnson, however, had been calmly smiling ever since the girl had arrived.

"That's right. We were lucky to acquire such a fine 'ouse," she nodded, looking around at her basic yet homely kitchen.

"Oh yes," Irene agreed, following the woman's gaze, "It's most cosy."

"O'course, we were sorry 'bout… the little boy." Irene watched the woman's face turn sombre, her gaze falling to the floor as she began collecting up the plates and cups and took them to the sink to wash them. She spoke a little louder over the water, though Irene still had difficulty hearing her with her back turned.

"It were about six months after we moved in. Me 'usband saw a strange mark on one o'the trees out back, like a cross. Started digging, dunno why. Maybe he thought it were buried treasure or some such." Irene already knew that it was not gold nor jewels that Mr Johnson had found that day.

"O'course, we thought it were dog bones at first, someone's pet laid to rest. Never imagined it'd be a… Anyway, whoever he were, he's where he belongs now." Mrs Johnson dried her hands and returned to sit opposite Irene, her face back to its former calm countenance.

"The boy died in an accident," Irene explained, though she did not know why it seemed so important to say so. Perhaps because he had been so young or because he had not been given a proper burial. She did not want Mrs Johnson to think badly of the Darttons. They must have had their reasons.

Mrs Johnson reached across the table to retrieve a piece of paper and an ink pen, drawing a series of lines before handing it to Irene.

"The cemetery up by Fishergate," she said in a hushed voice, rising to her feet again to tend to her stew, "This is where 'e's buried, God bless 'im."

Irene thanked the woman and tucked the map safely into her apron, feeling the remnants of bread and cheese where they had been reduced to crumbs during her journey. She let herself out of the house while Mrs Johnson returned to the stove, frantically stirring the contents of the pot with her face part grimace and part smile as Irene said goodbye. She took one final look around the kitchen, the sense of memory still hovering in the air like a friendly ghost, before closing the door behind her. So many stories had happened there, in that very house, in the garden and along the street. Irene thought it most strange to be walking in the same footsteps as Mrs Holden and her family all those years ago. Strange, yes, but somehow comforting too.

When she had heard the tales recited by her father, Irene had pictured the Darttons vividly in her mind and created her own versions of the settings and characters, but to have seen the house itself through her own eyes had made the stories feel all the more real and Mrs Holden's demise all the sorrier. Though she desperately wanted to go to the graveyard and find Benjamin's final resting place, Irene could feel the nip in the air and noticed that day had already turned to dusk.

She could not be sure how long it would take her to reach home and hoped she could remember Mr Ainsley's finger-pointed map well enough to reach her front door before the last of the sun disappeared. Tracing the faint outlines of her shoes she had made earlier in the dusty road, Irene began her way home hoping that when she returned her father would be there, waiting with pride and anticipation to hear the revelation she had made that day.

Chapter Thirty-Four

Mr Michael had recognised the town of Helmsley at once. He had followed its calmly flowing stream admiring the quaint houses of stone and wood either side, the air humming with the faint echo of the small marketplace he knew to be in the square beyond the streets. Now walking beside his bicycle, he took in all the familiar sights including the very house where his daughter had watched her first cookery lesson. How time had passed since then and how much she had grown. He was torn between such happy memories and the nature of his return to the town. It was such a quiet and friendly place, he could not imagine it being the home of a murderer.

Mr Michael sighed as he walked beside the gently rippling water, beginning to enjoy the peaceful pace and chatter of birdsong until he saw something that took the air from his lungs. On the far corner of the street was a shop with small square windows and its door ajar. The outside walls were covered with objects big and small, from wash stools and chicken coops to nesting tables, enamel sinks, cloths, feathers, pokers, boots, sticks, pots, and even a small horse carved from wood. Mr Michael picked it up and traced the grooves with a fingertip. He knew this horse well. He had made it as a gift for Mrs Holden and Benjamin many years ago.

He replaced the object carefully back on the windowsill and wiped his brow with his handkerchief. Were his eyes deceiving him? Had he fallen asleep on his journey, or else woken in a different world? His heart beat wildly against his chest, thudding between excitement and terror. He half expected Mrs Holden to be inside, sat in her chair with a sock and needle between her fingers, the letter opener safely concealed by her side.

Mr Michael shivered, though he could not tell whether it was caused by the sight or by the bitter wind that had suddenly whipped up around him. Curiosity eventually trumped his confusion. He walked towards a window and licked his thumb to wipe away a corner of the mucky glass pane. He brought his eye to the hole and peered inside, instantly releasing a dry strangled sound from his throat. His heart felt as if it had stopped. He was seized by disbelief, made numb by despair. There within the room amid the bowing bookcase and ornament cabinets and chamber pots stacked up by the fireplace was a bird, a black crow with a chip in its beak. As it turned its beady eyes in his direction, it began to squeal in alarm.

Though his mind told him to run, Mr Michael felt bolted to the ground. He heard a voice and cast his eyes around the rest of the room, the crow still cawing loudly. Opposite the chamber pots was an armchair almost identical to the one Mrs Holden had died in. A different old woman was heaving herself out of it, her face eerily familiar. She was looking up at the frantic bird, raising a hand with a piece of bread pinched between her fingers. As if hearing a noise or sensing an unwelcome presence, she swiftly turned to the window and stared at Mr Michael. He watched as her eyes widened with recognition, a devious grin spreading across her face.

Like Mrs Holden, she had aged well before her time, her skin sallow and wrinkled, the once dark tresses now streaked with shards of white and arranged in a tangled bun atop of her head. She was cloaked in dull layers of worn clothes, her movements slow and laboured as she shuffled towards the door. Her open palm reached out and a single finger beckoned Mr Michael inside. He followed, trying to still his thoughts and his thumping heart.

The woman returned to her armchair as Mr Michael stood turning back and forth, trying to make sense of the scene.

"It cannot be…" he managed to mutter, shaking his head as he looked at the many recognisable possessions gathered around him.

"In their rightful place," the woman spat, crossing her arms over her chest.

"But why? I don't understand."

"You never did. You never would." Her stare sent a shiver down Mr Michael's spine – not of fear, he now realised, but of familiarity. It had been years since he had seen her, but he would never forget those eyes – wide and dark like a startled fawn, their gaze making him feel powerless just as it had when he was a boy.

Mr Michael could still clearly remember the first time he had been taken to the other house. The girl had grabbed him by the sleeve of his shirt and pulled him into the garden while their mothers talked and had tea with biscuits in the kitchen. She had demanded that he chase her, running off across the grass squealing like a piglet. He could still recall her face as she had looked back at him over a shoulder, shouting 'follow me, follow me!' at the top of her voice, begging him to race after her, to catch her and kiss her. Bemused and a little afraid, he had stood there motionless while she kept sprinting and yelling. Eventually, reluctantly, he had conceded.

She had made him play this game at the start of each visit. As they raced, his legs would bandy about under him in an attempt to gain traction on the overgrown lawn at the back of the house, resulting in his new playmate winning every single time. She would jump and congratulate herself shrilly while Tobias panted, the hours feeling like years when all he wanted to do was to sit by the river in solitude.

After several months of this same activity, a new game was introduced; spying on the family next door. This seemed a pointless endeavour to Tobias, who knew his own neighbours as well as he did his family, yet it seemed thrillingly dangerous to his young companion. Peering through windows, sneaking into their back yard and rummaging through the rubbish offered him little enjoyment, but the girl seemed excited to the point of mania with every so-called secret they uncovered. She was especially curious about the neighbour's daughter, and it was as they were watching the girl in the garden that Tobias noticed the workshop nearby. One day, he summoned the courage to wander in and watch the carpenter at work, never to return to the girl and her games.

Reflecting on the memory, Mr Michael could not recall the last time he had thought about the playmate, but here she was: Margaret. Older, sterner, and now surrounded by a scene identical to that of her former neighbour's shop. It was all too much to believe. Just as Mr Michael was on the cusp of airing his many confused and conflicting questions, Margaret tucked a hand down the side of her armchair and pulled out a long thin blade with a strange emblem on the handle.

"That does not belong t'you," he cried out, resisting the urge to lunge and swipe the object from Margaret's evil grasping mitts, to shout and swear and tell her what he thought of her cold-hearted robbery and the unholy murder of an innocent woman. Yet Mr Michael could do nothing. It was as if he had fallen under a spell, an enchantment which Margaret alone could control. The crow clicked its beak, mocking him from its perch.

"It is mine. Always was. I were the one that gave it to 'im," she croaked, the voice unmistakable to Mr Michael's ears, pulling on long-forgotten strands of his memory.

"You stole it! An' you murdered 'er with it! My friend, Mrs..."

"Sit down an' shut up, you blabbering fool!" Her words were so sharp and her gaze so fierce that Mr Michael did as he was bid, pulling up one of the milking stools and sitting facing the woman in the only available space amid all the objects.

Margaret took several moments as if composing

herself before beginning the tale she had kept hidden for nearly all her life. Now she would reveal the real story of Mrs Holden and the letter opener, the little boy and even the crow; all the many pieces to the puzzle that Mr Michael had been struggling to understand. Margaret would share with him the memories that she had had to live with, the many demons that she had had to endure day and night alone. It was time for the truth.

Part Four

Chapter Thirty-Five

Some would say that no girl of fourteen years could truly know what it was to love a man, but Margaret knew. She had known from the moment she had set her eyes on him. He was not like the boys at school, nor the skinny shrimps she passed in the poor lanes, nor that useless playmate she had had to spend her childhood with before he went off to chip at bits of wood in the neighbour's workshop. This boy was different from all of them. She had never met anyone so confident and comfortable talking about their life and the lives of others. He was the first person to tell her she was pretty, funny and clever, in her own sort of way. He made her feel so much more than a wayward child, a forgotten daughter, a silly little girl. On his arm she was someone, and when the time came for them to marry, then the whole sorry town would realise just how special she was. She would be Margaret Holden; beautiful bride, doting wife, wonderful mother. She would finally be wanted.

While many of the local girls had no choice but to begin their working lives at a young age, Margaret had been given the opportunity to attend school instead. Her mother had told her of the domestic servants, washer women, factory girls and street sellers she could have become, or those unfortunate creatures who had to stay at home and care for their households like the girl next door. Unlike them, Margaret would have better prospects. She would be educated and marry well, bringing her parents the pride and security they were sorely lacking from their only child. They also hoped she would finally understand the concepts of discipline and obedience, turning her from a sullen and sour-faced girl into a dutiful and docile housewife.

After careful consultation between her desperate parents and the dubious headmaster, Margaret had eventually been accepted to the local school with lessons every weekday morning alongside seventeen other children of varying ages. It was a long walk there and back, and she had to wake before the sun had risen on most days of the year, but her parents left her with no alternative. No child of theirs would waste their life away crawling under contraptions or living off their parents. It was time for Margaret to begin making her own life in this world.

Duly ushered out of the front door one Monday morning, she made her way along the river towards school and spotted a young man sat on the embankment. As she approached, she could see his hairy muscular arms were exposed below rolled-up shirt sleeves. They flexed and pumped as he peeled the skin from an apple with a knife, cutting chunks off to throw into the water beyond. He looked on, amused by the ducks pecking helplessly on the surface as the lumps floated down into the murk. He spotted the girl stood motionless on the path a short distance away. He kept his attention fixed on her as he continued to eat the apple, his eyes running up and down the length of her body in a way that made her feel both vulnerable and womanly. She had returned his gaze before walking off, swinging her basket in just the right way as to make the hem of her skirt bob up and down around her ankles.

Margaret thought about him all through her lessons – his eyes, that smile, the way he had slipped the pieces of fruit onto his tongue. She received three thwacks of the birch across her left palm at the end of the morning for her daydreaming. When she walked back along the path, the man was still there. He followed her all the way to her door. The chance meeting became a regular occurance, and the pair began to pass the time of day with one another before progressing to longer and more illuminating conversations, though Margaret received a scolding for being late to school each time. She found out his name was Matthew and that he lived in Ogleforth, which she knew from her parents was a particularly well respected and wealthy part of town. Though his clothes did not look all that different from her own, she could tell that he was not a ruffian like the rest of them. His hair was always combed, his face free of whiskers, his teeth impeccable. Clearly, he was well bred. They would make a handsome couple one day, Margaret decided.

It took only a few weeks for Matthew to confirm his love for her, which she promptly reciprocated. Their first kiss was the sweetest nectar she had ever tasted, his arms strong and firm against her lower back. He would walk her to and from school as often as he could, and she would repay him with playful fumbles by the riverbank or in the woods. Sometimes he would accompany her home and they would sneak into her room and frolic on the bed, the window open to listen for her parents' return.

When the sickness came, Margaret laughed at the sight of the stringy bile in the wash basin. She had heard that love could make you feel ill, but she had never imagined it to be so literal in its truth. While she vomited every morning before and often on the way to school, she was also uncharacteristically ravenous during the day. If she spotted Matthew with a bit of bread or a bag of scraps, it would be out of his hands and hastily consumed before he could protest. He would bring gifts of sweet nuts and glazed buns that she would gobble greedily, leaving not a single crumb. Better yet were the sweets, eaten on sight without a thought of sharing them. At home, she could consume bowl after bowl of stew and would slather slices of bread with spoonsful of butter and jam. Her hips broadened and her stomach began to spill out. Not even her generous smocks could hide the change in her appearance. While her father worried, her mother shrugged. She was of that age and perhaps becoming a woman would finally make her behave like one.

As they walked along the riverside one sultry early evening, Matthew swung his beloved onto the grassy bank and began kissing her neck, his hands shuffling under her dress as he explored her tender flesh. His palm rested on her stomach, round yet taut, like his sister's had been some months previous. She had made him feel it to see if the baby would kick. He had torn his hand away then just as he did now, covering Margaret up again before swiftly lifting her to her feet. She had simply giggled at the look on his pale face as he stormed off ahead without her, though later she thought back on the incident and wondered what had caused his reaction.

She waited the next day for him to accompany her to school but he did not show, nor the day after that, nor for the rest of the week. She searched for him in every place they had visited together. She even went to Ogleforth and asked every man, woman and child on the street for him, but no one seemed to know a Matthew, nor even a Holden. The sickness worsened, her stomach grew, and eventually her mother explained what was happening to her body. Despite being barely out of infancy herself, Margaret was with child. Feeling nervous but eager, she knew that once she told Matthew the joyful news, they would be reunited and form a family together.

Some weeks later, she saw her dashing lover walking down the lane with a bunch of wildflowers in one hand. She changed her frock, swiped a brush through her thick waist-length hair and waited for the knock on the door. She waited and waited until she feared something dreadful had happened to him outside. Caught under the wheels of a passing trap perhaps, or ravaged by a wild animal? What she saw as she leaned out of the window was far worse. There on the low wall outside sat Matthew Holden, his face filled with a wide grin as Agnes Dartton sat opposite him with the flowers in her arms.

While the child grew inside her, Margaret endured

the sight of her beloved charming the girl next door. She grew too big to attend school without everyone discovering her secret, so she stayed at home hidden in her room while her mother forced her to recite Latin verses and stitch endless garments for the child. This was not how her life was supposed to be. She had wanted a wedding and a home, then later children while her husband worked. She was going to prepare delicious suppers and clean her divine house in Ogleforth. Instead, she had been cast aside like a stray dog, driven mad with the torment of knowing Matthew was now with the ugly whore next door.

One day, Margaret managed to sneak from her room and tiptoe outside. She found the courting couple in the old man's workshop. Standing silently by the door, she observed them as Matthew leaned down to drop something into a small pen on the floor. She hid herself as the pair departed before creeping in to see what they had left. When she looked, it was a kitten exactly like the one she had always longed for. She had even dreamed of its existence, recalling its description to Matthew during the halcyon days of their early union. The real thing was even more adorable than she could have imagined. Overwhelmed with affection, she could not help but take the tiny creature into her arms and hug its warm silken fur to her face.

At the tiny mew of the docile kitten, something snapped inside her. Margaret took up a blade from the work surface and committed the deed before the thought had even fully formed in her head. She let the lifeless body slip from her hand and replaced the tool. Looking down at her sodden hands and dress, she wondered if it would be the same in a few weeks' time when her due date arrived. She forgot the kitten and her heartbreak, taking to her bedroom until it was time.

The birth was painful in the extreme, her body still so young and with no midwife on hand, but Margaret managed to bring a beautiful baby boy into the world. Her father took away the bloodied bedding and brought more hot water while her mother sliced the umbilical cord with the nearest tool she had to hand; an old letter opener the family had received as a gift when they first moved into the house.

Margaret loved the child immediately – now her life made sense and her heart was whole once more. As her mother tended to the screaming infant, she fell into a deep sleep after twelve hours of exhaustive effort. She dreamed of a joyous future with just the two of them, playing and singing with no need nor want for anything or anyone else in the world. They would make their way together.

When Margaret awoke the next day and felt the empty bundle of blankets next to her bed, she thought she was still asleep. She roused herself and searched the house but she could not find her baby. She screamed at her mother and father, accusing them of murder and kidnap and betrayal. They calmly seated their daughter down and told her the truth. The boy was with a real mother now and had the chance of a better life. Margaret had been freed the responsibilities of motherhood and could instead remain as a child for a few years longer, finishing her schooling before finding a job and a good husband. They made it sound so simple, so justified. Yet Margaret felt nothing other than agony and fury within her.

Even all these years later, Margaret was still surprised by how well she had taken the news. There were tears and screams and sleepless nights, of course, but she did manage to recover from the birth, to go back to school, to eventually marry and to move to a new home in the town of Helmsley, far enough away from her old life and the bitter memories. Perhaps if she had never seen the child again, she could have accepted her fate. Perhaps if she had known that he had grown up contented and cared for, she would have forgiven her parents. Perhaps if she had been able to take back the boy and bring him up herself, all might have been well.

Instead, she had had to watch him suffer, beaten to death by the same woman who had stolen her childhood sweetheart and future husband. There was only one reason why Margaret had never had the life she deserved. The reason was Agnes Holden.

Chapter Thirty-Six

The story Margaret had recited was so appalling that Mr Michael could not believe it to be true. He already distrusted the woman from the experience he had had as a child, and now the suggestion that Mrs Holden had been responsible for the boy's death, for the loss of Margaret's own child, could only have been an elaborate lie fabricated from years of jealousy and selfishness. She had painted a picture so cruel and so despicable that he wanted nothing more to do with her. She was obviously mad and had somehow managed to steal all Mrs Holden's possessions and arrange her demise as revenge for a crime he knew his friend could never have committed. She had loved little Benjamin, of that Mr Michael was certain. Whatever had happened to the boy and wherever his body may have been buried, Agnes Dartton had been the sole positive force in that child's short and sorry life.

After Mr Michael had shared his opinion through clenched teeth, Margaret gave a sad sort of smile and shook her head. She was right and he was wrong; he was a fool if he chose not to believe the truth. Mr Michael was once again plagued by many questions, but he would not trust any answers from Margaret. Instead, he would go straight to the police and tell them about the house and the woman who still hated Mrs Holden. He did not care what would happen to her after that. He owed her nothing except his pity.

As he turned to leave the room, Mr Michael heard footsteps approach behind him in the corridor, thick and firm – the plodding of a burly male. The door opened to reveal a muscular chap who at first reminded Mr Michael of the descriptions he had heard of the late Matthew Holden. This character was of a similar height and build with a square jaw and straw-coloured hair swept to one side. He was wearing a sullied apron over a shirt and trousers with braces, his hands gnarled and blackened from whatever work he had been attending to. He was so unassuming in his appearance that Mr Michael could not remember if he had ever seen him before. Yet as soon as he had entered the room, he had felt a peculiar twinge in his gut that was growing ever stronger.

"Mr Michael, this is me 'usband, Adam," Margaret's voice bellowed, a faint trace of humour to it. The man too was smirking as if they shared an amusing secret. "You might not recognise 'im without his moustache."

Adam began chuckling low and loud like the rumbling of thunder, making the knot in Mr Michael's stomach even tighter as his mind raced through the remnants of his memory. The moustache, the waistcoat, the oversized boots and the strange coat. He could see it now, crystal clear. They were all the disguises of this man.

Now face to face with the likely culprits, Mr Michael experienced the true meaning of fear. He fled the room, leaving the front door wide open as he departed, hauling his bicycle out from the frosted bracken before pedalling as fast as he could in the direction of his home city.

The sun was fading rapidly, the roads already etched with ice, the air bitter against his face as he rode. Mr Michael recited over and over in his mind what he would tell Inspector Falmer, how all the pieces had suddenly come together. The belongings, the letter opener, the mystery man and the real criminals, but there was one question he still did not know the answer to. Who was really responsible for the death of the little boy?

As his legs grew tired and his energy waned, Mr Michael paused at a pub on the outskirts of York and ordered a large ale, slipping into a booth with the Bar Walls beyond barely visible in the dimming light. He sipped at his drink, rubbing his numb hands over his aching thighs in an attempt to soothe them, the fire a comfort but not quite reassuring enough. He had missed the opportunity to visit the police station, but at least he now had the evening to go over the story. As he calmed his breathing and tried to organise his thoughts, Mr Michael found himself contemplating his brief conversation with the pub landlord at The Shoulder of Mutton all those weeks ago. He berated himself for not having asked more questions, particularly about the fellow who had purchased the painting. Perhaps he was friendly with Adam. They could even have been in it together.

By the time he had finished his drink and agonised over his memories, night had fallen over the city along with a fine coating of snow. Not wanting to wake his wife and daughter at such a late hour, Mr Michael pushed the bicycle up to his workshop a short distance from the pub and made a bed for himself there with a few hessian sacks on the floor. He steadily chewed through the wedge of bread he had taken from the kitchen earlier that day before setting his head down on the makeshift mattress, succumbing to the deep sleep that had been alluding him for months. Little did he know that there was no one back home to disturb, for as his wife slept soundly, their only child was still wandering the streets alone.

After leaving the former Dartton residence, the taste of Mrs Johnson's exceptional jam still lingering on her burnt tongue, Irene made her way up the wide dirt track she had taken from the town. Mr Ainsley's directions had been simple enough to follow on the way there, imprinted as they were within her mind, but now that the light of the day was dimming, she could not be sure that the roads and turnings were quite the same. None of the buildings seemed familiar and the further she walked, the more frightened and confused she became.

She looked behind but the house had disappeared. She could not even see or hear the river; she had somehow managed to lose her way home. Though Irene had lived all her life in York, she had rarely explored beyond her front door, the local market and the school up on Fishergate. She had never visited anywhere at night, always making sure she was home in time to finish the housework and to prepare the supper, or even earlier if her mother was ill and she needed to tend to her.

Trying to conceal her panic, Irene walked swiftly up and down as many streets as possible, recognising not even one until finally, miraculously, she saw a bridge and knew she was near the river. She was unsure as to whether she should follow it up or down, so instead she headed towards where she could see a little light and hear people. Surely someone would take pity on her and be able to guide a young girl back home? She knew the street name where she lived and hoped it would be enough.

Despite her hopes, the strangers Irene met were not like the friendly faces she usually encountered. These were mostly men, each reeking of some foul substance – alcohol, tobacco, liquorice root, stale sweat, and other unpleasantries she could not identify. They all stared at her with sinister sneers across their faces. Some tried to grab her arms or her waist, whispering filthy words with coarse throats, their teeth blackened or missing. The women seemed to be even worse; raucous, audacious, spouting obscenities that would make the devil himself blush. Their skirts pulled up, their flesh hanging out, they showed no concern for their behaviour or its effect, letting men touch and tug them at will, garishly cackling as they saw Irene's shocked expression as she tried to hurry past them.

Her nimble steps quickly became a vigorous race as she pounded the pavements looking left and right for any sign of familiarity, the night growing ever darker, the air crisp with the threat of frost. Just when she thought she saw the entrance to the market or the roof of a neighbour's house, she found herself mistaken and had to keep going. Irene thought she must have traced every possible street but somehow she still could not find her own.

Tired, helpless and shaking with both fear and cold, she eventually came to the river again, the road across it still busy with people. As a few drifting snowflakes fell and melted at her feet, she clung to the railing trying to catch her breath. Gazing up, she could just make out the faint outlines of the ornate iron decoration highlighted by the gas lamps. She was sure she had heard her father describe such a structure and could even recall its name: Lendal Bridge.

As she stared anxiously around her, Irene tried to formulate a plan. Should she follow the river and hope to reach a point that she recognised? She could slip into a pub and ask one of the barmen to help her with directions home? Or would she be better off going to the Shambles and taking refuge in Mrs Holden's old house? She did not know what she would do, and now there was no kind and loving father to ask for advice. Spent of energy and hope, Irene slunk to her knees and began to cry.

A stranger's hand jolted her out of her solitude. She wiped her cheeks and looked up to see a man towering over her, though once she rose to her feet, she realised that he was actually short and stocky, built like a pit bull terrier. He had sharp little teeth too and a head of thin dark hair. She could almost have laughed at his canine resemblance, but his expression promptly subdued her amusement. He was watching her like she was a piece of meat ready to savour.

The man growled something inaudible and stepped closer to Irene, forcing her to shuffle back against the railing. He reached his hands forward and pressed them against her shoulders, pushing her further until she was pinned against the edge, the metal ice-cold against her back despite the many layers of her dress and petticoat. He continued to slur but she could not understand a single word. He smelled strongly of alcohol and his tongue was thick in his mouth, filling the space where his teeth should have been. Though there was no more room for her to retreat, he still moved up against her, his hands edging across her chest and around her throat.

The sparse passers-by Irene had seen on the bridge earlier seemed to have entirely dispersed, leaving her alone with this brute and his garbled chuntering under the now steadily falling snow. She remained silent, setting her stare determinedly on the man's eyes as she felt the hem of her skirt begin to rise on one side. His face was now close enough to hers that she could see coal dust filling the deep crevices of his face and a faded scar across his lower lip. His breath was hot against her cheek as he whispered into her ear. This time, she heard every word.

In one deft move, Irene reached her hand inside the pocket of her pinafore and produce the blade, plunging it into the side of the stranger's neck. He let out a gurgling shriek and stumbled backwards, pulling the knife out along with a violent spurt of blood before throwing it to the floor. Irene scrambled to reclaim it, wiping the blood on the inside of the cloth already stained from the night she had discovered Mrs Holden.

As the man collapsed to the floor still shrieking in pain, Irene kicked the toe of her boot into his shin before running back towards the town.

The night was now beginning to give way to the dawn, soft rays slowly filtering into the sky, illuminating the dusting of frost coating every surface of the city. The streets became a little more familiar, the drunks and criminals replaced by early risers on their way to work, smoke unfurling from the chimneys as fresh fires were stoked and windows opened in the hope of cool and refreshing air. Irene felt her shoulders relax and her pace ease until finally she saw the church and the square and the old curiosity shop, bare but unmistakable on the corner of the Shambles. How she wished Mrs Holden were there at this moment. She would know just what to do and what to say. Irene wiped away another tear and continued along the street, her feet crunching in the thin film of ice beneath as she made her way home.

Irene flung open the front door and looked wildly around the kitchen before racing upstairs. Her mother seemed safe in her slumber, perhaps never having realised her daughter had been gone for so long, but there was no sign of the man of the house. Irene longed to see him. She returned silently downstairs, catching her breath and composure by the empty fireplace, a wedge of bread waiting for her on the table, though she could not bring herself to eat it.

She stood to remove her apron, peering into the pocket before carefully taking out the contents – a bloodied knife, a pattern on a piece of paper, and several crumbs. She surveyed them in turn and placed them on the side, observing each one as if it were the clue to a mystery. Irene had formed her own sordid story now. She did not know what she would say to her father about her unlawful behaviour, but she still wished he would walk through the door. She had never needed him more.

Chapter Thirty-Seven

Awakening to the soft light illuminating his carpentry workshop, Mr Michael took a moment to admire the unusual sky outside, an off-white that was almost yellow, before savouring a few more moments on his makeshift mattress. The events of yesterday now seemed so far away, as if he had woken from a dream or conjured them from his mind. If only it were that simple. If only his imagination could have made and then forgotten the discoveries revealed by Margaret and the horrors he had heard.

Somewhere between sleep and reality, Mr Michael had decided not to go to the police just yet. Margaret and her husband would not be going anywhere with such lucrative loot to protect, and there were still too many troubling points that Mr Michael wanted to resolve, for his own peace of mind as well as to finally put Mrs Holden to rest. He knew the former neighbour was manipulative, deceitful and hateful, but she was also one of the very few people who knew about the little boy. She may even have been his real mother, if her story were to be believed; surely she would want only the best for his memory?

Rousing himself from his bed, Mr Michael tidied the workshop and ran his hand through his hair before retrieving the borrowed bicycle to make his way back to Helmsley. Thankfully, the snow had not settled and the cool morning air helped to awaken his mind and strengthen his resolve. He pedalled harder and faster, the wheels occasionally slipping across an icy puddle or a patch of mud, but still Mr Michael rode on. A few hours later, he spotted the stream with its quaint stone bridge coming into view outside of the town. His heart racing and his hands aching as they clenched the handlebars, he knew exactly how he would approach Margaret this time around. He would be strong and determined, with honesty and loyalty on his side. He would discover exactly how Benjamin had died, why Margaret and her husband had stolen Mrs Holden's belongings, and who had really killed his friend. There was nothing to lose.

Unlike York, the town seemed still to be sleeping. There was no sign of the wintery weather Mr Michael had left behind, yet there were only one or two people milling about the streets, nodding politely as they passed him. He hid the bicycle in the bushes as before and adjusted his hair and clothing before knocking on the door of the shop. Looking up, he saw a wooden sign swinging above that he had neglected to notice before. It had curled letters that read 'Crow's Haunt' and the tiny silhouette of a black bird underneath. A woman's voice from within made Mr Michael jump, followed by a long inhuman screech. The shop's namesake was evidently still inside.

As he knocked and entered, Mr Michael cast his eyes around the room once again. He had spent the night in disbelief at what he had discovered, wondering if his eyes had somehow deceived him. Returning a second time, he knew it had been no vision or fiction. Every object looked indistinguishable to those he had seen so many times in Holden's Haunt. The bookcase, the chamber pots, even the crow and the armchair. Each was identical and so very unnerving. There amid her empire was Margaret, the one woman whom Mr Michael never wished to meet again, but the one person who might be able to bring answers to his seemingly endless questions.

Margaret greeted him with a twisted smile more malice than welcome. She had changed into an oversized frock of deepest grey, almost the same colour as her hair, which she now wore down like rat tails around her neck and shoulders. In her hands she held the letter opener, stroking its blade and emblem mockingly, not taking her eyes from her guest. The bird made a sudden swoop in Mr Michael's direction, barely missing his head as it lunged at a piece of bread on the floor before returning to its perch with the morsel in its chipped beak.

"Don't be stupid, o'course t'isn't the same one," Margaret snapped, even though Mr Michael had not spoken. He had been watching the crow greedily swallowing the lump. It had brought back the memory of the rescued fledgling, the gift from Mrs Holden for the little boy's fifth birthday present. Somehow Margaret had read his thoughts and responded.

"I took the little thing 'ome when Benny passed away. Brought it up in me own room, feeding it mushed this 'n' that. Twenty-two years, I 'ad it. Longer than my boy got. Ain't life cruel?" She rose to leave another scrap on the floor, but this time the bird stayed put.

Mr Michael turned his gaze back to Margaret, ignoring the shiver of discomfort that ran down the length of his spine. He seated himself on a milking stool, more to settle his trembling limbs than to make himself comfortable.

"Tell me more 'bout Benjamin…" he began to ask tentatively, but his query was cut short. Margaret rose from her chair in a burst of rage, stabbing the tip of the letter opener into the top of the wooden mantlepiece with a sharp thud.

"Benny! His name were Benny!" she shrieked, her eyes wide with fury. She released her grip and the blade stuck in the wood vibrating slightly, the emblem catching the light from the window, twinkling enticingly.

Mr Michael muttered an apology and averted his eyes. He did not want to upset Margaret at this point when there was so much he wanted to know, to understand. He needed to be tactful, even cunning. He shifted his sight back in her direction, feigning courage.

"I'd like t'know 'bout that little boy… your little boy… if you please."

"Oh, if you please, eh! Away with yer airs an' graces, they're no good t'me," she replied, batting her hand in the air as she returned to her armchair, "I know why yer 'ere. S'cause you want t'know the truth. And you've nowhere else t'go. So, listen carefully. That Mrs 'olden were a murderer."

The word hung in the air turning the atmosphere cold. Mr Michael shifted on his seat and slackened his collar with a finger. His hands were sweating and he could feel droplets forming on his brow, but he did not move nor look away. He locked eyes with the piercing gaze from across the room, nodding, ready to listen and prepared to learn the truth.

Chapter Thirty-Eight

They say that appearances can be deceptive, and Margaret was the queen of disguise. After her initial heartbreak, she acquired a renewed strength to attain some normality to her young life, completing her school studies with reasonable success before acquiring a decent position as a laundry girl for a wealthy household in none other than Ogleforth. During her first few months there, she had asked anyone she passed on the street the whereabouts of the Holden family residence. Not a soul had even heard of the name. She forced the rage and humiliation to sink deep within. She had grown used to the pain by now.

Though she still lived at home, when Margaret was not working she would attempt to socialise with other young women in the city. She had attended the theatre on a few occasions and had even joined an amateur dramatics group. Her gift for drama was hardly surprising given the fact that she had managed to spend the previous five years hiding her true emotions from everyone who knew her. On the outside, she appeared to be a charming and most amiable young woman, but within she held nothing but contempt and malice for the evil hag that had stolen her life, Agnes Holden. Even the words on her lips were like poison.

As soon as she awoke, before she went to bed, and in every spare moment in between, Margaret would choose one of her hiding places and watch the family next door with her darling boy, her very own son, wrenched from her life before she had even had time to name him. It was the girl who had chosen to call him Benjamin, but to Margaret he quickly became her Benny, the word she would whisper into the wind and watch as he turned his head back and forth trying to discover its origin.

She imagined that he would view her as a spirit or even an angel, and that one day they would be reunited. Their bond, she knew, was unbreakable. It was only a matter of time before Benny would grow old enough to realise this himself and would beg to be with his true mother once more. She could not count the number of hours she had recalled that very moment, wrapping her own arms around herself as she imagined her child's embrace, his happy face buried into her bosom, them both sobbing with joy. It would be on his fifth birthday, Margaret had decided. On that day, he would be hers again.

She had kept a small diary in which she noted down every event in Benny's life that she had been able to witness. His first walk outside, the night he slept all the way through to sunrise without crying, his lost teeth, new foods, caught fish, bee stings and, of course, birthdays. Every moment she was able to watch was a tiny miracle, a gift from God reminding her that she was still his mother and that Benny in turn would always be the most important person in her life. Ringed with inked hearts was the boy's fifth birthday, the diary page now so worn that it had several rips and two torn corners. Five years she had waited for this day; finally, it arrived.

For several weeks Margaret had watched the grocer's boy bring ever bigger bundles of food to the house; breads, meats and cheeses, chickens and ham joints, fruits and vegetables, even packets of expensive-looking biscuits and confectionary. She had seen Agnes too out in the garden picking flowers and leaves and bits of wood – for what purpose, Margaret did not know, but it riled her all the same. She had snuck outside and hidden under the neighbour's window, which when opened released the most delectable smells – pies and pastries, cakes and jams – the sound of the girl's sweet singing tinging Margaret's rage with jealousy.

On the boy's birthday itself, Margaret had crept to the same spot and peered through the window into the vacant kitchen. She saw the table laid out with a gluttonous selection of plates piled high, the limited space in between stuffed with foliage and small bundles of wrapped gifts. Agnes herself then appeared dressed in a hideous garment, her hair loose and dishevelled like some filthy gypsy child. She watched her make a few adjustments to the table before retrieving some blankets and leaving out of the back door towards the garden without putting any shoes on. Margaret was appalled. How could such a despicable whore be left to care for such an innocent and beautiful child? It had filled her with a fuming fury for years, but now, on Benny's birthday, it would all come to an end.

She herself had dressed handsomely for the event, though she had no intention of being seen by anyone other than her son. She had chosen a shift of light blue with a pristine white pinafore and had plaited her ebony hair into a long braid behind her back. There were her own sweet treats to prepare too, including candies, dried fruits, and her absolute favourite, hot chocolate. She had saved up her earnings to buy Benny a teddy bear with two bright red buttons for eyes. As well as the boy, she had every intention of taking back the letter opener too, which she had found gone without a trace from her room along with her child all those years ago.

The morning seemed to stretch out into one long performance, Mr Dartton and his daughter doting on the infant as if he were incapable of attending to himself. Margaret believed that to spoil a child was a sin and a cruelty. While she knew she would be a kind mother, she had already vowed never to mollycoddle him to the extent that Agnes did, treating him like just another of the wretched creatures she rescued from the woods. It was pitiful – disturbing, even.

By some coincidence, she had even given a poor demented fledgling as a gift for the boy, though what he was supposed to do with a bird that could not even feed let alone fly, she did not know. It was strange, to feel so much love one moment as she caught sight of Benny's smile to only be swiftly replaced by malice when she saw or heard Agnes with him. Margaret had to console herself with the reminder that this would soon be another memory, that it would be the girl next door watching in envy instead of her.

Eventually, they reached a point in the day when Mr Dartton had to carry his ill wife back to the house where they remained. Agnes attended to Benny in the garden for a while longer before leaving him to clear up in the kitchen. This was Margaret's chance. She had decided to keep the gifts and delicacies for later; instead, she would speak to him in the garden and give him a cup of her special hot chocolate. She was sure Benny would be delighted. Perhaps it would be his very first taste and she would be able to write this in her diary. She could feel herself filling with motherly pride at the thought.

From her open back door, Margaret listened as cautiously as a wild animal. After a few moments, she felt certain that Agnes was well within the confines of the house, unable to hear or see anything taking place in the garden. Margaret took the cup of hot chocolate and walked across her own lawn to the neighbouring space, smiling warmly at the little boy playing. Sensing her presence, Benny looked up from his games and watched the stranger striding towards him. He was intrigued but not frightened. Margaret sank to her knees in front of the boy and held out the drink with both hands as if it were some magical potion. She told him her name and explained that she was a friend. She had decided to tell him later about her true identity. For now, it was enough to simply be beside him.

Benny peered into the contents of the cup and gave a low hum of approval as he smelled the enticing scent of cocoa, sugar and a hint of honey – Margaret's secret recipe. He took the offering and said thank you before a sudden snap made the pair of them turn to look in the direction of the house. There was only time to run a fingertip down the length of the boy's cheek before Margaret rushed away, returning to her own house where she ducked down behind a bush near the door. She watched the boy like a hawk, her breathing now short and sharp, her body trembling as her heart raced. Silence. She raised her head further, just enough so that she could see Benny taking his first curious sip of hot chocolate.

Agnes called to him from the house, the wrong name from the wrong mother. Margaret slunk back down and listened intently as the name was repeated, growing louder and more insistent. Soon it became clearly audible a short distance from where she crouched, followed by the soft thud of bare feet on damp grass. There began other noises that Margaret could not identify – certainly not warm and friendly. It sounded more like choking and coughing, then slapping and muttered exclamations. She did not dare reveal herself, but the sounds became so extreme that she had to raise her head.

There she saw Agnes kneeling on the ground, Benny thrown over her thighs as she slammed her palm into his back over and over again, bringing him up to shake his shoulders, ramming her fingers into his face. It was the ghastliest display of cruelty Margaret had ever witnessed, yet she could do nothing to prevent it. She peered over the foliage, her own fist in her mouth as she stifled a scream. Benny collapsed into Agnes' arms like a rag doll, his head lolling towards the grass, the cup drained and forgotten beneath him.

Consumed by shock, Margaret slumped down and curled herself into a tight ball as she tried to forget the nightmare she had just witnessed, her mind repeating the scene continually against her will. As much as she wished it were otherwise, she had no doubt as to what had just happened. She had seen Agnes Holden killing her son. The girl next door was a murderer.

Chapter Thirty-Nine

When Margaret had finished her retelling, she was drenched with sweat and her fingers had left a series of red crescent moons where they had dug into her palms. Her eyes had been fixed on Mr Michael for the entirety of her speech, but now her pupils looked glazed and unfocused as if she had been in another place or time. She shivered lightly though she was sat beside a roaring fire. Neither spoke, the room instead becoming filled by the growing noises from outside as the town finally awoke. A mild breeze rattled the objects hanging outside the shop as a horse's hooves trotted merrily along the dusty street outside. A few jovial voices called out to one another, their words intelligible, and a dog began to bark playfully then stopped.

Margaret seemed oblivious to the sounds and to her surroundings. Mr Michael watched her carefully, his anger slowly subsiding into pity and curiosity. He did not know whether he could believe the woman's stories, yet the expression on the face before him seemed entirely genuine. She had wrapped her arms around her chest to try to stop herself from shaking, her eyes blinking furiously as if holding back tears. Finally, she rose her gaze to Mr Michael, her piercing stare inviting his response, but he could think of no words to say. Margaret had quite clearly loved the child. His death at the tender age of five must have hurt her as much as it had Agnes Holden.

While Margaret may have seemed fully grown at the time, in reality, she had only just come to the end of her own childhood, and a traumatic one at that. She had been largely ignored by her parents, forgotten by her lover Matthew Holden, then denied the joys of motherhood. Through it all, she had come to the conclusion that the girl next door was to blame – her rival, her enemy. Margaret's years of loneliness and isolation must have made the devastation of that day all the more painful. She had had to live with it all her life, unable to confide in a single soul. If only she had known the truth, thought Mr Michael. It may have prevented her from becoming the hateful person he was now cautiously locking eyes with.

"I know 'bout the boy, Margaret," Mr Michael began, trying to make his voice calm, though it still wavered with fear. "I were told the story. It came from Mrs 'olden's… from Agnes' lips 'erself," he continued, hoping she would understand, "But it's not true. It were not murder. It were an accident."

Margaret's face contorted with fury again but she did not speak. She had evidently heard this conclusion before, perhaps had even tried telling herself as much, but she was adamant. Her boy had been taken before his time and someone was to blame. Someone had had to pay.

Mr Michael leaned forwards a little on his stool, his hands clasped together as if pleading. He felt almost as if that were the case as he wished Margaret would listen and see reason, that she would finally forgive Agnes

Holden for a crime she did not commit.

"I was told by a doctor that the boy might 'ave 'ad an allergic reaction. A fit or summat. Couldn't breathe, couldn't speak. Poor lad were choking an' Agnes were trying t'help. She were rescuing 'im, Margaret, don't you see?" The woman took a great inhale of breath, clenching her hands against the sides of her armchair.

"All I saw were a murdering cowardly slag!" she screamed, rising from her seat with a look of pure outrage, the letter opener in one hand.

She took two strides towards Mr Michael with the blade elevated, but he was already on his feet, the stool tumbling back and falling over in his haste. He towered over Margaret but it did not seem to deter her. She thrust the letter opener towards his chest, crying out in anguish, her eyes clamped shut as tears streaked down her cheeks. She stabbed in any direction, not even seeming to care whether her actions were inflicting any damage, her wails growing louder as she began to shake.

Mr Michael managed to block her blows and eventually took hold of her shoulders, steadying her firmly until she lowered the implement. Margaret's whole body quivered, his grasp holding her upright as her legs threatened to give way. She was mumbling between weeps, random sounds and attempts at speech escaping her gaping mouth as more tears fell. Finally, she slipped from his grip and fell softly to the floor like a wilting plant drained of life. The letter opener scuttled along the floorboards, coming to rest against the foot of a dresser as Margaret wept into her open palms, helpless and broken.

Mr Michael crouched beside her, softly resting a hand on one shoulder. The old woman was oblivious, rocking and crying almost inaudibly now, lost to her memories and regrets, consumed by the guilt of her dark deeds. As he watched her with sympathy, Mr Michael heard footsteps on the stair behind and the sound of the door creaking open. As he turned to look, he saw only the unusual pattern of a waistcoat before he fell heavily to the floor, a sudden sharp stinging sensation at the back of his head before wet droplets slipped down his face and onto the floorboards where his head lay. The room turned black.

When Mr Michael regained consciousness, he found himself in an unfamiliar interior, slumped in a worn though comfortable oak chair with a tall wide back and a padded seat. It was one he could remember admiring at Holden's Haunt. His hand went instinctively to the back of his head where a large lump had formed and something had clotted in his hair. As he removed his hand, he saw dried blood dusted across his fingertips.

Surveying the room, he realised they must be in the back kitchen of Crow's Haunt. There was a small stove, a square wooden table, four mismatched chairs, and a heavily chipped white enamel sink below the squat square window. Outside was a small but idyllic garden, neat rows of what looked to be vegetables along the left-hand side and a chicken coop with a border of flowers on the right. On the table where he sat was a scrap of fabric and a cup of water.

"Sorry 'bout the 'ead," came a voice from behind. It was the man he had met yesterday – Margaret's husband, Adam. He watched the man in his distinctive waistcoat walk round the table to sit at the opposite side before nodding at the cloth and the drink in encouragement. Neither his tone nor expression were particularly friendly, but he did not look like he was about to deal his guest another blow, or worse.

Mr Michael sipped the lukewarm water and splashed a dreg onto the rag to clean his hair. He winced as the injury stung under the pressure of his hand. He did not blame Adam for protecting his wife – he himself may have responded in a similar fashion on seeing such a commotion – but now he was ready to go home. No more conversations, no more confessions. Mr Michael had now exhausted his energy on pursuing the mystery and had decided that Margaret was mad, stealing the objects before killing Mrs Holden purely out of revenge for Benjamin's death. He would return to York, inform the inspector, then leave the police to deal with this sordid affair while he went home to be with his wife and daughter. If this experience had taught him anything, it was that his family were the single most important thing in his life. It was time he honoured that.

As he finished mopping his head, Mr Michael noticed that there were no sounds from the rest of the house. Perhaps Margaret had fallen asleep with the exertion of her attack or had even run off in a fit of rage. Either way, he had no wish to find out. A voice interrupted his thoughts as Adam broke the silence.

"My wife, she ain't well," he sighed, running the

edge of one fingernail under another, "Not just now, like, but fer a long time. Maybe since she were a kid. She feels things more than other folk do. She 'urts more."

He rose to reach into a cupboard, pulling out a half-empty bottle of whisky. He filled a mug for himself then tipped a quick splash into the cup Mr Michael had emptied. The smell was so strong that it caught in his throat. He coughed into the damp and bloodied cloth while the other man downed his drink in one before pouring himself another. Mr Michael remained silent. He sensed Adam could be just as volatile as his wife, especially with the aid of liquor.

"Once we were wed, we didn't 'ave any kids of our own. Tried like, but it never 'appened. She were so upset. She told me, said about the boy she'd had, what she saw that day, all them years lost. It were awful. I never seen no one break down like that. So I said I'd help 'er…"

Adam and Mr Michael met one another's gaze, both knowing where the tale would lead – the robbery, the murder, the real culprit finally revealed. So Margaret was not the only one to blame. Resisting the urge to voice the multitude of musings that now fluttered through his mind, Mr Michael waited for Adam to continue. He watched him finish the second drink of whisky and smack the emptied mug back onto the table. Then the story began.

Chapter Forty

For four years, Adam had been part of a happy home. His family enjoyed a life of modest comfort in the heart of York where his father and his uncle Thomas saw to the business on the ground floor while he and his mother occupied the upper rooms. She was a charming woman and doted on her firstborn, spending hours with him looking at books, playing games and singing songs together. Adam remembered that time fondly; the glory years, as he called them. It was when he was four that his brother was born and suddenly the life he once knew evaporated.

After that, Adam barely saw his mother as she cared for the new baby, with his father and uncle becoming even more absorbed by their grand schemes for the grocery shop. The house suddenly felt cramped and unwelcoming, his toys and books taken away to be given to the younger child. Adam was told that he was too old for such things and would soon have to start school and focus on his education, not on play.

Adam learned that life was cruel and that love was fleeting. Nevertheless, the brothers grew up together quite amicably and tried to assist their father with the business in any way they could. Their mother had become involved in local campaign groups promoting fairer working conditions for women, which caused her sons no end of taunts at school and from their former friends who lived on the street. While the brothers never formed a close bond, they rubbed along well enough until they reached their early twenties.

It was a day like any other when the pair were awakened by the sound of shouting from the shop floor, their father and uncle deep in a heated argument. They came downstairs just in time to see the first punch thrown, their father collapsing in a heap on the floor clutching his bloodied nose. Shortly afterwards, Uncle Thomas packed his possessions and left the shop, never to return. Their father took over the business and promptly continued as if he had always been an only child, while the two sons mourned the loss of their second father. They had grown up in his constant company and his sudden absence was as painful as it was mysterious.

Their father remained tight-lipped and evasive about the event, with Adam and his younger sibling silently continuing to help with the orders, deliveries, shelf-stacking and customer service in the shop each day. The old man was weakening and had begun to use a stick, though he remained bright and cheerful despite his ailing body. As his children grew into men, he became closer to his youngest son and ever more dependent on his support and diligence. He quickly decided that it should be this boy who would one day inherit the company, confident in his capabilities and commitment. While no one in the family would admit it, the father's favouritism was clear and keenly felt by both brothers.

Ever since he was old enough to walk and talk, the younger boy had proven himself to be sociable, considerate and well-mannered, always waking up early and staying up late to help his family with anything they needed, with no chore or request refused. He had even been caught in the early hours of the morning carefully scouring one of his mother's handkerchiefs, speckled with blood from a coughing fit. He had returned it to her spotlessly clean only for the woman to die three days later.

Already grieving for their vanished uncle, the loss of their mother made the two boys even more emotional, though in opposite ways. While the youngest grew more sensitive and empathetic to others, the elder drew away from his family and the few friends he had made, becoming an angry and resentful loner.

Now a single parent, their father was even more reliant on his sons, but it was only the younger man who was happy to help. Adam, on the other hand, aspired to have a different and better life. He did not want to waste his time and energy spending all day shoving tins of fruit onto a dusty plank of wood. He longed to be part of something more stimulating, more demanding, with higher wages and the chance to meet new people and have adventures. York was dull and predictable for someone with his ambitions.

For all the talk among the neighbours of progress and innovation, Adam could see little hope of opportunity or excitement in his hometown. He knew there were better prospects out there in the wider world and he would not hang around with his elderly father and boring brother waiting for fate to call. Instead, he decided that he would find his uncle and ask him for help with a new life and career. Wherever Thomas was, Adam knew he would have made a success of himself and would likely be more than happy to encourage his favourite nephew to do the same.

As the idea grew more and more plausible in his mind, Adam continued quietly with his work in the shop to earn some easy money, spending his free time asking locals and acquaintances for information regarding his uncle. Once he knew where the man had moved to – for he was convinced that he would not have remained in York – he would find him and make him a proposition. He could begin as a paid apprentice in whatever industry Thomas had joined, then perhaps become a partner in a company before one day taking over the business himself. Finally, he would be rich, successful and happy. It was the only thing that encouraged Adam out of bed and into the shop each day.

During his later school years, Adam had sought every opportunity to rebel, frequently receiving shouts and smacks, cane whips and detentions, along with numerous weeks at home when he was expelled. In desperation, his father had visited the headmaster and pleaded for help with his wayward son, but between them they could not come up with a suitable solution nor punishment. The youth was simply stupid and ignorant, the headmaster had concluded, despite the father's insistence that he was still a good boy. He had tried talking to his son, then shouting at him, then giving him more work in the shop as a way of occupying his mind. All his efforts came to nought.

Eventually, the school recommended that Adam

take on full-time employment in the family business. His father tried to give him more responsibility, but Adam was not interested. He would frequently turn up late or miss a shift entirely, relying on his brother to work the missing hours. Sometimes Adam would make deliberate errors, even in front of customers. He knew his brother would be watching and that was part of the fun. His father did not know what to do, alternating between frustration and sadness that he did not seem to be able to appease his eldest. The brother tried to reason with Adam, warning him that his misdemeanours would only lead to trouble of a more serious kind. Adam would reply with laughter.

Occasionally, the two brothers would assist with delivering groceries to a handful of residencies on the outskirts of the city. It proved a useful way to occupy the troublemaker, allowing the younger brother to keep an eye on his sibling while their father could tend to the shop without constant worry. Adam enjoyed the excursions as they allowed him to escape his father's watchful and concerned gaze and gave him the opportunity to ask more of the locals about his uncle.

One of the locations they often visited was the first of two houses stood side by side just beyond the city walls, surrounded by a handful of workshops and grazing land with the river and a small wood at the back. Adam recognised the girl who lived in the house where they made the deliveries. She used to come into the shop herself once or twice a week, but she was not much to look at nor to talk to – not like some of the lasses he had seen with bosoms the size of marrows.

His brother, however, seemed keen on the girl and would flush violently whenever she opened the door to take the parcel of groceries, a strange urchin of a boy usually wrapped around her legs. There was no sign of a husband or any other family living there.

After two or three visits, Adam noticed that they were being watched. While his brother delivered the groceries, he spotted a younger girl emerging from the entrance of the house next door. She had a round face framed by thick hair as black as night, with wide eyes that looked better suited to an animal than to a girl. While she was not pretty, there was something appealing that attracted Adam, and he would feel strangely intoxicated by the captivating intensity of her unwavering stare.

Though she seemed to be hiding, she made a poor show of it and would grin brazenly whenever Adam spotted her on his visits. After a few more sightings, he decided to speak to her and offered a handful of nuts from the delivery. She took them readily, using only her grip to crack open the shells before picking through the remnants to retrieve the treats inside. As she ate, her keen gaze never moved from Adam's eyes. It would draw him back again and again. Their friendship quickly developed, until Adam became convinced that she was the one.

As luck would have it, their romantic union proved more beneficial than Adam could ever have hoped. During supper with the girl and her parents, he discovered that they had heard of a man named Thomas who lived in Helmsley and worked for the local tannery firm there. After a few more well-chosen conversations with other individuals, Adam was finally able to find out the address of his uncle. He had moved into a property right in the centre of the small town the very year he had disappeared from York. Finally, everything seemed to be falling into place.

With her parents' blessing, Adam swiftly married his young sweetheart with the assurance that he would soon be able to provide a better life for them both. He had worn a tatty waistcoat he had found in his uncle's old wardrobe, while she had been given a fusty cream gown that had belonged to his mother. The rings too were from the family, though Adam had not been given permission to take them. Ever since he was small, he had always remembered where his mother had kept her most precious jewels, and there they had remained since her death, stowed away in a wooden box underneath the bed. He reasoned that they in part belonged to him and that his mother would have been more than glad to see them on the finger of her eldest son's bride. He also took a few of the other pieces of jewellery to add to the sum he had been able to save from working at the shop. With money and a wife, Adam could now make his move to Helmsley and find his uncle.

Before his departure, Adam supplied his new wife with a small allowance and instructed her to take a trap and join him in the town exactly one week later. He did not say goodbye to his father and brother, packing only a few belongings before turning from the family home and business hoping never to return. Luckily, the information Adam had been provided was true. He found old Uncle Thomas living quite comfortably in a small cottage in Helmsley, just a stone's throw from the stream, the marketplace and the local pub.

Thomas had secured himself a steady job at the tannery and had a reasonable income along with his own property, both of which he was happy to share with his long-lost nephew. Though Thomas did not have a particularly enviable job, he was nonetheless respected and admired for his hard work and jovial nature, despite the often unsanitary conditions. He was even on first name terms with the tannery owner, Mr Stewart. When approached by his favourite employee, Mr Stewart had been more than glad to offer young Adam a job starting with a two-week trial period, after which he would receive regular wages as well as one meal per working day.

From his very first morning toiling alongside his uncle, Adam already felt that his life held more value and potential than it ever had back at his father's shop. The little cottage was gradually beginning to feel more like home too, and he was sure his wife would make it even more welcoming and comfortable once she arrived. His uncle lived simply with barely any furniture or possessions, but the simplicity suited Adam and he quickly learned to ignore the constant draughts, imposing low ceilings and incessant scratching as the mice scurried through the thatch. He had already begun making improvements to the small garden, something that only the wealthiest houses would have back in York. He had wedged a spade into the thick peat in one of the far corners, thinking it would make a suitable perch for his bride's pet crow.

The woman in question arrived dutifully enough a week later and the pair were provided with the smallest room at the top of the house furnished only with a bed and a small wardrobe, but which was theirs nonetheless. For several months, the three inhabitants lived together quite amiably until the tragic day when Uncle Thomas was discovered stiff and stone cold in his bed. The coroner confirmed that it had been a heart attack and the couple promptly went into grieving, with Adam permitted to take two days from work to arrange the funeral and deal with his uncle's affairs.

Though Adam was grateful for his job at the tannery and had worked with the same determination as his uncle, the newlyweds had not been able to accumulate enough savings to be able to purchase their own property. They had never spoken to Thomas about a will as he had always seemed so healthy and carefree, yet they now found themselves at his mercy. If he had not left them his house or at least some money, they would have nowhere else to go. Adam would rather they live on the streets than be forced to return to York and beg at his father's door.

As fate would have it, luck was on their side. As Adam's wife began clearing through the old man's scant belongings, she found what they had been dreaming of – the will, made a month before the death and suitably certified, with Thomas' nephew and wife to inherit his property, his possessions and his life savings. They had been saved.

Adam returned to his job at the tannery while his wife

preoccupied herself with tidying the house, learning to cook and preparing for what she hoped would soon be a large family, but her hopes were never realised. She was unable to conceive and eventually forced to confess the possible reason behind her failure to her husband. Between choking tears one evening after supper, she informed him of the child she had given birth to when she was but a girl herself, the event hastily concealed by her own parents and the infant given away that same day. Much to Adam's surprise, the baby had been raised by the very girl his own brother had doted on with his deliveries, Agnes Dartton.

Adam absorbed his wife's pain and anger, knowing he could never replace her loss but still desiring nothing more all the same. But from the moment she had admitted her true past, his wife had changed. While she had always been confident and outspoken, her words were now laced with poison, her demeanour unashamedly selfish and conceited. She began to view her existence as a constant battle against the world with Adam as her accomplice. In sickness and in health, he had promised, until death us do part. A decade later, his vows were put to the test.

It was a rare day of absolute summer, the sky a perfect band of blue as the air hummed with heat, bringing smiles and laughter to the townsfolk as they emerged from their homes into the warmth. With no work that day, Adam suggested that he and his wife enjoy a trip out together, eventually deciding on York as their destination. They had quarrelled time and time again over her desire to visit their former home while he had always refused with the same excuse; under no circumstance did her ever want to see his father and brother again, not even for their funerals. Yet there was something about his wife's determination and the beauty of the day that finally convinced him otherwise, so to York they travelled.

His wife had grown up an only child, prohibited from entering the city's Bar Walls except to attend school. Even as an adult, she only saw her workplace and the two or three roads that ran between it and her home. She had missed out on so much excitement, the real York and all the places that people talked about – the market, the railway station, the factories, the bridges. She wanted to see them now, fully-grown and with her husband on her arm. Adam assured her it was all a mass of ugly people choking through thick smog and open sewers, but she did not believe him.

So there they were, on a horse and trap, rolling steadily through the countryside back to their home city. Adam directed them to all the places his wife wished to see, staring up in awe at the intricate patterned masonry of the minster, the endless traffic shuttling up and down the streets, followed by the bustling market that consumed the city centre. They both stood on the periphery staring in wonder at the number of stalls clumped side by side – the market was at least twenty times the size of the one in Helmsley with a seemingly endless variety of produce.

As they rightly suspected, the dirty air caused their throats to swell and their eyes to water, but they quickly grew used to the discomfort as they had in their younger years and eventually ceased to notice. It was such a pleasant day after all; they were both just glad of the chance to experience something new. They visited almost every location except the family grocer's on Coney Street, with the final destination being perhaps the most famous: the Shambles. Neither had walked down its slippery cobbles more than once or twice in their youth, so it was somewhat of a surprise to find the street so commonplace despite its reputation.

As they reached the far end, Adam felt his wife suddenly pull on his arm. She was falling, fainting, weak with disbelief at the sight in front – a shop called Holden's Haunt. With her breathing double its normal pace, Adam had to assist her to the end of the street where she could rest in the shade of the church. Perhaps, he reasoned, it was the heat of the day, the unsanitary air or the excitement of exploration. No, she told him. It was something else. Something awful. The shop beyond and its owner. Holden was the married name of Agnes, she said, the girl she had told him about. The one who had taken her only child away. Adam was stunned, unable to believe that such a villain did indeed exist, and that she was inside that very shop. He had to see for himself – the curiosity was too great to resist.

Leaving his wife seated on the low wall of the graveyard, Adam returned to the Shambles and spent a few moments casting his gaze over the curious collection hung up all along the walls outside. He tried to peer through the windows but they were thick with grease, so he made his way into the shop itself, wondering what his wife's former neighbour might look like. Everywhere he turned, there were items for sale crowding the floor, stacked against the walls and even hanging from the ceiling. He cast around until his eyes fell on a woman sat in an armchair by the fire. There she was. The woman who had destroyed his wife's life, her sanity and her harmony. The reason they would never have a family. Agnes Holden herself.

Reaching for the whisky bottle to top up his cup, Adam paused in the story and waited for Mr Michael to absorb what he had heard.

"So, you're Adam Ainsley? Brother of Stuart Ainsley Junior? Of Ainsley's Grocery on Coney Street?"

Adam rolled his eyes in response, re-corking the bottle before swigging down half the contents of his cup and belching loudly.

"Was," he clarified with a hoarse throat, the alcohol strong on his breath, "Not that it means much round 'ere, gladly."

Mr Michael nodded slowly, chewing over the narrative in his mind, trying to work out how it all fitted together. Though he knew he was edging ever closer to the answer, he was now fearful of discovering the truth.

Chapter Forty-One

Despite the dawn, Irene wished for nothing more than to be in her bed. Exhausted from her dramatic adventure, she had heaved her mattress once more onto the floor of her mother's room, hoping the sound of her breathing would soothe her heavy heart. They may only have spoken a few words in the past month, but simply knowing she was there was a comfort to Irene, one she desperately needed as she tried to fight against the memory of the man on the bridge, his words, and his fallen body. She could still feel the imprint of the blade in her hand, could still hear his strangled cry as she had removed it from his neck. Ignoring the sounds of neighbours emerging from their homes, she pulled the blanket up over her head and clenched her eyes closed, praying for sleep to take her.

When she finally awoke, the room was filled with a soft dappled light and Winifred was sat up in bed with her face lit by a single ray. Her mother's eyes were closed but she was fully awake, a small smile playing across her lips. She was basking in the rare warmth of the winter sun, feeling refreshed and ready for breakfast. The imaginary smells of tea and toast wafted around her nostrils, distant memories suddenly recalled after months of being muted.

Irene slowly came to her senses, rubbing her tired eyes as she exhaled a slow sigh of relief, glad to be at home and safe. She almost did not recognise her mother's voice when she wished her a good morning. She rose from the floor and climbed onto Winifred's bed, tucking herself against her side as if she were still a small girl. Closing her eyes, she snuggled into her mother's loving embrace, taking long deep inhalations of her scent, wishing they could remain this way forever.

Winifred enfolded her daughter into her frail arms and nestled her nose into her hair, which did not look like it had been washed in weeks. There was an odd odour beneath the grease and smoke, hints of tobacco, beer, and something else that was familiar, almost like… blood. She stroked the girl's head then heard a soft whimper from below her chin. Irene was quietly sobbing, tears soaking through the worn muslin fabric of her mother's nightdress. Winifred took her daughter's face in her hands and used both thumbs to wipe away her sadness. Though she knew she had not earned Irene's trust, she wanted more than ever for her to be able to confide in her mother and for she in turn to be able to help. It was a rare opportunity to fulfil her role as God had intended.

She implored her daughter to speak the truth, to reveal what it was that made her weep so, her face too distraught to belong to someone so young. Feeling as if she had at last found a friend, Irene revealed the events of the previous day and the full extent to which she and her father had been pursuing Mrs Holden's case. Winifred listened patiently, nodding as her daughter flew through a myriad of memories that seemed both fantastical and disturbing. Among the garbled recollections was one sentence that Irene kept repeating. Winifred quickly realised that this was the source of her child's devastation, yet she could not believe it to be true. How could her little girl have possibly killed a man?

After her confession, Irene's cries became frantic and her despair all the more evident. She buried her face further and further into Winifred's chest as if to hide from the world and somehow erase the deed with her tears. The bloodied apron had been left to soak overnight in the kitchen sink and the knife had been cleaned. She could not be certain whether anyone had seen her, nor whether the man had indeed died from his wound. He could have survived and reported the incident to the police. But there was also a chance that he had not, or that he had fallen into the river, or been run over on the road. Irene felt despicable for having such thoughts. What had become of her? A criminal, a degenerate – the same scum that had murdered Mrs Holden. Her father would be ashamed of her.

Winifred held her daughter close, clutching her head and hushing softly. No, her mother insisted with a determined voice unfamiliar to Irene, she was a good girl. She had been trying to help Mrs Holden and her father until the man had disturbed her. It was fear that had driven her to protect herself. It was what any other human being would have done. She had nothing to feel guilty about, Winifred insisted. She had done the right thing.

The right thing, Irene repeated as she wiped her face dry and mustered the last remnants of her courage and self-belief. The right thing would be to go to the police, to leave the house this instant and to confess her crime to Inspector Falmer, then to accept whatever punishment was appropriate. Her mother narrowed her eyes and shook her head, her face paling again, though her eyes were sharp and alert. She would not let Irene give herself in. She would not let her daughter put her life in the hands of an incompetent inspector and his band of dithering officers.

Irene could not help her mouth twitch upwards at her mother's words. She nodded in agreement and decided to instead wait for her father to return. He would know what to do. The girl reluctantly left the room to retrieve some warm water and soap for her mother so that she could wash herself. It was usually Irene who bathed her each day, so it seemed strange to be leaving the bowl by the bedside. Strange, yes, but also a relief. She went down to the kitchen instead to make tea and toast with fried eggs, her mother's favourite, taking the two platefuls up to the bedroom so that they could eat together.

Irene had to cut up the meal and help steady her mother's hand as it wavered towards her mouth, but otherwise it felt like a perfectly normal family occasion and she was so very glad of it. Her mother had put on a pretty yellow dress that had not been worn in months, the colour making her look even more radiant. She had even brushed her hair, which hung down to her waist in thin coiling wisps. As Irene helped her form a neat bun with the curls, they both jumped at the sound of a knock on the door. Mr Michael had taken a key and they were expecting no visitors.

Winifred grew pale and her hand dropped, the brush released and clanging loudly against the floorboards before rolling underneath the bed. Irene had not moved as she listened intently. The knock repeated, sharp and insistent, as if belonging to someone of rank. Someone like Inspector Falmer. The thought rose to their minds at the same time and they looked to one another with horror etched on their faces. Winifred opened her arms to receive her daughter in the hope of protecting her, though she did not know how, but Irene remained where she was. She had grown up more than her mother could ever have known and she was not about to hide from her fate.

Irene decided in that instant that she would take full responsibility for the crime, for it was through her own choice that she had found herself on the bridge alone and at night. She had no one to blame but herself. She kissed her mother tenderly, making a mental note of her kind face and bright eyes. Perhaps it would be the last time Irene ever saw her mother again. She tried to dispel the thought before the tears formed.

Leaving the room and heading downstairs, she shuffled on her shoes and wrapped a thick woollen shawl around her shoulders, its weave warm from where it had been resting in the fallen light from the window. She felt an urge to take a personal possession with her in the belief that she might never return home; in her haste, she pocketed her favourite knife from the kitchen counter. The thunderous banging continued, causing Irene to grow ever more fearful with each repeated blow. She finally opened the door, holding her breath as she came face to face with Inspector Falmer.

Still wearing his helmet along with a look of mild impatience, the inspector gave his customary greeting and twitched his moustache against the sudden stench of a chamber pot being emptied into the gutter behind. The neighbour raised her eyebrows at Irene, who in turn flinched further behind the door, gripping onto the wood until her knuckles were white. As she watched the woman retreat, a vivid recollection of her bloodied hands flooded into her mind and she suddenly realised what she was carrying – the weapon itself. She could not dispose of it now. She could almost feel the cold metal of the blade against her thighs.

The sound of Inspector Falmer's voice brought Irene to her senses. With grave reluctance, she stepped out onto the pavement leaving the door slightly open behind her, biting her lip fiercely to conceal her distress. The inspector removed his helmet and tucked it under one arm, hooking the opposite thumb into his lapel.

"Miss Michael, if I could have a few minutes of your time, please?"

Irene did not dare raise her gaze for fear of the truth tumbling from her lips, but she was struck by the tone of the inspector's voice. He sounded quite calm, jovial even. The neighbours around them had gradually paused in their business and stood twittering among themselves wondering what the latest scandal could be.

"Shall we perhaps take a seat for a moment, Miss Michael?" The inspector stepped around Irene and led the way back inside the house, the rabble of voices growing louder and more animated as Irene closed the door.

Still convinced she was about to be taken to prison, Irene paced the narrow space in front of the empty fire and waited for the inspector to continue. He looked around the gloomy cramped kitchen with a barely concealed grimace, hugging his helmet to his stomach rather than risk placing it on any of the worn surfaces. After a few uncomfortable minutes, Irene took a seat at the small table and poured herself a glass of water to steady her nerves. The sound of the chair scraping across the floor caused the inspector to start. Recovering his composure, he idly picked a fleck of debris from his helmet then began.

"I believe you may have heard of a Mr Stuart Ainsley Junior?" he asked, pronouncing each part of the name loudly as if there could be the possibility of error. Irene swallowed the lukewarm water uncomfortably and returned the cup to the table. It had not been the question she was expecting. Perhaps the inspector was just establishing the wider scenario before she would be made to confess the murder, she thought. Wiping a sleeve across her mouth, Irene gave a soft nod.

"I do," she began, trying her best to compose her voice and still her emotions, "He's a kind 'n' gentle man, I liked 'im a great deal."

Recalling her encounter, she realised the truth of her words and wished more than anything that she had just returned home after her visit that day. Instead, she had headed off on her own, foolish and naive, thinking herself some kind of budding detective. She had proven to be nothing of the sort. Quite the opposite.

The inspector cleared his throat using a navy handkerchief retrieved from his trouser pocket and ran a hand over his helmet in thought. He was watching Irene intently, his concern growing as she grew ever paler and her hands trembled. The girl seemed most out of sorts. Little did he know that she was desperately trying to think of a way to replace the knife before the inspector found it.

"We've been speaking with Mr Ainsley and he's provided some rather interesting details about his brother, do you know him?" he continued. Irene shook her head.

"No, I thought as much. He's in Helmsley now, you see."

Inspector Falmer took a step back as Irene leapt out of her seat faster than a whippet round a track, causing him to loosen the grip of his helmet so that it went clashing to the floor and rolled under the table. Irene hastily crawled below to recover it, surprised at its weight despite the soft texture of the surface. With quaking fingers, she plucked at the balls of dust and dirt that had adhered to its surface, giving her time to think through this new information. It had revealed a different direction, an alternative possibility that finally seemed to offer some significance to the mystery.

"Inspector," she began with caution, "Are you meaning t'say that this man… this man were involved?" Her anxiety had been replaced by energy, her posture now confident, her expression keen and alert. Inspector Falmer furrowed his brow, both at the girl's changed behaviour and at the state of his helmet. He took it from her hands and placed it on his head, filth and all.

"Indeed," he nodded curtly, "And I am to depart to Helmsley within the hour. I had hoped your father had returned, but I heard the bicycle he borrowed was still missing." Well well, thought Irene, the officers had certainly been doing some thorough investigation of late – and about time too.

"Me father's in 'elmsley," she replied, heading towards the front door, "An' you're to tek me with you." It was given as an order and not a request in a manner even Mrs Holden would have been proud of.

Inspector Falmer knew better than to protest, so together they left the house then the street and eventually the city, both equally determined to find Mr Ainsley's brother, Mr Michael, and finally, the truth.

Chapter Forty-Two

Adam inhaled and exhaled slowly as if readying himself. He cracked the knuckles of each hand and wiped his palms against the length of his hair, slicking it back from his face. Bringing his drink to his mouth once more, he drained the contents then upended the cup onto the table with a sharp thud. His eyes were surprisingly focused yet with a glint that would have unnerved even the calmest of men. Mr Michael attempted to swallow, his mouth and throat dry from the combination of alcohol and anxiety. Despite his unease, he had to know. He had to hear the truth.

"So… Adam Ainsley. The shop, when you saw Mrs 'olden that day… what did y'do?" There was a pause as the last query hung in the air, not quite accusatory but nevertheless uttered with a tone of suspicion and concern. They shared another knowing look before Adam took up the story once more.

On entering Holden's Haunt, Adam was struck by the sheer volume of objects that were crammed into the small room, making it feel both claustrophobic and endless. An old woman – Mrs Holden, he presumed – was sat in a well-worn armchair in the corner working away at a woollen sock with a large hole in its toe. She was obviously well aware of his presence but had chosen to say nothing, occasionally glancing upwards at the stranger with a blank expression that at best showed indifference and at worst irritation.

Unperturbed, Adam began to pace the room. Like so many visitors before him, he could not keep his eyes from roving around trying to seek out something even more curious and more impressive within the collection. He pottered around for ten or perhaps even twenty minutes, just him and the silent Mrs Holden. There seemed to be no sign of a husband or of any children, no evidence in the house of people actually living here. Maybe it was just a business after all, and she had been left in charge for the day.

Eventually, another customer came in carrying two ceramic jugs he had found outside. He began bartering over the price, which offered Adam the opportunity to watch, listen and learn. Though her body, clothes and voice were that of an old woman, her eyes suggested she was far younger in years than she appeared. Perhaps not much older than he, Adam thought. Yet something had happened to her. She had clearly suffered some kind of illness or emotional trauma, the consequences of which were visibly evident. From her long bony fingers to her sour wrinkled face, this was not a woman who had lived a life of joy and laughter. There was heartache, Adam realised, not unlike that which had ailed his wife.

The customer left with both jugs and Mrs Holden emptied the coins into the pocket of her pinafore, two steely eyes watching Adam as she did so. He continued with his search, squeezing between towering bookcases and squat chests of drawers until he finally saw something of interest. It was a little wooden rabbit, intricately carved in a way that brought the quality of the grain to the surface. It reminded him of the ones he often saw around Helmsley, nibbling their way at tufts of grass along the hedgerows. He took his purchase to Mrs Holden and did not argue when she finally suggested a price, which was more than reasonable in his opinion. Working his fingers over the soft indents of the figure, he handed the money across and returned to the throbbing tidal mass of shoppers on the Shambles. He looked up at the sign above, its gold lettering glinting in the sun. It was as if he had just entered and returned from another world altogether.

Adam found Margaret where he had left her, the colour now returned to her cheeks and her breathing back to normal, though her eyes were roaming back and forth between the shop and the people passing by with an odd speed and unnatural intensity. She asked only 'well?' with a hiss then listened intently as her husband tried to recall the exact details of the shop and its contents, though he knew his words could never do justice to the variety of goods nor the unique atmosphere of exploring what was on offer. He handed her the rabbit and she backed away with a sudden jolt as if he were holding some implement of the devil. Adam slipped it into his pocket, reluctant to let it go just yet. His wife, meanwhile, did not wish to spend another minute in York. Adam tried to persuade her to take a second walk around the market, or to visit the river to watch the cargo boats, or perhaps even see some of the famous City Walls, but she shook her head like a petulant child at each of his suggestions.

They promptly returned to Helmsley and continued life as if the visit had never happened, with Margaret refusing to speak about the day whenever Adam passed comment or attempted to put the wooden rabbit on display. While this might have been enough to protect Margaret from her memories, there was an odd occurrence that ensured she would never forget their excursion to York. On the day of their visit, her beloved pet crow had vanished from its usual favoured perch in the front room on the dresser by the window. On returning home, Adam had searched the town for any sign of the animal but it was nowhere to be found. His wife pretended not to care.

Some months later, Margaret turned the evening topic of conversation to Holden's Haunt. They were attempting to finish a burned and barely edible supper of hare and turnips, which Adam was forcing down in between sips of stale ale after a hectic day at work. Most abruptly, Margaret asked her husband to recall every detail of what he had seen in the shop, casting a stern gaze as he coughed out a mouthful of meat. Even though it had been some time since their visit, he still found he could remember many of the items he had seen in precise detail, particularly the ones that he imagined were worth a fair price. Margaret nodded as if these were the exact words she had wanted to hear. She had been doing her own reconnaissance too and had learned that Agnes was indeed widowed and barren, the shop now her only source of income.

For the first time in years, Adam saw his wife smile, though it was not a pleasant experience. As her eyes locked with his, she grinned almost manically, malice etched across every crease in her skin and radiating from her wide wild eyes. She took her husband's hands and clenched them tightly.

"My love, I 'ave 'ad an idea. We're to end it fer Mrs 'olden." Her voice was filled with glee, her eyes growing ever larger.

"End it? 'ow?" Adam could feel a lump forming in his throat. He knew from his wife's behaviour and voice that the solution would not be a happy one for her former neighbour.

Much to his surprise, the answer was not murder nor even to hurt the woman. Margaret was not even the one to suggest they rob the place, or not in so many words, at least. What she wanted instead was something far greater in value and much more detrimental in its effect.

"We'll mek 'er know what it feels like t'watch yer own life endin'. We'll mek 'er feel like I did watchin' me bairn die in 'er arms. We're going to destroy 'er."

Each word was metered out with such venom that Adam pulled his hands away and slumped back in his chair, the meal forgotten, his wife still smirking. Whatever Margaret had in mind, Adam could sense that it had already somehow begun.

As Mr Michael readied himself to hear just exactly what Margaret had proposed to Adam that day, the kitchen door swung open and there stood the woman herself, hands on hips and her face a picture of disgust. She looked between her husband, who had paused open-mouthed mid-story, and Mr Michael, the enemy, drinking her whisky by the look of it. She snatched up his empty cup and took a sniff, shaking her head.

"'aving ourselves an afternoon gossip, eh?" she chimed with fake merriment, her eyes mere slits as they darted between them, her teeth clenched. She grabbed the nearly empty bottle by the neck and poured the remaining liquid into the cup, downing it just as her husband had before releasing a soft burp. She sat down at the table, the men muted by fright.

"Now then, my love," she said to Adam, eyebrows raised in expectation as her hand caressed his, "Carry on! Let us 'ear how dear ol' Agnes met her demise, hm?"

Adam looked as pale as snow, his hand frozen solid where it rested beside the empty bottle.

Margaret had indeed grown up since their childhood acquaintance, thought Mr Michael, though she had not become a lady. She was villainous to the core, but could she really have killed another person? He no longer knew what to believe and was growing increasingly troubled by the story that was gradually unravelling. He was beginning to wish he had never gotten himself involved in the first place.

There was a look of relish on Margaret's face as she smacked her lips and folded her arms across her chest awaiting their full attention. Mr Michael and Adam remained silent, their fates entirely in her hands. With a staged sigh, she continued the story she had heard her husband reveal, relishing the opportunity to share the next chapter in her own words.

Margaret had not known precisely where the idea had come from, but once it had arisen in her mind, it had dug itself in there like a fierce tic, a persistent itch that would not cease. She would have to be clever, she knew, but with the help of her husband she was certain the pair of them would be able to achieve the unthinkable – to ruin Agnes Holden and bring some form of justice for her evil deed and the broken-hearted mother it had left behind.

While Margaret had tried year after year to push the incident from her mind, there had not been a day when she had not thought of her darling Benny and wished that he were by her side. What a fine young man he could have become, with both a mother and father as well as a comfortable home in Helmsley. There had been so much hope, so much potential and possibility, but every one of her dreams had been snatched away in an instant by that wretched girl. It had not been the sunny weather nor her nagging husband that had persuaded her to go to York that day, Margaret realised. It had been fate. Now she had to restore the balance.

The idea was simple enough – to own a shop so successful that it would drive Holden's Haunt out of business, leaving Agnes with nothing but the clothes on her back. She would have no income, no customers, no family or friends to comfort or support her. She would be entirely alone. Finally, she would know the true feeling of emptiness, as Margaret had done nearly all her life. It was Adam who had taken the proposal one step further, suggesting that they take every possession from the Shambles itself and turn their Helmsley home into the new retail venture. With the skills he had acquired from his father's grocery business and with no children for Margaret to care for, it would be easy for them to set up trade right from their front room once they had their stock in place. They could hope to earn themselves a decent profit while leaving Agnes bankrupt in the process. It seemed the perfect scheme, and they began its progress the very next day.

Fishing out some gaudy clothing from Uncle Thomas' old belongings and making a few subtle differences to Adam's appearance with a little rouge, some boot polish and a few tufts of animal hair, Margaret created a number of different disguises, choosing the most convincing for her husband's first excursion to York. They both doubted that Agnes would remember him, but they did not want to risk the possibility.

Adam cycled to York, leaving his bicycle in the nearby churchyard before adjusting his attire. He entered the shop as calmly as he could, browsing around briefly before daring to make a few passing comments to Mrs Holden who, as always, was far too busy darning in her armchair to notice him. After fifteen minutes, he left the property with a pewter bowl, three silver spoons and a handful of costume jewellery, all of which he stuffed into the large pockets Margaret had sewn inside his baggy coat. No one had entered the store nor looked through the window, with Mrs Holden remaining unaware.

As he hurriedly left the Shambles, Adam buttoned up his jacket to keep the contents safe and concealed as he mounted his bicycle. The objects jangled noisily against one another as he made his way across the cobbled streets and out of the city, pedalling with all his might. He eventually reached Helmsley just as the sun was beginning to set, his breathing laboured by the long journey and the excitement of his success. Margaret was delighted with his initial haul and the apparent simplicity with which the deed had been committed. At this rate, they would have a thriving business in a matter of weeks. She spat on and polished each item in turn before carefully placing them on an empty shelf in the front room, which she had dusted and rewaxed especially for the occasion. Her shop was beginning to take shape.

Over the course of several more visits, Adam managed to gradually take every article from Holden's Haunt. The old woman was so oblivious to the fact that he had even slackened his efforts with the costumes, going out before Margaret had awakened with just some old boots or the trusted overcoat to hide his identity. Life on the Shambles moved so quickly that few people seemed to take notice of anything or anyone other than themselves. With every fruitful steal, Adam became all the more confident of his wife's plan and the possibility of their much-improved future. It may not have been the life they had intended, but it would do.

A new energy and vigour engulfed Adam as he became addicted to the game and its rewards, spurring him on to make even bigger and more impressive thefts. He had been able to persuade a couple of colleagues from the tannery to take time off work to assist him with the larger pieces of furniture and borrowed a horse and trap for the deed, allowing his accomplices to claim whatever goods they fancied as means of payment. A few missing items would not make a difference to his business once it was officially opened. He had already calculated an approximate value for the possessions now sitting in his cottage in Helmsley and it was more than he could ever have dreamed of possessing.

Margaret meanwhile was becoming increasingly impatient regarding what would be the most important item of her new collection: the letter opener. Every time Adam returned from his trip, she would hunt through the produce of his pilfering seeking the distinctive symbol, but day after day her search would prove unsuccessful. Adam would wring his hat in his hands like a disobedient child, mumbling some excuse and trying to make the best of whatever objects he had managed to take. But it never seemed good enough for Margaret. The more time that passed, the more desperate and demented she became.

On a couple of odd occasions, Adam had stayed long enough in the shop to have seen Mrs Holden with the letter opener. He had a favoured spot behind an old bookcase from which he could see both the old woman and the entrance, giving him ample time to pick and choose without being noticed. There had been a glimmer of light shining across the wall and when he had looked, there was Mrs Holden with the letter opener in her hands. As he edged out to try to gain a better view, the floorboard let out the faintest of creaks. Mrs Holden had quickly slipped the blade between the fabric of her chair, but not quickly enough for Adam not to have seen it. It had been the emblem on the handle that had produced the shimmer, its shape branded into his mind forever more. No wonder Margaret coveted it. This letter opener looked like none he had ever seen.

Fresh from a morning scalding from Margaret, Adam had taken the decision to try to encourage Mrs Holden outside of her shop, thereby allowing him the opportunity to retrieve the blade. The weather, the flooded river, the royal family and the price of fish all entered into his conversation, but no amount of talk could persuade the old woman to move from her chair. Adam had even tried to use the bird as a distraction until it seemed to recognise him and flew down to perch on his shoulder. Mrs Holden had narrowed her eyes with curiosity as Adam flapped his hand to rid the crow from his person. A few days later it had flown home, taking to its usual spot beside Margaret. He had found her stroking a single finger over its slick black body, the same question barked at him as he came through the door.

"So where is it, eh? I want that letter opener!" Adam stared at the creature nestling into his wife's hand, a peculiar chill creeping up his neck.

He knew this would not be over until Margaret had what she wanted, yet he was beginning to feel that her vindication was much more than simply revenge. For Margaret to have suffered so cruelly, she seemed strangely keen to have the memories of that loss all around her – the objects, the letter opener, the crow, each one a memory of her past, a reminder of her suffering. She had even decided to use her maiden name for the shop rather than her married title. She seemed to want to be little Margaret all over again, though it could never bring back her son. Nothing could.

Chapter Forty-Three

It was early October, 1872. The leaves of the trees lining the River Ouse were beginning to turn golden and crisp, the traffic below them as fervent as ever. The fog had grown thicker and more pungent with the increased industrial production and the ever-expanding transport networks both churning out clouds of sullied smoke. Business was indeed booming; all except for one proprietor. Holden's Haunt was closed until further notice. It had been robbed right down to the nails in the beams. The police were baffled, the neighbours stunned. Mrs Holden had been left entirely helpless.

Meanwhile in Helmsley, a new curiosity shop had opened on a clear and sunny morning, a queue of eager customers already lined up outside. Margaret and Adam made several decent sales during their first day, though most visitors had come simply to look around the place and marvel at the many mysterious objects arranged haphazardly in the front room and across the outer walls. Even the garden had offered a few choice items, with Margaret pottering between the spaces as she talked to her patrons and noted their purchases in her smart new ledger. To any stranger, it appeared that she had worked in a shop all her life. Adam too felt content for the first time in years, until later that evening when Margaret closed the door on their final customer.

After finishing dinner, Margaret screamed at her

husband in desperation. She wanted – no, she needed – that letter opener. If he was not going to help her then she would depart for York the following day and reclaim it for herself. Adam tried again and again to explain the difficulty of doing so and the potential dangers of her travelling alone to commit such an act, but his wife would not hear of it. He was made to sleep on a pile of blankets in the kitchen, where he awoke the following day to find the fire cold, the laundry abandoned, and his breakfast plate empty. He was alone. Margaret had risen before dawn and taken the first trap heading to York. Adam could only hope that she would return unharmed.

On reaching the city, it took Margaret some time to regain her bearings. She now realised that it had been Adam that had led them around the streets that day and she was finding it difficult to retrace their steps. She climbed onto the Bar Walls, twisting her head this way and that as she followed the route trying to gauge a familiar sight. With her feet sore and her stomach murmuring, she returned to the city centre and purchased a currant bun from a baker's stall, asking the kindly gentleman serving where she might find the Shambles.

Having eaten her treat, Margaret eventually managed to locate the square by the church, the shop just visible on the corner beyond. She did not yet know what she would do or say to Agnes Holden, though she had thought of little else for many weeks. She knew the crime had been severe and ungodly, and she possessed no sympathy for her former neighbour. What she had yet to resolve was whether she should – or indeed if she even could – kill her enemy in cold blood. Knowing that the woman would not willingly give up the letter opener, it seemed the only option, and Margaret would not return to Helmsley empty handed.

Eventually, she summoned the determination to walk towards the shop and assess the outside, once crammed with various curiosities and now completely barren save for a few rusted nails and two small squares for the windows, each covered with a thick layer of filth. Margaret licked her thumb and circled it across a pane of glass, just enough to be able to see Agnes in her chair talking with a man whose face she could not see.

She watched the pair intently for some time, not even noticing the street beginning to empty and the light slowly fading. Her cheeks flushed against the increasing chill but she could not move. Her neighbour had not aged well, she noted, though her eyes were the same. For many years, Margaret had hoped she would never have to see her rival again, but it had not helped the memories to fade.

Thanks to the flicker of a gas lamp inside, Margaret could see that Agnes and the stranger were discussing something of importance, though a sock had briefly been passed between them. The knife had not appeared but she knew it was there, tucked beside the armchair. She watched as the old woman's face changed from indifference to disinterest, then most unexpectedly to distress and even pain. The man seemed to be listening to Agnes telling a tale – the sorry story of the missing possessions, perhaps?

The noise from the street resumed, this time full of leers and warbled songs, men already drunk travelling to and from the pubs, a couple of women with revealing dresses and overly rouged lips winking and nudging them as they passed. Margaret knew she could not remain outside for much longer but she could not bring herself to leave, especially not now that the stranger inside the shop was heading for the door. She turned to watch him go, wondering who he was and how he had come to know Agnes. Surely a pathetic old woman like her did not have friends?

Peering back through the window, Margaret was convinced that no one else remained. Agnes was alone. Several minutes passed as she watched, just an old woman in a decrepit armchair lost in thought, until she saw a hand reaching down the side of the cushion. Out it came – the letter opener. Margaret bit her lower lip, her fingertips clawing at the window ledge as she strained to see through the murky glass. She was not mistaken. There it was, its blade moving back and forth causing shadows to dance on the ceiling. Was Agnes remembering Benny as she held it? The boy she had killed, the boy that had belonged to Margaret, the boy whose death would shortly be avenged.

With a sudden rush of energy, Margaret marched into the shop and locked the door behind her. She entered the room and watched as Agnes paused in her fondling, aware of a presence though she did not look up. Instead, she called a man's name, perhaps the person who had just left. Margaret did not know nor care. She was too preoccupied with the magical talisman before her. The letter opener looked even more beautiful than she remembered. How easy it would be to snatch it away and run, to race far away from this evil woman and her ugly little house, but Margaret had waited too long for this moment. She wanted to talk. She needed the chance to tell her side of the story, to finally hear Agnes confess to the misery she had inflicted, to hear her say, 'I killed that little boy'.

Margaret said the words for her. "You killed my baby," she called out, a faint echo sounding across the room.

Agnes looked up, though her eyes did not focus. They were directed at where Margaret stood but they were as white as flour and swimming with moisture. Margaret waited to be identified but the face turned to her was completely blank. She then realised that Agnes Holden was blind.

"It's Margaret," she continued, waiting until a glimmer of recognition flashed across Agnes's face, "And you've me t'thank for yer sorry state. Now y'know how it feels t'be completely alone."

Margaret began pacing around the room, her shoes clicking sharply against the bare floorboards as Agnes hunched further into herself, her face growing ever paler. She remembered her neighbour and she knew why she had come.

Margaret paused in front of the chair and reached out to touch the emblem of the letter opener where it sat in Agnes' lap. The old woman flinched as she felt the extra weight and could sense the warmth and the smell of straw and dust from the stranger. There was a small sound, barely a whisper: "Why?"

Why… Mrs Holden could not be sure if the word had fallen from her own lips or from Margaret's. She gripped as firmly as she could to the letter opener, though she knew that she would not be able to defend herself if Margaret wished to take it. She had already somehow managed to steal every other possession from the shop right from under her nose. More than that, she had been robbed of her livelihood, her reason for living. While she had not until now known who had ruined her business, Mrs Holden had grown to suspect their motive. Someone somehow must have seen her that day when Benjamin died. They must have witnessed the terrible scene and had come to the same conclusion as she had herself so many times. She had unintentionally caused the death of a child, the little boy she had come to think of as her son, her own flesh and blood. Now God had seen fit to punish her.

With the demise of her parents, the stillbirth of her daughter, the accident that had taken away her husband, and the theft of everything she owned, it seemed there could be only one possible ending to a life already stripped of its purpose. Mrs Holden knew she was about to die. What she now wondered was whether Margaret would be the person to commit the deed. Did this once brash and determined little girl have it in her to become a murderer? Had she really witnessed the events of that fateful day when Benjamin had died? Or was there someone else involved, someone who had watched and told, the two of them conspiring their revenge for years and years afterwards?

Mrs Holden did not have any answers, only more questions, but she was weak in body and mind. She was tired of fighting, of clinging onto courage. What good had it ever done her? What hope did she have left now? Her fingers loosened their grip, the knife slipping softly into her lap. All the while, Margaret stood before her, eyes ablaze, her fists clenched into two tight white rocks. She laughed, cold and piercing, the sound resonating around the room.

"Why? You ask me why? You killed 'im! You killed me son!" Margaret spat, the twisted grin vanishing as she loomed over the armchair, "He were mine and you took 'im. Five years I watched you, with me little boy and me letter opener. Then that day when y'cruelty an' jealousy overcame yeh. I saw it all." She stood upright again, combing her fingers fiercely through her thinning hair, her breath heaving as the old woman cowered ever lower into her seat.

So it had been Margaret all along, Mrs Holden thought. The witness and the true mother. They had experienced the same grief. If only she had known Benjamin was her neighbour's child, perhaps she would have acted differently or have made other choices. Would she have loved the boy less or even have given him back? Mrs Holden did not know, but it was too late and too painful for any more regrets. She shook her head softly with both disbelief and empathy, truly sorry for what had happened.

"Margaret, forgive me," she began, her eyes watering

even more than usual, "I didn't know." She tried to focus ahead, to finally see what the woman who ruined her now looked like, but she could not see anything other than faint blocks of light and shade.

"But I did love the boy as me own," she continued, hoping Margaret would understand, "And when he… died… it were an accident. That's the truth."

As the words left her mouth, Mrs Holden realised that she believed them. She now knew in her heart that she could never have murdered Benjamin. Every action she had taken that day was for his benefit, to try to help him, an attempt to save his life that had failed. She was not to blame. She had done the right thing, she was sure of it. Almost.

While Mrs Holden felt a sense of calm pass through her, Margaret experienced the opposite. Every muscle was tight with fury, her eyes streaming uncontrollably, her body quaking as she tried to hold in her emotion, but it was too much. She wrenched her hands from her head, pulling away wisps of black and white hair before stamping a foot against the floorboard with rage.

"You liar!" she screeched, suddenly lunging forward towards Mrs Holden and snatching the letter opener from her lap. Margaret held it aloft with the blade directed towards the old woman's face, the two milky orbs of her eyes rotating round and round in panic. For what seemed like several minutes neither moved, each momentarily lost in their memories of the same little boy and his cheerful smile.

Dragging herself back to the moment, Margaret embraced the anger in her heart and swiftly took the old woman's arm, pinning her by the wrist to the armchair, the blade still suspended mid-air. Slowly it descended, almost of its own will, carving a deep and neat line from the base of Mrs Holden's palm until it reached close to her inner elbow. There was a pause before the blood began to seep, a trickle at first before flowing freely, flooding the skin with colour. Mrs Holden could feel the warmth and smell something akin to metal coins, but she made no attempt to move nor to defend herself. Fuelled with an intensity she believed to be justice, Margaret watched with satisfaction as the red liquid slowly spilled. She noticed that Mrs Holden had her other arm rested in the same position, as if expecting her to mirror the injury, so she did. Another careful slice, in and through the flesh, scraping past the bone from the hand up the arm. It looked almost like suicide.

Margaret wiped the letter opener and her hands on the armchair before the blood oozed out over it, covering the smudges and running down to the floor where it pooled. Mrs Holden sat there, her arms open, her head rested back on the chair. She had known so much death that she no longer feared it. She had suspected for many weeks now that her time was to come; at least she had had the luxury of knowing, unlike her loved ones.

Her former neighbour stepped back further and further until she felt the wall behind her, where she slumped down into a heap on the floor. She had the letter opener now and the old woman would soon be dead. She would sit here and wait until sunrise, then head back to her new shop in Helmsley and try to live her life with the knowledge that Benny's death had finally been atoned for. She pushed aside the voices in her head that had begun questioning whether it had been murder or if it could have been an accident, like Mrs Holden had said. What use was wondering now? The deed was done.

At the first sight of daylight, Margaret unlocked the door of Holden's Haunt and made her way to the railway station where she found a young man in a trap heading towards Helmsley. She was not stopped nor even looked at, just another face in the early morning crowd. Soon enough, she was sitting at her kitchen table in a clean frock with a cup of tea, her speechless husband sat opposite having put his wife's soiled clothes in a bucket to soak. Neither spoke as their eyes remained fixed on the beautiful bloodied blade that rested on the table between them.

Chapter Forty-Four

In a mirror of that very night, the letter opener now appeared in the centre of the table, Margaret, Adam and Mr Michael leaning closer as they each stared at its haunting power and strange beauty. Mr Michael could not help but wonder how much trouble and sadness had been caused by such a remarkably simple object. He felt horrified to look on it now and know that it had been used to end Mrs Holden's life. It had not been enough to warn his friend. He should have taken the blade for himself or have been there to protect her. He should have discovered the truth before all this sordid mess had begun to unfold.

Despite their successful plot, the two culprits did not appear proud of their achievement. While Margaret looked as sullen and enraged as she had as a child, Adam seemed distinctly ashamed and even scared of the woman he had married. How could two people commit such a deed and continue their lives in contentment? They had only themselves to blame for their suffering, and that would have to be justice enough for Mr Michael. As he scraped back his chair to stand, Margaret did the same, swiftly taking up the letter opener and holding it aloft as she had earlier.

"Leaving so soon?" she questioned with an unnerving sing-song tone to her voice, "Let's mek ourselves comfortable in the front room, eh?"

She jabbed the point of the blade in Mr Michael's

direction and he obeyed, walking from the kitchen back through to the other room and taking a reluctant perch on the milking stool once more. Margaret seated herself in the armchair with Adam standing by the door like a sentry. Perched atop a bookcase in the corner, the crow ruffled its wings, its beady eyes still managing to unsettle Mr Michael.

"See, you'll be off t'tell that inspector o' yours 'bout what 'appened, won't yeh?" She nudged the point of the letter opener into the fabric of the chair. "But there ain't a chance in hell I'm fer the rope!"

Despite such a solemn acknowledgment, Margaret rocked her head back and released a croaking cackle, part triumph and part madness. There seemed no possibility of Mr Michael escaping now. He remained seated in silence, patiently allowing the game to unfold just like when they were children.

"You'll find life becomes quite meaningless when yeh lose the only thing that mattered. And my Benny, he were the only thing that mattered t'me," she sighed with what seemed genuine emotion, tracing her fingers over the knife's emblem just as Mrs Holden had. A single tear fell onto Margaret's cheek, swiftly wiped away by a calloused and wrinkled hand.

She stood and walked over to Mr Michael, the letter opener swinging at her side before she stopped and pointed the dull tip of the blade to his throat. She knew he could quite easily overpower her in an instant, but she also knew fear when she saw it and the man before her was as frightened as a mouse. The letter opener, the possessions and Agnes Holden dead in the ground where she belonged – she was not going to lose everything she had worked for because of some carpenter and his pathetic sense of duty.

Margaret held the letter opener firmly against Mr Michael's neck, watching with wide eyes as he edged back from her blade, his shoulders heaving as his breath quickened. She pushed it further, the indentation close to puncturing the flesh – still, he did not react. She could almost imagine the blood seeping out like that night with Mrs Holden.

As the memories of the murder flooded her mind, the crow gave an almighty squawk, causing Margaret's hand to jolt and the knife to slip from her grip. She turned behind her to see the bird hopping along the length of the bookcase, sounding its alarm in distress, before a sharp knock at the front door reduced it to silence. Margaret and Adam looked at one another, their faces drained of colour. Finally, thought Mr Michael, he was saved.

With the letter opener replaced against his neck, Margaret instructed her husband to answer the door, a low and formal voice emanating from the other side. Adam tried to peer out of the entrance to politely decline their visitor, but the door was swiftly forced open. He watched helplessly as a policeman stormed inside and through to the front room, a strange girl following behind. Both stopped in their tracks at the scene – Margaret with her blade poised, Mr Michael trembling beneath, and the crow crying out once more.

It happened almost simultaneously, each person trying to predict and respond to one another. Adam flung himself at Inspector Falmer, the pair falling to the floor in a skirmish. The crow swooped down towards Margaret and appeared to be clawing at her head rather than attempting to perch on its mistress. Mr Michael ducked low on his stool to avoid the blade while Margaret tried to bat away the bird with one hand and stab her victim with the other. Irene did not know what to do, but all she cared about was the safety of her father. It took her only a moment to respond to his cries of distress. She reached into the pocket of her apron and produced her own knife, swiftly launching it in the direction of her father's assailant. It impaled Margaret's hand with perfect precision through one side to the other, causing her to drop the letter opener, which went spinning across the floor to Irene's feet. She picked it up and pocketed it, watching as Margaret stumbled back into her armchair howling in pain.

On hearing the commotion, two workmen had come into the house and had Adam pinned to the wall while Inspector Falmer recovered himself, shortly followed by three police officers whom he instructed to arrest Margaret and Adam for their multitude of crimes. Mr Michael tucked himself into the furthest corner of the room clinging tightly to his daughter, the pair watching as the two offenders were hauled away protesting their innocence. The floorboards were speckled with tiny splashes of blood from Margaret's injured hand, leaving a trail as she was dragged away.

Inspector Falmer directed his officers outside the house before returning inside to check on Mr Michael and Irene. Both looked shocked and confused but otherwise unharmed. The inspector went through to the kitchen and brought back some water and bread, watching with care as the two shaken victims paused their panting breaths to refresh themselves before he began taking their statements. They were seated on the cold hard floor surrounded by upturned and broken furniture, small pools of setting blood, and a few fallen black feathers.

Irene listened in shock as her father recalled the latest news regarding Mrs Holden's robbery and death. It seemed to belong in a book, not real life, but finally the truth had been revealed. After Inspector Falmer had made ample notes from Mr Michael's narration, he arranged for a trap and personally escorted them back to York, promising that the case would now be well and truly laid to rest thanks to both their help.

Just as they reached the bridge leading out of Helmsley, Irene spotted a strange shape in the sky that seemed to be moving towards them. Eventually, the wide wings, bright eyes and crooked beak of the crow came into full view. It followed the trap as they traversed the countryside before landing softly by the girl's side just as they were approaching their hometown.

Irene stroked a single finger along the length of its head, wondering whether it could really be the very same bird that Mrs Holden had rescued as a girl. If only animals could talk, she thought, what stories this creature would be able to share.

Mr Michael watched wearily, still unnerved by the bird's presence, but he could see how much it meant to Irene and supposed there was room enough for one more member in his family home. Though it had never been his favourite feature of Holden's Haunt, it had become a part of its magic and myth, capable of bringing back memories of happier times that had recently begun to feel very far away.

The sky grew ever darker as their journey continued and Irene became agitated and frightened, curling up beside her father for comfort. She knew that they must be nearing the city centre, yet everything seemed so unfamiliar, so large and looming, as if they had somehow taken a wrong turning and found themselves in London or Manchester, not York. The trap approached a wide road across the river, its daily traffic replaced by the idling couples, dawdling drunks and shady-looking characters of dusk. It was a scene Irene had witnessed once before and had hoped never to set eyes on again. She grew smaller, shrinking as far as she could into her father's side as the trap began to cross Lendal Bridge.

Inspector Falmer replaced his hat as if preparing for official duties and eyed the pedestrians with a steely gaze as the horse slowed to make way for the people crossing its path. Irene shivered as she watched them pass. This was where she had found herself lost that night, the road dusted with frost, the river flowing like mud beneath, the unwelcoming glares of strangers… and there he was. She held her breath and squeezed her father's hand as the trap rolled to a stop, the stout and sour-faced man she had stabbed standing right beside the carriageway.

Irene tucked her face out of view, afraid that she would be recognised. She peered out with one eye as

Inspector Falmer looked down on the man and passed a few forced pleasantries, to which he received only scowled responses, hoarse and thickly accented. The man turned to point out the direction in which he was headed, towards one of the pubs where there would be no more fights, he solemnly promised the inspector. With his gaze cast yonder, Irene noticed a dark deep welt in the side of his neck. It was about half an inch long and surrounded by a fading bruise that looked sore and crusted on the surface. It was the same man, she was sure. She took another breath, trying to remain quiet and inconspicuous.

"'ere, you found the little blighter what stabbed me yet?" the man asked the inspector as he pointed to his swollen injury. Irene did not dare even breathe, slinking further against the bench as she felt her father's hand grip her own more tightly, as if he already knew what had happened.

"I think that's a lost cause, Mr Madden. No doubt you deserved it," replied Inspector Falmer raising one eyebrow. He nodded his head and the driver whipped the reigns with a flourish, setting the horse on its way again and leaving the angry man, the nightly crowd and the stagnant river far behind.

After what had felt more like a lifetime than a single day, Mr Michael and Irene finally arrived back at their home shortly after midnight. Winifred had stayed awake, too consumed by worry for her absent husband and daughter to be able to rest. Though neither of them looked their best, she was still overjoyed that her loved ones had returned home unharmed. Their skin was pale, their faces weary, but in their eyes Winifred could see an eager enthusiasm that reassured her of their wellbeing.

Across the kitchen table, father and daughter took turns in recalling the drama and revelations that had taken place at Crow's Haunt. They sipped the last of the homemade lemonade that Irene had made weeks ago for the funeral and feasted on wedges of leftover cheese, ham and fruit. It was by no means a banquet, but it was the first time that the three of them had shared a meal together in many years. Despite the challenges they had faced and the emotions they had endured, each knew in their hearts that it was a moment to celebrate, the beginning of a new chapter in their lives. The story was over, the mystery solved. The Michael family could now begin anew. Or so they hoped.

During the course of the following week, Inspector Falmer and his team of officers busied themselves with the resolution of what was hailed as the crime of the century, taking numerous statements and conducting rigorous interrogations of Margaret and Adam, but also of Mr Michael and Irene. Though lengthy and at times confusing, the interviews were not the harrowing experience Mr Michael had previously had to endure when he had been considered a suspect. On the contrary, father and daughter were on this occasion treated as valuable sources of information, shedding light onto the more unclear elements of the case that the police had yet to discover, though it seemed they had been informed of only a fraction of the story by the culprits.

The pair were never once asked about Agnes and

her brother Benjamin, nor the event of his birthday, leading them both to believe that Margaret and Adam had decided to keep the boy's existence and the woeful incident a secret, so Mr Michael and Irene did the same. Instead, a great deal of time was spent discussing the letter opener, which Irene had reluctantly handed over to the police, though she privately hoped she would be able to keep it for herself. Like Mrs Holden, she found something mesmerising about feeling the blade and the emblem beneath her fingertips.

During their questioning, the police officers were especially keen to learn where the object had come from and who it really belonged to. Despite her foul crime, Margaret had apparently begged for the letter opener's return, but could provide no reliable evidence of it having ever been hers in the first place. She could only remember seeing it in her parents' house as a child, until one day it had simply 'disappeared'. She was sure Agnes Dartton had stolen it, but the police were dubious of her tales. Mr Michael and Irene had no additional knowledge either, only the frequent memories of seeing their friend tucking the blade into the side of her armchair when she thought she was not being watched.

On reaching York, Margaret and Adam had both been taken straight to the infamous Castle County Gaol for imprisonment, while almost the entire contents of their home in Helmsley were gradually transferred back into Holden's Haunt. With a police department numbering just two men out in the countryside village, Inspector Falmer felt it appropriate that Mrs Holden's former possessions should be returned to the initial crime scene where they could remain under his watchful eye. It seemed his whole force were given some role to perform in the process, particularly as the winter weather made the roads ever more perilous and the officers all the more resentful of their task. Irene had been more than glad to volunteer her assistance, racing to the shop after school each day to advise the officers on the careful placement of each returning object. The crow would often accompany her, taking up its usual spot once the larger items of furniture had been placed back into position, but would always return with Irene to her home each evening.

Mr Michael meanwhile was working harder than ever in his workshop with the energy and enthusiasm of his former self, having secured numerous commissions in preparation for the festive season. His part in the finding and capture of the culprits had not gone unnoticed either as his heroic actions quickly became the talk of the town, with numerous elaborate accounts being shared across washing lines, shop queues and foaming pints regarding his discovery of Crow's Haunt. Whenever he was questioned directly, Mr Michael shook his head with quiet politeness and declined to comment – he had had quite enough storytelling for one lifetime. Now he wanted to focus on the future, free from Margaret and the misery she had caused.

He knew that several questions still remained unanswered, including how his daughter had escaped arrest following the attack she had admitted to on the night they had returned to York. It had played on Mr

Michael's mind for a few days before fading into a forgotten memory. Even if the police discovered Irene's crime or indeed already knew, he did not think Inspector Falmer would take the matter any further, as he too was looking forward to a quieter existence. Mr Michael tried every day to focus on the feeling of contentment that had finally eased his mind and restored his soul. He had helped to solve Mrs Holden's case and, in doing so, he had put to rest not only her memory but also his own demons.

On returning home, Mr Michael and Irene would greet Winifred warmly and prepare for a long and leisurely evening enjoying comforting meals and commonplace conversation, as if they had always been that way – a normal family. Though she continued to sleep long hours and would often look frail and delicate, Winifred was able to move around the house without assistance and had even begun helping Irene with the daily chores and cooking. During their chats, she caught up on her husband's and daughter's activities, riveted by stories that both shocked and amused her. While she had never met Mrs Holden in person, Winifred felt a fondness for the old woman created exclusively from the words, tones and expressions used by her loved ones in their tales. There were so many missed years that she could not atone for, but she vowed to make amends now that she was well again.

Having heard the joyful news about Winifred's recovery along with the astonishing adventures of Mr Michael and his daughter, Doctor Pruce was keen to renew his acquaintance. He was cordially invited to join the family, along with his wife and young son, for a supper of stewed meat and potatoes with cabbage – another of Irene's specialities. As they seated themselves around the small kitchen table, the doctor had difficulty taking his eyes off the transformed Winifred, who he watched enjoying a healthy portion of food along with a glass of cider as she conversed merrily with Mrs Pruce. He could not account for the improvement but was quite delighted to see it. Perhaps there was something to be said for faith after all.

As dusk began to fall, Doctor Pruce thanked the family for their hospitality and bid them goodbye, escorting his wife and son from the house and waving them off down the street while he waited behind. Mr Michael stood in the door frame while his daughter and wife headed upstairs.

"A brief moment of your time if I may, Mr Michael?" began the doctor once he was sure his words would not be overheard. The door was swiftly closed before Mr Michael ushered him into a vacant seat.

There was a pulsing energy surging through Mr Michael's body that he had not experienced in many weeks. He bowed his head, listening intently.

"You asked me once about an unusual case – an allergic reaction, I believe?" Mr Michael nodded, recalling the occasion when he had tried to find out more about the nature of Benjamin's demise. He had forgotten all about it.

"It occurred to me only quite recently," the doctor continued, his brow furrowed as he stroked his chin, "I had heard an almost identical story before. A man in the hospital here in York, some time around 1860, I seem to recall. He had been seriously injured in a masonry accident." Mr Michael kept silent as he remembered the few details he had heard about the death of Mrs Holden's husband. Could it be the same man Doctor Pruce was referring to?

"Well, he died in a manner that would suggest an acute allergic reaction, though it was entirely unrelated to his injuries. The cause seemed to have been his drink. The nurse had brought the man hot chocolate." The doctor stared into Mr Michael's eyes, a soundless code of understanding between them.

Hot chocolate – the same treat Margaret had given to the boy before Mrs Holden had found him, before he had died in her arms. Mr Michael mused the suggestion over before responding.

"But surely that's not a regular way t'die? Common, like?" He too had begun stroking his chin as he watched the doctor shaking his head firmly.

"Indeed not. Most unusual. Though there is some medical evidence that would suggest a hereditary link. That is to say, that a parent could pass the problem on to a child. However, it seems highly improbable that the man I had heard about and the incident you described were in any way linked. Food for thought, nevertheless."

Doctor Pruce gave the same knowing look before adjusting his spectacles and dusting down his already immaculate dress coat with both hands. He departed the house and hurriedly made his way down the street in pursuit of his family, with Mr Michael watching from his open door, his mind once again whirring as if made of cogs. Margaret, Benjamin, Matthew – could it really be true?

"O'course! It all fits!" came Irene's eager response later that evening when Mr Michael related what Doctor Pruce had told him.

With Winifred always the first to retire to bed, father and daughter were still able to enjoy their late night talks together, just the two of them in their customary positions by the fading embers of the fire, finishing off a last morsel of dinner over a hot drink. The crow would often listen in, positioned on the back of Irene's chair and watching its new mistress intently.

"And that's not all," Irene continued, shifting in her chair to retrieve something from the pocket of her apron, "Wait 'til you see this, father!" She had in her hands the letter opener, her eyes gleaming with excitement. Mr Michael added a little more wood to the fire, encouraging just enough light for another hour so that he could listen to Irene's latest news.

Chapter Forty-Five

Mr Michael smiled as he watched his daughter trace the letter opener across her fingers with the same delicate touch he had seen used by Mrs Holden. He was glad it had been given to Irene. She would be able to look after one of the few things that had made his friend's life bearable despite her suffering. Hopefully it would remind his daughter of happier times in her childhood too. The crow craned its head behind her having caught a glimmer of the mysterious symbol highlighted by the faintest source of light from the fire. Irene tilted the handle back and forth, making the jewel shimmer, before beginning to tell her father how it had come to be in her possession again earlier that day.

Irene had spent most of the day at Holden's Haunt assisting with the reclaimed items. Shortly after having returned home, she had answered a knock at the door and was greeted by an Officer Dunn, exceedingly tall like her father with thick sandy hair and a bushy moustache that obscured his lips entirely. After introducing himself and entering the house, Irene had sat at the kitchen table and watched as the officer produced the letter opener. While he and two colleagues had been moving a particularly heavy set of drawers back into the Holden property, a thin wooden panel had been loosened in the base, revealing a slim collection of paperwork. Most were receipts for items long since bought and disappeared, but one described a 'fine paper knife with runic button', which they believed to be a reference to the letter opener.

The receipt was from a local pawnbroker still trading in the city centre, and the name of the buyer had been Dartton, a Mr Edmund Dartton – Mrs Holden's father. Scribbled on the back of the paper in an inky scrawl were the words 'gifted to our new neighbours, the Crows'. As if recognising its own name, the bird had given a curt squawk and snapped its broken beak in reply. Irene had retrieved the letter opener from the table and admired its shape between her hands, thanking the officer as he departed. How curious, she had thought, that this very object had been bought by Edmund Dartton, given to his neighbours, and then given back again with baby Benjamin. It seemed it had belonged to Agnes Holden after all.

"An' that's why the shop were called Crow's Haunt!" Mr Michael chimed in, having been enraptured by his daughter's retelling. She nodded, but the small smirk was still etched on her lips. There was something more to reveal.

"There were one more thing 'bout that paper that struck me," she began, stroking her thumb across the handle, "That phrase, 'runic button' – odd, ain't it?"

Her father nodded softly, though he did not understand what this could mean, until he heard a sound. It was a tiny click, small yet sharp; it had come from Irene's hand. Mr Michael leaned in closer and saw that the mysterious symbol beside his daughter's thumb had slipped a fraction of an inch down the length of the handle.

"What in blazes..." he began, staring as the letter opener fell apart into two, revealing a cavernous space inside and what looked to be a long skinny twig concealed within.

Irene nodded eagerly as her father reached a hand forward. He picked up the pale object and realised it was paper, incredibly thin and wound tightly into a roll. He carefully prised it apart and gasped at the words headed at the top: 'Last Will and Testament'. Though he could not understand most of the contents, there were a few words he could recognise – the names Agnes Holden, Tobias Michael and Irene Michael. It seemed his old friend had not been so careless with her commodities after all.

The following day, Mr Michael and Irene took the letter opener and the will back to the police station where they quickly fell into the hands of Inspector Falmer. His face was a picture, as if all his Christmases had arrived at once, and he practically skipped as he commanded his officers to contact the relevant individuals. Soon enough, they had amassed an unusual assortment of local residents: Doctor Pruce, Stuart Ainsley Junior, Reverend Gannet, Sarah Johnson, and Arthur Manner, one of the Shambles' street butchers who owned the property next to Holden's Haunt. In their presence, the legitimacy of the will was confirmed. The house and its contents, including the letter opener, were to be entrusted to Mr Tobias Michael until the day when his daughter turned sixteen, at which point ownership would fall entirely to Miss Irene Michael. She would inherit everything Mrs Holden had ever owned.

Father and daughter returned home to tell Winifred the incredible news. As Mr Michael hugged his wife, Irene slipped away to begin preparing what would be a celebratory supper. She could not quite believe the outcome of the day, nor the story in its entirety. She had learned more within the past few months than a lifetime at school could provide. She had discovered so many sides of human nature; about love and hatred, friendship and families, how to live with loss, and how to make life's meaning one's own. She was quite sure that Mrs Holden had been the best teacher she could have wished for and her father the best of friends to have shared the adventure with.

As Irene finished slicing the onions and heated the pan on the stove, she slipped her spare hand into the pocket of her apron to check the letter opener was still there and to enjoy one more feel of the button under her fingertips. As she searched for the blade, she remembered what else she had once slipped inside the fabric – the fragment of paper Mrs Johnson had given her. For many weeks now, it had sat on a small wooden stool beside her mattress, tucked between a carved squirrel her father had made for her as a child and a doll's cup painted with roses that he had bought from Holden's Haunt. Though she had kept the map, Irene did not think that she would need it. She was fairly certain she knew its drawing by heart now. Even after watching Mrs Johnson create the image in Mrs Holden's childhood kitchen, Irene was sure her footsteps would know where to lead her in the cemetery itself. She decided that she was long overdue a visit.

The following day after school, Irene wrapped her thick shawl around her and headed through the snow up along Fishergate to the cemetery with the paper, the letter opener and a teaspoon in her pocket. Even though it was the depths of winter, the air had lost its usual chill and the sun was still able to softly illuminate the city with a pale glow that felt almost spiritual, especially once she reached the graveyard. As Irene followed the path on and on past the rows of headstones, she spotted the bald dome of a gardener's scalp across in the distance, bobbing and throwing up weeds as he worked. She kept the paper concealed and trusted her memory and instinct to find what she had come for. Soon enough she reached her destination; the final resting place of Benjamin Dartton.

Irene was suddenly overwhelmed with sadness. The headstone was so small and impersonal, seeming insignificant and forgotten among the hundreds of others that were all much more prominent and elaborate. There was no name and no dates engraved where Benjamin had been buried, just a phrase that Irene had never seen on a headstone before: 'Blessed sleep to which we all return'. She thought carefully about what the words might mean and decided that it was a most appropriate and kind quotation to have used. The little boy, who had been so loved, was merely sleeping, forever in a playful dream and perhaps now with Agnes by his side.

Irene wondered if the grave had ever been tended to, if she might even be the first, but despite the lack of visitors she still knew that Benjamin had been adored. She knelt and took the spoon from her pocket, digging down into the hard icy dirt to form a long thin furrow. She carefully placed the letter opener inside and replaced the soil across the top, reciting her own prayer. She gave thanks to Benjamin for bringing his new mother such joy, for though they may not have been related by blood, Irene was sure that the boy had loved Agnes as much as she had loved him, and that was the most important thing. As Mrs Holden had left her everything she owned, Irene had felt that she should give at least one token to the woman's son. What could be more valuable to both their memories than the letter opener? She felt at peace with herself as she slowly rose to her feet again, shaking off the dirt from the spoon and slipping it into her pocket.

As Irene turned to leave, she was startled by an unexpected presence behind her – the gardener, who had managed to sneak up unheard. The man smiled softly, his cheeks and ears flushed with colour from the cold. He had a bundle of muddy weeds in one hand and held out an object with the other. Irene took it and ran it through her hands. It was a carved wooden rabbit, very much like the ones her father made.

"Gentleman came t'other day, asked me t'leave it 'ere," the gardener said, nodding down towards the headstone, "Didn't say nowt else. Not much of a talker." He gave a little chuckle before heading on his way again, stooping on his route to pull up another rouge shrub.

Puzzled and amazed, Irene bent down to rest the

ornament at the base of the grave, just as her father had done with his carved cross at the Holden family burial. She could not determine how or who, when or why, but it did not seem to matter. The letter opener and the wooden rabbit were now somehow in their rightful places beside Benjamin. Irene returned home, but this time she decided to keep the story of her visit to the graveyard to herself. It would be a secret that only she and the spirit of Mrs Holden would share.

Chapter Forty-Six

The start of a new century marked many changes, though the self-contained world of the Shambles was slow to alter its historic legacy. The street remained dominated by its butcher's shops run by generations of the same families, with properties continuing to pass from father to son and retaining their reputations despite competition from the numerous new grocer's and stores that had started to appear. The inns on the street were among the most popular in the city, treated almost as second homes by their faithful bands of regulars who would amass to share gossip and dares over brews, and with the occasional brawl, just the same as it had been for decades previous.

Nevertheless, there were other businesses along the cobbles that had begun to embrace the latest commercial opportunities. The single bakery had developed a novel new recipe using oatmeal in their baps, the goldsmith's had acquired a fine selection of commemorative collectibles to mark the Queen's Jubilee, while the tobacconist's had begun stocking many of the coveted confectionary creations coming out of the still expanding Rowntree's, Craven's and Terry's factories. The market had many more stalls selling goods from places folk could barely pronounce, let alone find on a map. Even the locals themselves were starting to look different as more modern fashions came into vogue as worn by Her

Royal Highness and popularised by advertisements, newspapers and picturehouses.

There was one shop on the corner, however, that still retained its history. Routinely piled high with all manner of curiosities both outside and in, the business had blossomed since the new owner had taken charge several years earlier. Whenever one item was sold, it would swiftly be replaced by another, with many visitors coming purely to see the changes rather than to purchase anything new. The proprietor did not seem to mind. She enjoyed welcoming everyone and anyone to look round her shop, holding a keen understanding of their appreciation and always responding with thanks to their kind comments. It was an institution, she knew, with its heritage as much a part of the city as the marketplace, snickelways and celebrated buildings. It had been ingrained in the shared narrative of every local resident thanks to one person: Mrs Agnes Holden. Her legend had grown even more since her death, and the coveted few who could remember the original Holden's Haunt were often called upon to recollect their memories.

Lanky Luke and Dan Chelten had long since left the city, but their fables had lived on along with a handful of the original items which were now purely for display and nostalgia. Littered around the shop, one could still discover a few carved wooden ornaments, several stained chamber pots, and even the original bowing bookcase complete with a crow perched on top, who would be regularly fed by the neighbourhood children with berries, seeds and nuts they had found along the river. Irene would watch them happily from the comfort of her counter in the corner, encouraging the children to hold their tiny hands out flat and wide so that the bird could swoop down to pluck up the treats. Their gleeful cries brought joy to her heart, along with the many customers and visitors she was so grateful to receive on a daily basis. Since she had inherited the shop at the age of sixteen, she had only closed on Christmas Eve. On every other day, it had been an open and welcoming haven.

With so many people coming in and out of the shop, Irene never felt lonely. Indeed, there were even days when she looked forward to nightfall just to be able to have a few moments of peace to herself. She could now understand why Mrs Holden had been so content here, despite the personal losses she had suffered. A single conversation with an appreciative customer would always serve to brighten a dull day, and it gave her great gladness to see one of the objects go on to a new home.

As yet unmarried and childless, these items had become part of Irene's family, their presence as familiar and comforting as any person or pet. There had been several suitors, of course, but the world was changing and ideas along with it. She did not feel any need to rush into a romance when she had so many more interesting occupations at present.

Of course, there were her parents too, who visited regularly. Though they were both beginning to show signs of old age, they remained cheerful and sprightly as if they had only just fallen in love. The pair had stayed in their property on Fossgate and now shared a room together for the first time in decades. Whenever their daughter paid a visit, the house would be filled with the smell of baking and the sound of wood being worked. She herself was no stranger to domestic comforts either, making her famous pies to sell as well as teaching herself how to carve wooden love tokens with a little help from her father. They were always a popular purchase before Valentine's Day.

Occasionally, her mother would look after the shop while Irene and Mr Michael took flowers to the graves of Mrs Holden and her loved ones. Sometimes when they visited, there would already be a fresh arrangement or a small gift – an object, a handwritten note, a knitted baby boot. They did not know who the well-wishers were but were nonetheless comforted by the thought that the old woman and her family had not been entirely alone nor unloved. Friendships could be formed in the most unusual of situations and between the most unlikely of people.

This, Irene believed, was the most important lesson she had learned from Mrs Holden, and she was reminded of the fact every time she looked up at the sign of her shop. Created by Mr Michael, it was the shape of a shield and painted deep green with gold detail, a runic emblem at the top and curled lettering below that read 'Agnes and I'. Two women, past and present, who from a single business had created a whole new world; a place of excitement and intrigue, of possibility and opportunity, but above all, a place of hope.

Lightning Source UK Ltd.
Milton Keynes UK
UKHW040842121021
392077UK00001B/28

9 781914 560101